PUFFIN BOOKS

ALDRIN ADAMS
and the
CHEESE
NIGHTMARES

PAUL HOWARD

ALDRiN ADAMS
and the
CHEESE
NiGHTMARES

Illustrated by Lee Cosgrove

PUFFIN

PUFFIN BOOKS
UK | USA | Canada | Ireland | Australia
India | New Zealand | South Africa

Puffin Books is part of the Penguin Random House group of companies
whose addresses can be found at global.penguinrandomhouse.com.

www.penguin.co.uk
www.puffin.co.uk
www.ladybird.co.uk

First published 2021

001

Text copyright © Paul Howard, 2021
Illustrations copyright © Lee Cosgrove, 2021
The moral right of the author/illustrator has been asserted

Text design by Lizzy Laczynska
Printed and bound in Great Britain by Clays Ltd, Elcograf S.p.A.

A CIP catalogue record for this book is available from the British Library

The authorized representative in the EEA is Penguin Random House Ireland,
Morrison Chambers, 32 Nassau Street, Dublin D02 YH68

ISBN: 978–0–241–44167–1

All correspondence to:
Puffin Books
Penguin Random House Children's
One Embassy Gardens, 8 Viaduct Gardens
London SW11 7BW

For my wife, Mary.

PROLOGUE

It was the **darkest of dark, dark nights**.

And Habeas Grusselvart was in a very peculiar mood indeed.

He should have been happy – ecstatic even. On his gigantic wall, full of TV screens, he could see hundreds and hundreds of people experiencing the most **horrible, HORRIBLE nightmares!**

Like Asafa Mitchell from Brewin Drive, who was at that exact moment being chased home from school by a pack of snarling dogs. In an effort to escape their snapping jaws and dagger-like teeth, he turned down an alleyway – only to discover, too late, that he'd run into . . . into a dead end!

'MUMMMYYYYYY!!!!!!'

Over on Adelaide Road, little Amy Twamley was getting ready to celebrate her sixth birthday with a huge party, to which all of her friends were invited. She was standing in front of the mirror, brushing her hair, when she smiled at her reflection. It was then that she saw that all of her teeth had fallen out – and in their place were hundreds and hundreds of . . . disgusting maggots!

'DADDDYYYYY!!!!!!'

And, on Waterloo Terrace, poor, frightened Frankie Fidderer was trapped in the upper branches of a very tall tree. Terrified of heights, he clung to the trunk like his life depended on it. Which, of course, it did. Then, out of nowhere, a wind started to whip up. It quickly grew in strength until it raged with the force of a hurricane and shook the tree so violently that the branch on which Frankie stood suddenly **snap**ped – sending the boy plummeting, head first, towards the hard ground below.

'AAARRRGGGHHH!!!'

All over town – and, indeed, in towns like this all over the world – children were waking up and

screaming for their mums and dads. And so were quite a few grown-ups, for adults aren't immune from the terrors of the night.

Usually, this thought would have filled Habeas Grusselvart with great delight. He was, after all, a supervillain, and this was his supervillain *thing* – creating blood-chilling nightmares to spread anxiety and unhappiness throughout the world, so that he might one day rule the entire planet through fear.

And he was very, **VERY** good at it.

But tonight, for reasons he couldn't quite put his finger on, his work gave him no pleasure whatsoever.

All he felt was a strange sense of unease.

He pressed the button to summon his personal assistant, Beddy Byes.

'Something is wrong,' he told him. 'It's just . . . a feeling I have.'

'A feeling?' Beddy Byes asked. 'What kind of feeling, Oh Great and Masterful One?'

'Almost a disturbance,' Habeas explained. 'Like something is about to happen. You see, if I didn't know better, it's almost as if . . .'

But then his voice **trailed off** and he didn't allow himself to finish the thought.

PART ONE

CHEESE FOR EVERY MEAL

Most people have a happy place – a favourite spot that fills them with warm, fuzzy feelings of joy. For Aldrin Adams, it was his mum and dad's cheesemonger's shop. It was called *C'est Cheese*, and everyone agreed that it was the best cheesemonger's for miles and miles around.

To Aldrin, though, it was far more than just a shop. He found comfort and delight in the smells, the colours and the shapes of the hundreds of different varieties of cheese that Cynthia and Doug Adams laid out with loving care each day.

There were white cheeses, orange cheeses and yellow cheeses. There were brown cheeses, blue cheeses and even green cheeses. There were cheeses covered with brilliantly coloured wax – fire-engine red,

 6

dark chocolate brown and bright tangerine. There were cheeses filled with holes, cheeses dusted with charcoal and cheeses marbled with mould.

There were wheels of cheese the size of car tyres, some stacked flat on top of each other, others standing on their sides like books in a library. Some were cut in halves or quarters. There were cheeses shaped like barrels and cheeses shaped like pyramids. There were cheeses shaped like footballs, and rectangular slabs of cheese that looked like tombstones.

There were cheeses that smelled of fresh-cut grass and cheeses that smelled of – revolting as it

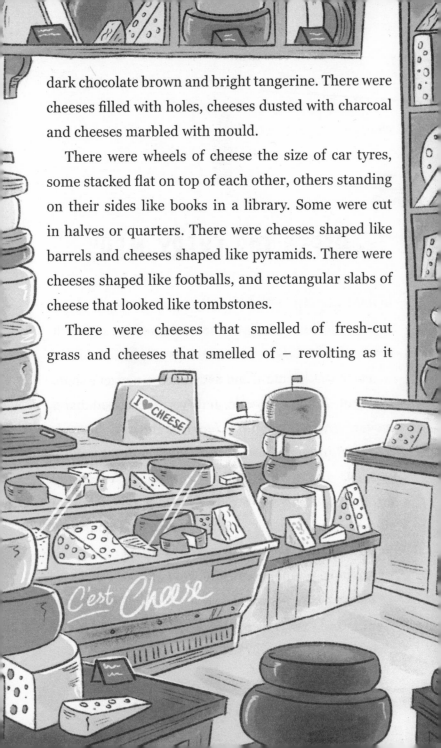

sounds – sick! There were cheeses that smelled of – equally disgusting – sweaty feet and cheeses that smelled of butterscotch ice cream!

There were cheeses that crumbled when you cut them and cheeses that **oozed**.

To Aldrin, it was just a magical place.

He even loved the language of cheese – the colourful words his mum and dad used to describe to customers the textures of all the different varieties they sold: *brittle, grainy, oily, chewy, fluffy, runny, springy, sticky, flaky, chalky, dense, dry, firm, smooth, pressed, spreadable, creamy, supple.*

They had a whole other set of words to describe the different flavours: *fresh, fruity, yeasty, garlicky, sweet, grassy, perfumy, earthy, musty, buttery, floral, pungent, sour, funky, ripe, oniony, soapy, gamey, fermented, mushroomy, chocolatey, lemony, limey, complex, herbaceous, tangy, milky, meaty, nutty, rustic, smoky, almondy, peanutty, walnutty, spiky, winey, zesty, sharp, ripe, rich, persistent, peppery, outdoorsy, barnyardy.*

He was sure his mum had made up one or two of those words herself – especially 'barnyardy', which didn't sound like a real flavour at all.

Aldrin loved spending time in the shop, especially at this time of the day, when the final customer had left and Cynthia had turned the sign on the door to **'CLOSED'**. Because that was when he got to handle all these weird and wonderful cheeses. Every one had to be removed from the wooden shelves and wrapped in plastic shrink-wrap, before the shelves were swept of crumbs and scrubbed clean.

He had watched his mum and dad do this from the time that he was a baby, crawling around on the tiled floor of the shop. And now that he was older, he was allowed to help.

Aldrin Adams was – how to put this sensitively – a bit **heavier** than the average eleven-year-old boy.

What made him that way was his inability to resist eating his mum and dad's stock. And with all that earthy Cheddar, and grainy Parmesan, and nutty Edam, and salty feta, and caramelly Gouda, and creamy Gruyère, and buttery Brie, and mushroomy Camembert, and milky mascarpone at his fingertips – well, who could really blame him?

Aldrin *loved* cheese the way other children loved chocolate, or hamburgers, or ice cream. A perfect day for him would be one in which he could eat cheese for every meal. And, in between, he would snack on those little round Babybels that his mum absolutely adored and insisted on stocking, even though cheese snobs would turn their noses up at them and say that they didn't belong in an artisan cheesemonger's.

Cynthia was standing on a stepladder, taking down a block of delicious, grassy Montgomery's Cheddar.

'I was thinking,' she said, 'we might *all* go to the London Festival of Cheese this year – we've never been as a family. You'd love it, Aldrin.'

'**Mmm,**' he replied.

'Cheesemakers from all over the world come to display their wares. You can have a free sample of absolutely anything you want.'

'**Mmm,**' Aldrin repeated.

Cynthia was surprised by his less-than-enthusiastic

response. She looked at her son over the top of her glasses.

'Aldrin Adams,' she said, 'what are you eating?'

Aldrin didn't answer her. He couldn't, because at that moment his mouth was stuffed with burrata, a soft and stringy cheese that tasted a little bit like yogurt and just so happened to be one of his absolute favourites.

'Mmm-mmm,' Aldrin said, which was meant to sound like, 'Nothing.'

'You're absolutely sure there's nothing in your mouth?' she asked. 'You didn't, by any chance, eat that burrata that was there, did you?'

Aldrin felt his face redden. He shook his head again. But suddenly he could feel that delicious cheese melting on his tongue and the urge to actually chew it became too great.

Cynthia laughed.

'How are me and your dad supposed to make a living if you keep eating **EVERYTHING** in the shop?'

Doug chuckled as he checked the temperature gauge, just like he did every half-hour. The shop had to remain cool at all times to prevent the cheese from spoiling, which is why it was usually colder *inside* than it was *outside*.

'Sorry, Mum,' Aldrin said through a mouthful of

creamy mush. 'It just looked so good!'

'There are *other* foods in the world,' she reminded him. 'Most kids your age like sweets, or chips, or cream cakes.'

'I just love cheese, though.'

'Well, make that your last piece for the day,' she told him. 'We don't want you having nightmares.'

'Cheese doesn't give you nightmares,' Doug said. 'That's just an old wives' tale.'

'An old wives' tale?' Aldrin said. 'What exactly does that mean?'

'An old wives' tale,' his dad explained, 'is a story that lots of people believe to be true, even though it has no basis in scientific fact.'

'And *you've* been eating the Manchego,' Cynthia said, pointing at the giveaway crumbs of butter-coloured cheese that had lodged themselves in her husband's enormous walrus moustache.

'Guilty!' Doug laughed.

They finished cleaning the shop and wrapping the cheeses, then they took a moment to admire their work before they switched off the lights and went upstairs to their flat for the evening.

'By the way,' Aldrin said, 'in case you didn't hear my answer, I would **LOVE** to go to the London Festival of Cheese.'

His mum smiled at him, but in a sad way.

'What's wrong?' he asked.

'Come here,' she told him.

Aldrin walked over to her and she enveloped him in a warm hug.

'You're a very special boy,' she whispered, planting a kiss on the top of his head.

'What do you mean?' he asked.

'You have a rare gift, Aldrin. You don't know it yet, but you're going to do extraordinary things in your life.'

Aldrin suddenly opened his eyes. He was back in his bedroom. He'd had that dream again. It was his favourite dream – reliving their last truly happy day together as a family, before he found out about his mum's cancer. He wished sometimes that he could stay locked in that dream forever. But he always woke up to the reality that she was gone now.

His eyes adjusted to the darkness of the room. He was staring at the vintage *Fromages de France* poster on the wall at the foot of his bed, featuring pictures of fifty famous French cheeses that looked so real you could almost taste them. Fruity Morbier, and tangy Roquefort, and fudgy Boule de Lille, and herby Pouligny Saint-Pierre.

He thought about what his mum had said to him that day. A very special boy with a rare gift, who was going to do extraordinary things in his life. Did she really mean that, he wondered? Or was it something that all mums said to their kids? A year after her death, he was still confused by it.

Aldrin threw back his covers and swung his legs out of bed. Today was a big day. His first morning in a new school.

He pulled on his dressing gown, said good morning to his pet frog, Silas, then headed for the kitchen. Dad was already downstairs, unwrapping the cheeses and preparing the shop for the day.

Aldrin opened the fridge and took out a block of Comté, a firm cheese that was buttery in colour, smelled of warm croissants and tasted sweet and nutty. He took the stainless-steel cheese plane from the drawer, shaved a thin slice from the top of the block and nibbled on it while he searched for his class timetable.

It had arrived in the post two days ago, but Aldrin hadn't seen it since then, so he looked in the bottom drawer, where all the clutter usually ended up, from junk mail to loose batteries, and from bits of string to remote controls for electrical items they'd thrown out years ago. He eventually found a white envelope and pulled out the piece of paper inside it.

But it wasn't his class timetable.

It was a letter from the bank, addressed to his dad. And, while he knew it was wrong to read someone else's post, once he started, he simply couldn't stop himself.

It seemed that Doug hadn't made any mortgage repayments on the shop and the flat for the past six months. The letter was full of big words and grown-up language, but Aldrin understood all too clearly the final line – and it sent a chill through him:

Unless all of your outstanding debts are met within the next thirty days, you will be evicted from your business premises and your home.

'Morning, Aldrin!' Doug called as he tramped up the stairs to the flat.

Aldrin shoved the letter back into the drawer and quickly closed it.

'Morning, Dad,' he replied.

'I thought I'd give you a lift this morning,' Doug said as he popped his cheery face round the kitchen door, 'seeing as it's your first day and everything.'

'I was just, um, looking for my class timetable.'

'Oh, I put it in your schoolbag. Did you have your breakfast?'

'I'm having a slice of Comté,' Aldrin said, showing him the cheese.

Doug's moustache bristled.

'You'll have to eat more than that,' he insisted.

'I'll have a second slice if I'm hungry,' Aldrin told his dad.

'What I mean is, you've got a big day ahead of you. You should have cereal or something. You can't survive on just cheese.'

Aldrin thought about the letter from the bank. And, in that moment, he realized just how right his dad was.

A NEW SCHOOL

Doug parked the ***C'est Cheese*** refrigeration truck outside St Martin's Grammar School, then switched off the engine.

Aldrin stared out of the window as dozens of children – some older than him, some the same age – made their way through the iron gates and into the large white building.

'It's much bigger than my last school,' he said.

'It only seems like that because it's new to you,' Doug assured him. 'You're not worried, are you?'

'No,' Aldrin said. 'Not about school anyway.'

'Is there something else on your mind?' Doug asked. 'It's just you barely said a word during the drive here.'

'When I was looking for my class timetable,' Aldrin

confessed, 'I accidentally saw the letter – the one you got from the bank.'

'Oh,' Doug said. 'I suppose you read it, did you?'

Aldrin nodded in reply.

'Look,' Doug said, 'it's nothing for you to worry about.'

'How can you say that?' Aldrin asked. 'It said we might lose the shop – and the flat!'

Aldrin knew that business had been slow since his mum died. Cynthia had been the heart and soul of the shop. She had known everything there was to know about cheese, having served her apprenticeship at the famous Farlowe's Cheesemakers in London under the legendary Frenchwoman Madame Lacombe. People used to come from miles around to ask for Cynthia's recommendations and advice. Since she died, the number of customers passing through the door of *C'est Cheese* had slowed to a trickle.

'It's not your problem,' Doug insisted. 'It's my responsibility to turn things around, and that's what I'm going to do – OK?'

'But how?' Aldrin wondered.

'By not giving up,' Doug said. 'That was always your mum's advice, whenever business was bad. Keep doing the right things, she'd say. Get up early, set up the shop, then clean it in the evening after we close. The customers will come back.'

Aldrin was quiet for a long moment.

'Will there ever be a day when I'm not sad?' he asked. 'About Mum, I mean?'

'Of course there will,' Doug said. 'When you lose someone you love, Aldrin, it leaves a very big hole in your life. That hole never goes away. But, over time, you just get used to the fact that it's there. Does that make sense?'

Aldrin nodded.

'She'd be so proud of you if she could see you now,' Doug told him.

'Would she?' Aldrin asked.

'Absolutely. You're just like her in so many ways. The way you're always thinking about others. The way you're never frightened of anything. Go on now. You don't want to be late on your first day.'

Aldrin took a deep breath, then he opened the passenger door of the refrigeration truck and prepared to jump out. His dad repeated the words that astronaut Neil Armstrong said just after he set foot on the moon:

'That's one small step for man . . .'

Then Aldrin completed the line as his feet landed on the ground:

'One **giant** leap for mankind!'

It was one of their little jokes. Doug loved all things related to space. Aldrin was named after Buzz Aldrin, who was one of the crew of Apollo 11, the first manned mission to land on the moon.

'Have a good day, son!' Doug called after him.

'You too, Dad!'

And then slowly, and a little warily, Aldrin walked through the giant iron gates of his new school.

As he made his way across the playground, he spotted a familiar face. Or, rather, he spotted a familiar head. Frankie Fidderer was kind of hard to miss, since he was completely bald. Aldrin and Frankie had been at the same primary school. And while Aldrin enjoyed making brand-new friends, it was nice to see an old face on his first morning in St Martin's.

'All right, Aldrin?' Frankie asked. 'How was your summer, mate?'

'It was, um, good,' Aldrin replied, because, while he was sad in his heart, he always tried to put on a brave face. 'I was working with my dad in the shop every day. How was yours?'

'**Unbelievable**,' Frankie said. He looked over his left shoulder, then his right. 'Except I can't tell you nothing about it. Be more than me life's worth, see.'

Frankie Fidderer was a boy with a very overactive imagination. As a matter of fact, his nickname in their last school was Frankie Fibberer – on account of all the lies he told.

'You don't *have* to tell me,' Aldrin assured him. 'Probably none of my business anyway.'

'OK, I'll tell you,' Frankie conceded, 'seeing as you twisted me arm and everything. I was working for MI5 the whole time.'

'MI5?'

'As a spy. Spent the whole month of August operating behind enemy lines, didn't I? Had to jump out of an aeroplane at twenty thousand feet – me parachute didn't open neither.'

Behind him, Aldrin heard a girl's voice say, 'You're lying, Frankie Fidderer.'

He turned round. Standing there was a tall, wiry girl, with black hair tied in pigtails and train-track braces on her upper and lower teeth.

'I ain't lying,' Frankie told her.

'You weigh – I'm guessing – six stone,' the girl said.

'An object of that weight falling from twenty thousand feet would hit the ground having reached a terminal velocity of one hundred and twenty miles per hour. Which would mean you'd be dead.'

'I had a soft landing – in a hayfield.'

'You'd still be dead. Now I'm going inside. Assembly is starting in five minutes.'

And, with that, the girl walked off. Aldrin couldn't help but laugh.

'Who was *that*?' he asked.

'*That* was Sisely Musa,' Frankie told him. 'She's my next-door neighbour and she's a mathematical genius, by the way.'

'Yes, I sort of gathered that,' Aldrin said.

They followed Sisely into the school.

'She's got a photographic memory as well,' Frankie said. 'She just has to read something once and she remembers it forever.'

'Wow!' Aldrin exclaimed. 'I could see how *that* would come in handy.'

'Sisely's nice – except, well, she tends to just blurt out whatever she's thinking. Which can sometimes hurt your feelings. She doesn't mean it, though. That's just the way she is.'

The building seemed even bigger on the inside than it did on the outside. They followed the herd through the entrance lobby and up a flight of stairs to a large hall. It was already packed with boys and girls chattering excitedly about the summer just gone and the year ahead.

They spotted Sisely. She was sitting in the front row and they joined her.

'This place is absolutely massive,' Frankie said.

Sisely shushed him. 'I don't want to miss anything because you're talking,' she said.

Frankie turned to Aldrin and smiled.

'See what I mean?' he mouthed.

Aldrin heard a small voice say, 'Excuse me – is this seat taken?'

Standing beside him was a short, skinny boy with a pudding-bowl haircut and thick, round glasses that looked like swimming goggles.

'Er, no. Sit down,' Aldrin said. 'I'm Aldrin Adams. This is Frankie Fidderer. And that's Sisely Musa.'

'Hi, I'm Harry,' the boy replied. He pulled an asthma inhaler from his pocket, put one end of it in his mouth and pressed down on it with his thumb. 'Harry Stiles.'

'Harry Stiles?' Aldrin repeated. 'What, do you mean like the pop singer?'

'Yes!' said Harry impatiently, as if he had to explain it a hundred times a week – which, in fact, he did. 'Although I'm obviously not *the* Harry Styles. *I* spell *my* surname with an **I**; *he* spells *his* with a **Y**.'

He sat down. Aldrin noticed Harry's school diary in his hand. On the front cover there were pen-and-ink drawings of Batman, Spider-Man and Wonder Woman.

'Wow!' Aldrin exclaimed – because they *were* excellent drawings. 'Who did these?'

'I did,' Harry said. 'Do you like superheroes?'

'Of course,' Aldrin replied. 'Doesn't everyone?'

'Speaking of superheroes,' Frankie said, leaning forward in his seat to talk to Harry, 'I'm actually a spy.'

Harry stared back at Frankie, wondering what kind of spy would drop a line like that into an introduction.

It was at that moment that Mr Maskell, the headteacher, stepped on to the stage. He was a big, burly man in his mid-fifties, with jet-black hair, which Aldrin presumed was dyed, and eyebrows that looked like big furry caterpillars. He wore a brown corduroy jacket, which had patches on the elbows and chalk marks on the pockets, and sandals with socks.

'Silence!' he shouted into a microphone – and the chatter stopped immediately. 'For those of you who don't know me, I am Mr Maskell, the principal of this institute of learning. I trust you all had an enjoyable summer break and are looking forward to getting back to your school books?'

There were loud groans from the back of the room.

'OK, try not to sound *too* enthusiastic!' he said. 'I would like to extend a very hearty welcome to all of our new Year Seven students. I'm sure the school feels like a big and scary place at the moment, but you'll find your feet in no time. I would also like to welcome to the school a new member of our teaching staff. Mrs Van Boxtel, would you mind joining me on the stage, please?'

'Mrs Van Boxtel?' Harry said, looking at his class timetable. 'I think we have her this morning – for English.'

A woman walked slowly up the steps and on to the stage. Everyone goggled at her. She was an elderly, frail-looking lady, with tiny, rat-like eyes, a long nose and an even longer chin. She had an **enormous** mop of grey hair that reminded Aldrin of a dandelion puffball. It was the kind of hair that made you worry about sneezing around her, just in case the entire thing blew away!

She wore a purple cardigan, a tweed skirt and brown, fur-lined ankle boots – the type that grandmothers wear. And, most noticeably of all, around her neck was a thick white surgical collar, suggesting that she'd recently been the victim of some kind of whiplash injury.

'Hello, boysh and girlsh!' she said.

That was another thing that was rather unusual about Mrs Van Boxtel. She was from a country called the Netherlands. And while her English was very, very good, she pronounced every 's' sound as if it was a 'sh'.

'It ish a great pleashure to be here at Shaint Martin'sh

Shchool,' she said. 'I am very much looking forward to having shome of you in my clash. I can promishe you that our time together will be fantashtic fun, ash well ash a wonderful, wonderful adventure!'

Behind him, Aldrin heard a snigger. He turned his head and saw a tall, older boy with floppy blond hair laughing behind his hand. Straight away, Aldrin had a **very bad** feeling about him.

Then he accidentally caught his eye.

'What are you looking at?' the boy snapped. 'Turn around, Fatty.'

Yes, a **very, VERY** bad feeling.

3

A NEW FRIEND

'So, who's your favourite superhero?' Aldrin asked Harry later that morning.

They were rambling along a seemingly endless maze of corridors, looking for Room A13, where Mrs Van Boxtel would be teaching them English every day.

'My *absolute* favourite?' Harry replied. 'That would have to be Agent Cunning. He was a comic character from the 1930s. He had the power of psychokinesis.'

'What's psychokinesis?' Aldrin wondered.

'It's the ability to move things without touching them. He could use his mental powers to pick up a bus and throw it! Or even stop a bullet! *And* he had telepathic abilities.'

'What, he could communicate with other people, using his mind?'

'That's exactly it. He could also teleport himself, meaning he could go anywhere he wanted to go just by thinking really hard about that place.'

'How do you know all this stuff?'

'Me and my dad collect old comics. Agent Cunning was in one called *The Defenders*. We have the very first edition – the one where he discovers his superpowers.'

'He sounds amazing.'

'He *is* amazing. By day, he works as a gentleman's tailor in New York City – then, by night, he becomes . . . Agent Cunning, Fearless Protector of the City and its People!'

Harry pushed his glasses up his nose with his finger. Aldrin noticed they tended to slip down when he got excited.

'He also has a sidekick,' Harry told him, 'a woman named Linda Dale, who works in the New York Public Library. She's kind of the brains of the outfit.'

Aldrin looked around him.

'Where are we?' he asked.

'Er, I don't know,' Harry said. 'I was following you.'

Aldrin had been so engrossed in the conversation

that he'd managed to walk straight past their classroom. And now all of the other children were in lessons and the corridors were empty.

'That's Room A22,' Harry said, 'so it must be back the way we came.'

They turned round and retraced their steps.

'Who was that boy in assembly?' Harry asked. 'The one who said he was a spy.'

'Oh, that's Frankie Fidderer,' said Aldrin. 'He was at my last school. He's not *really* a spy, by the way.'

'Yeah, I kind of guessed that!' Harry laughed. 'So how come he's bald?'

'He has a condition called alopecia,' Aldrin explained. 'All of his hair fell out when he was five years old and it never grew back again.'

'That's awful,' Harry said.

'It doesn't really bother him,' Aldrin said. 'I think he kind of likes standing out.'

'That's very un-spylike!' Harry said.

Aldrin laughed.

They had arrived outside Room A13. They listened at the closed door.

'Oh, no,' Aldrin said. 'The class has already started.'

He knocked, then he pushed the door. It gave way

to a large classroom containing thirty desks laid out in five rows of six. Aldrin spotted Frankie and Sisely. Like all of the other children, they had their heads down and they were writing in their exercise books.

Mrs Van Boxtel was standing at the back of the class.

'Good morning,' she said. 'Why are you late for clash?'

'It was *my* fault,' Aldrin explained. 'I made Harry late because I was asking him –'

'What ish your name?'

'Aldrin,' said Aldrin. 'Aldrin Adams.'

'Aldrin? Like Buzsh Aldrin, the ashtronaut?'

'Yeah, that's who I'm named after.'

She turned to Harry then.

'And what ish *your* name?'

'Harry Stiles.'

Everyone in the classroom laughed.

'Harry Shtilesh?' said Mrs Van Boxtel. 'What ish sho funny about Harry Shtilesh?'

'He's a pop singer,' Frankie shouted.

Mrs Van Boxtel looked Harry up and down.

'You are a pop shinger?' she asked.

'No, he's talking about a different Harry Stiles,' Harry told her. '*He* spells his name with a **Y** and *I* spell mine with an –'

'I don't have time to lishten to thish,' Mrs Van Boxtel said, cutting him off. 'Find a sheat, then copy down the lettersh I have written on the board.'

Aldrin sat down at a free desk next to Sisely, while Harry sat down at the desk in front of him. Aldrin stared at the board. On it, there was an **A**, an **E**, a **K**, an **L**, an **M**, an **R**, an **S** and a **Y**.

'Did you say you wanted us to write down the letters?' Harry asked.

It seemed a little bit beneath them.

'That ish correct,' said Mrs Van Boxtel. 'Practishe writing each one, over and over again, with the utmosht care. Why are *you* not writing down the lettersh?'

Mrs Van Boxtel was talking to Sisely, who was sitting there with her arms folded.

'I knew the letters of the alphabet when I was still in my cot,' she told the teacher. 'What exactly are we supposed to be learning here?'

'What ish *your* name?' Mrs Van Boxtel asked.

'My name is Sisely.'

'Well, Shishely, what we are learning ish to *love* the lettersh of the alphabet.'

'To *love* the letters of the alphabet?'

'That ish correct. Now, pick up your pen and write

down the lettersh from the board.'

Aldrin did what he was told. But, in his boredom, it wasn't long before his mind began to drift. Suddenly, he was remembering the letter from the bank, with its threat of grave consequences if his dad couldn't find some money soon.

Dad had promised that he'd turn things around, but Aldrin didn't see how he could. People just weren't coming into the shop any more – not in the numbers they once did.

'A is for Arrears,' he thought as he slowly and deliberately drew the lines that made up each letter.

'E is for . . . Eviction.'

After a few minutes, Harry turned round in his seat and placed a piece of paper on Aldrin's desk. It was a picture he had sketched of a man in a black boilersuit with a brain motif on the front. He was wearing enormous red gloves, a red eye mask and red knee-high boots.

Underneath, Harry had written: *Agent Cunning! Fearless Protector of the City and its People!*

In that moment, Aldrin found himself wishing that he had superpowers. Nothing special. He didn't want X-ray vision, or the ability to fly, or even a cloak of invisibility.

All he wanted was the power to save his dad's cheesemonger's.

A FAR FROM ORDINARY NIGHT

'So, how was your first day at your new school?'
Doug asked.

He was standing behind the long refrigerated
counter of *C'est Cheese*. Aldrin was standing on the
other side, where the customers usually stood.

'It was fine,' Aldrin answered. 'Frankie is in most
of my classes. And I made a new friend – he's called
Harry Stiles.'

'Harry Styles?' said Belinda, looking up from the
celebrity gossip magazine she was reading. Belinda
was Doug's assistant. She was a stoutish woman,
around Doug's age, with brown hair, a pretty face
and a pair of sunglasses perched permanently on top
of her head. 'Has his solo career not worked out then?'

'No, not *that* Harry Styles,' said Aldrin. 'A different one.'

'Oh,' Belinda said disappointedly, then she returned to her magazine.

'So, how was business today?' Aldrin asked. 'Did you have many customers?'

'Oh, a few,' Doug said breezily.

'A few isn't a number,' Aldrin pointed out. 'Dad, tell me the truth.'

'Not many,' he admitted. 'But then Monday is always a slow day, isn't it?'

'Every day is a slow day,' Aldrin said sadly. 'How are you going to repay all the money we owe when no one is buying cheese?'

'I told you not to worry about that,' Doug said, then he changed the subject. 'What about your teachers? What are they like?'

'They're mostly all right,' said Aldrin. 'Except for my English teacher, Mrs Van Boxtel. I think she might be a crazy person.'

'Van Boxtel?' Doug said. 'What kind of a name is that when it's at home?'

'It's Dutch.'

'Hey, do you know what else is Dutch? Gouda. And I

got a fresh half-wheel of it this morning. It's five years old! Shall I cut some for you?'

'Definitely!' Aldrin said, his face brightening.

Gouda was another one of his all-time favourite cheeses. It came coated in yellow or bright red wax to help preserve it. Inside, it was sort of yellowy-orange in colour with a slightly crunchy bite to it.

Doug took the half-wheel down from the shelf and brought it over to the cutting block. Attached to the block was a steel wire with a wooden handle on the end, which was used for slicing cleanly through hard cheeses. Doug brought the wire down on the wheel, cutting off a triangular-shaped wedge like a piece of birthday cake. From that, he cut off a thinner slice and handed it to his son.

Aldrin bit into it.

'Whoa!' he exclaimed. 'It's very caramelly, isn't it?'

'That one's made with goat's milk,' Doug told him. 'Adds an extra layer of complexity to the flavour, doesn't it?'

'Definitely,' Aldrin agreed. 'Could you give me some for later?'

'Oh, I don't know,' Doug said. 'Your mum wouldn't

have approved. "No cheese before bedtime −" I can hear her saying it − "or he'll have nightmares.'"

'But you always said that was an old wives' tale,' Aldrin reminded him. '**Come on − please, Dad!**'

'OK,' Doug said. 'As long as it doesn't become a habit,' and he cut off three more slices and wrapped them in some wax paper. Aldrin popped them into the pocket of his school blazer for later.

While this was happening, an elderly man shuffled into the shop and up to the counter. Belinda barely looked up from her celebrity gossip magazine.

'We're closed,' she snapped.

The man make a big show of checking his watch. 'Er, not quite yet,' he said. 'Aren't you open until six?'

Belinda put down her magazine and rolled her eyes.

'What do you want?' she asked.

Belinda was famous for being the **Laziest** and **Most Unhelpful Shop Assistant in the Area** and **Maybe Even the Entire Country**.

Cynthia's motto in business had been: *Never serve a customer without a chat!*

Belinda's was: **Never serve a customer without a pained sigh, a roll of the eyes, or a rueful shake of the head − or, if the mood really takes you, all three.**

And while Cynthia had done her best to improve Belinda's customer-service skills, Belinda had fallen back to her old habits since she'd died.

'Could I have some goat's cheese?' the man enquired.

'What kind?' Belinda asked. 'There's loads of different kinds – unfortunately.'

'That one over there looks rather nice,' the man said. 'The Humboldt Fog. Could I have about ten ounces of that, please?'

Belinda **huffed**.

'You had to go and pick the one that's furthest away from me, didn't you?' she said. 'You know I'm going to have to stand up now and walk over there to get it?'

While Doug liked Belinda, he wasn't so well off for customers that he could afford to have them take their business elsewhere. They'd had only four people in the shop all day – and one of those was just looking for change for the parking meter.

'Er, Belinda,' he said, 'perhaps you might allow *me* to serve this gentleman?'

'I knew he were trouble the second he walked in,' she said bluntly.

'You can go home if you like, Belinda. See you tomorrow, yes?'

Belinda **sighed** and rolled her eyes, removed her apron, sighed again, shook her head, rolled her eyes again, sighed one final time, then headed for the door.

'I'm sorry about that,' Doug said to the man. 'Now, did I hear you ask for some Humboldt Fog?'

'Is it good?' the man wondered.

'Oh, it's delicious,' Doug assured him, cutting off a piece of the white, crumbly cheese for him to sample. 'It was actually a favourite of my late wife's. It's quite bloomy.'

The man tried it.

'Oh, that's absolutely divine,' he said. 'Yes, I'll take ten ounces.'

Doug cut off a larger piece and dropped it on to the scales. It weighed twelve ounces.

'It's a bit over,' Doug said, 'but I'll let you have it for the price of ten. I'll also let you into a little secret. I've always found that little cubes of crystallized ginger go wonderfully well with goat's cheese.'

'Thank you,' the man said, handing over the money. 'You've been very helpful indeed,' then he shuffled out of the shop.

Doug turned the sign on the door to **'CLOSED'**, then he and Aldrin set about the job of sweeping the shelves and wrapping up all of the cheeses for the night. This, Aldrin had to admit, was not as much fun as it once had been. They worked mostly in silence now. Once or twice, Aldrin would notice his dad staring off into the distance, and he knew that he was missing Mum.

When the work was completed, they went upstairs to the flat for what Aldrin presumed was going to be just another ordinary night.

But this night would turn out to be **FAR** from ordinary!

Aldrin ate his dinner, did his homework and watched some TV with Doug, before his eyes began to feel heavy and he decided it was time for bed. They went through the same little comic routine they performed every night.

'*Sweet dreams* –' Doug said.

'**– are made of cheese,**' Aldrin replied.

'*Who am I* –'

'**– to diss a Brie?**'

It was based on an old pop song that Doug liked called 'Sweet Dreams (Are Made of This)' by a group called the Eurythmics.

'Night, son.'

'Night, Dad.'

It was just as he was nodding off that Aldrin remembered the delicious Gouda that Doug had given him for his supper. He jumped out of bed and retrieved it from his blazer pocket. Then he got back under the covers, peeled open the wax paper and started to eat.

As he did so, he thought about his first day at St Martin's. He thought about his new friend, Harry, and the picture of Agent Cunning that he'd drawn for him, which Aldrin had pinned to the noticeboard above his study desk. He thought about crazy Mrs Van Boxtel and Sisely daring to question the wisdom of her teaching methods. He thought about Frankie and his story about being a spy parachuted behind enemy lines.

He chewed the Gouda until it was just a sweet-tasting ball of mush in his mouth . . .

And *very quickly* . . .

without even realizing . . .

that it was happening . . .

his eyes started to feel . . .

very,

very

heavy . . .

And then . . .

he was suddenly . . .

out

for

the . . .

5.

A NIGHTMARE

Aldrin found himself walking through a dense forest. It was night-time and the only sounds he could hear were the low **chirr**_{**up**} of insects, the **hoot** of an owl and the **snap** of twigs beneath his feet.

He walked for what felt like twenty minutes across a clearing, under the dim, milky light thrown down by the moon. Then he stopped and sat down on a fallen tree. And that was when he heard it. It was faint and seemed to come from the far distance.

It was the sound of a boy . . . crying for **help!**

Aldrin jumped to his feet. He listened closely. The sound was coming from the direction from which he'd come. He took off, retracing his steps, as fast as his feet would carry him.

After a few minutes of running, he heard the screams again – louder this time and more urgent.

'**HELP!**' a boy's voice yelled. '**HEEELLLPPP!**'

Aldrin followed the sound through prickly undergrowth that cut his hands and thwacked painfully against his face.

He was very close now:

'**SOMEBODY! PLEASE HELP ME!**'

He pulled aside a bush and found himself in a small clearing. Straight in front of him was a large tree. The cries for help were coming from high in its upper branches.

'**HEEELLLPPP! HEEELLLPPP!**'

Aldrin squinted upwards. A hundred feet above him, he could just make out the outline of a figure standing on a branch and clinging to the trunk of the tree. It looked like . . .

Frankie Fidderer?

Aldrin cupped his hands round his mouth and shouted: '**FRANKIE? CAN YOU HEAR ME?**'

Frankie looked down at the ground.

'**ALDRIN?**' he called back, sounding surprised. '**WHAT ARE YOU DOING HERE?**'

'**I'M GOING TO TRY TO HELP YOU!**' Aldrin said.

'**I'M GOING TO FALL!**' Frankie told him.

'YOU'RE NOT GOING TO FALL, FRANKIE! I'M COMING TO GET YOU!'

Aldrin studied the tree for a moment. He was almost certain that he could see a route up. He took a firm hold of one of the lower branches and he pulled himself up on to it, then he reached for the limb immediately above it, and suddenly he was clambering his way up the tree towards his terrified friend.

It was then that Aldrin heard a low rumble that sounded like distant drums. A wind started to blow. Very quickly, it grew in strength and shook the tree to its roots.

Aldrin quickened his pace.

He was about halfway up now.

He looked up and saw that the branch on which Frankie was standing was swaying violently under the force of the wind.

'IT'S GOING TO SNAP!' Frankie cried.

'JUST HANG ON!' Aldrin shouted. **'I'M COMING FOR YOU, FRANKIE!'**

Aldrin knew he had no time to waste. He couldn't think about how far he was from the ground, or the raging wind that was trying to send him back down there. He kept on climbing.

Moments later, he had almost reached his friend. He grabbed hold of the final branch, the one on which Frankie stood, still desperately hugging the trunk of the tree. As he pulled himself up on to it, he heard the ominous sound of wood splitting.

Frankie turned and looked at him.

'THE BRANCH IS GOING TO BREAK!' he said, still shouting to make himself heard over the yowling wind.

'IT'S GOING TO BE OK!' Aldrin said. **'IT'S JUST A BAD DREAM, THAT'S ALL!'**

Aldrin walked along the branch towards his friend. He could feel it threatening to come away from the trunk under their combined weight. Aldrin could see that Frankie was trembling.

'IT'S BREAKING!' Frankie shouted. **'WHAT ARE WE GOING TO DO?'**

'WE'RE GOING TO JUMP!' Aldrin told him.

'JUMP?' Frankie said, shocked. **'ARE YOU MAD? THE FALL WILL KILL US!'**

'IT'S JUST A NIGHTMARE I'M HAVING!' Aldrin pointed out. **'I CAN DECIDE HOW IT ENDS!'**

'I'M NOT JUMPING!' Frankie said, not even daring to look down.

'I'M MAKING YOU A PROMISE, FRANKIE! NONE

OF THIS IS REAL! HERE, GRAB MY HAND!'

The branch bucked beneath their feet. It was seconds from snapping off completely. In desperation, Frankie let go of the tree trunk and he took Aldrin's hand.

'ON THE COUNT OF THREE,' Aldrin said. 'ONE . . .'

Frankie shut his eyes.

'TWO . . .' Aldrin continued the count.

'WE'RE GOING TO HIT THE GROUND,' Frankie said, 'AND GO SPLAT!'

'THREE!' Aldrin shouted.

They leaped from the branch at the very moment they felt it give way beneath their feet. They heard it go crashing towards the forest floor and land with a deafening **crack**.

A second or two later, Aldrin tapped Frankie on the shoulder.

'It's safe to open your eyes now,' he told him.

Slowly and nervously, Frankie pulled his eyelids apart. He looked around him. His expression quickly changed from fear to wonder. They were standing in a large wicker basket. Above their heads was a huge red-and-yellow-striped balloon.

'We're . . . we're in a hot-air balloon!' Frankie said.

'I know!' Aldrin laughed.

Frankie peered over the edge of the basket. He could see the tree below him.

'How . . . how did you do that?' Frankie asked.

'I just thought about a hot-air balloon,' Aldrin said, 'and one appeared.'

'What, just like that?'

'It was just a bad dream, Frankie, that's all.'

The wind lifted them upwards until they were above the clouds and all was quiet and peaceful.

'A bad dream,' Frankie repeated.

'Exactly,' Aldrin said.

Then, with a sudden start, Aldrin opened his eyes and found himself lying in the darkness of his bedroom. His heart was beating hard and his mouth and throat were dry. He was soaked in sweat, yet shivering with the cold. And his head was pounding.

He sat up in the bed.

What a weird, WEIRD dream, he thought.

Perhaps his mother was right after all about eating cheese before bedtime.

6

'WHO IS THAT BOY?'

From the plush comfort of his secret lair, Habeas Grusselvart was watching.

Habeas Grusselvart was **ALWAYS** watching.

A tall, powerfully built giant of a man, with a pale complexion, a wild mane of black, curly hair, hooded eyes, a crooked nose and dark sideburns that ran down to his chin, Habeas was a picture of pure, hard-hearted evil. He wore a long black coat, even when he was indoors, buttoned right up to his neck, with the collar standing up, and everything about him was cold, including the breath that emerged from between his thin blue lips.

This, as it happened, was *his* happy place – standing proudly in front of his **Wall of Torment**,

with its hundreds upon hundreds of TV screens, each one relaying live footage from some of the millions upon millions of horrifying nightmares that he had created.

He could see little Jada Wilmot from Albert Road, who at that precise moment was dreaming that her bedroom floor was crawling . . . with rats!

He could see young Liam Ramsey from Cedar Court, who was being chased through a haunted house by an evil-looking ventriloquist's dummy!

And he could see poor, unfortunate Kofi Moore from Ashlawn Park, whose entire body, from his head down to his toes, was covered in nasty, stinging wasps!

Night after night, he watched these ghastly dreams unfold, and he never grew tired of them. To see children, as well as grown-ups, experiencing genuine, toe-curling, teeth-chattering terror while they slept filled Habeas with warm, fuzzy feelings of joy.

'When people are afraid,' he liked to say, 'you can do absolutely anything.'

Beddy Byes stepped into the office, partially blocking Habeas's view of the Wall of Torment. Thin like a broom handle, with dark, slicked-back hair and black horn-rimmed glasses set upon a large nose, and dressed in a dark suit, with a red bow-tie, Beddy Byes was every inch the dutiful personal assistant.

'Good news, Your Lordshipfulness,' he said. 'Another twenty cheese shops closed in England this week.'

'Twenty?' Habeas chuckled. 'Oh, that *is* good news.'

'Internationally, cheese consumption is down fifty per cent on this time last year. Even in France, Ireland, Italy and the Netherlands – countries that are famous for their cheesemaking – people are eating less than at any time in history.'

'Because of the nightmares!' Habeas declared.

'The data would most certainly support that view,' said Beddy Byes.

'**Excellent! EXCELLENT!**'

'But I decided to save the best news until last, Oh Great and – dare I say it? – Fragrant-smelling One!'

'What is it? Spit it out!'

'The London Festival of Cheese . . . has been cancelled this year!'

'Cancelled?' Habeas repeated, a smile erupting across his cruel face.

The London Festival of Cheese was the oldest and once the biggest cheese festival in the entire world.

'It seems there just isn't the same appetite for it any more,' Beddy Byes told him. 'According to all the indicators, cheesemaking is now a dying trade. And the once-famous cheese festival is going to be replaced by – wait for it – the London Festival of Strawberries!'

'Strawberries?' Habeas said, before summoning up an evil, hacking laugh. 'Oh, that's absolutely wonderful! **WONDERFUL!** Everything is going exactly the way I –'

But then Habeas forgot what he was about to say. Because, suddenly, he spotted something that chilled him to the marrow.

'Who is that boy?' he asked.

'Which boy?' wondered Beddy Byes.

He followed Habeas Grusselvart's line of vision to one of the hundreds upon hundreds of TV screens.

'*That* boy!' said Habeas. 'Climbing up that tree.'

Beddy Byes narrowed his eyes. 'He shouldn't be there,' he said.

'I know he shouldn't be there!' Habeas growled. 'So what on earth is he doing in Frankie Fidderer's nightmare?'

'It seems he's attempting . . . to rescue him!'

They both watched in appalled silence as the mystery boy, apparently undeterred by the furious, howling wind, climbed all the way to the top of the tree. Instantly, Habeas discovered the source of the unease that he'd been feeling over the past few days.

'He's one of *them*,' he said, his voice dripping with disgust.

'He can't possibly be,' Beddy Byes replied. 'He's . . . just a boy.'

'**AND I'M TELLING YOU**,' Habeas fumed, '**HE IS ONE OF *THEM*!**'

They watched wide-eyed as the screen was suddenly filled with a red-and-yellow-striped hot-air balloon. Frankie and his unknown rescuer stood in the basket, looking around them, as the balloon climbed higher and higher until it rose above the storm.

And that was when Habeas lost control completely. '**NOOOOOOOOOOOO!!!!!!!!!!!!!**' he screamed.

He tipped over his desk, spilling everything on to the floor. Then, in a blind fury, he lifted his office chair above his head and he threw it at the Wall of Torment. The TV screen on which Frankie's nightmare was being transmitted shattered in an explosion of sparks. Habeas kicked over every piece of furniture in the room. He pulled pictures from the walls and smashed them to the ground. He picked up his computer monitor and threw it through the window.

Beddy Byes backed out of the office. He knew better than to stick around to witness one of his boss's famous rages.

From outside, he could hear the sounds of glass breaking and wood splintering and Habeas banging his head on the wall and screaming over and over again,

'NO! NO! NO! NO! NO! NO! NO! NO!'

7

IMPOSSIBLE

Aldrin and his classmates couldn't believe what Mrs Van Boxtel was asking them to do. They were standing outside, in front of the whitewashed gable wall of the main school building, and she had handed Frankie a can of red spray paint.

'You want us to . . . write on the wall?' Frankie stuttered.

'Yesh,' Mrs Van Boxtel confirmed, 'that ish absholutely correct. And make shure to shake the can before you shpray, yesh?'

'But that's vandalism,' Sisely pointed out.

'Cavemen expreshed themshelves by writing on wallsh,' Mrs Van Boxtel told her, 'long before paper wash even invented.'

Harry gave Aldrin a sideways look.

'She's stark raving **MAD**,' he told him out of the corner of his mouth.

'I know,' Aldrin replied.

Frankie shook the can.

'And you're absolutely sure that I won't get into trouble?' he asked.

'I am shimply trying to give you a love of the language,' Mrs Van Boxtel said. 'And for ush to love the language, we musht firsht learn to love all the lettersh of the language. Sho I want you to write shomething on the wall – big and proud, yesh?'

'What do you want me to write?' Frankie asked.

'Anything you want,' Mrs Van Boxtel told him.

'Can I write Chelsea?'

'Chelshea?'

'Yeah, they're my favourite football team. My dad had season tickets when we lived in London.'

'OK, sho what ish the firsht letter of Chelshea?'

'It's a C.'

'A shee! That ish correct! And shee ish a *beautiful*, *BEAUTIFUL* letter!'

Frankie aimed the nozzle of the spray can at the wall and started to trace the wide, circular arc of a **C**.

'**SHTOP!**' Mrs Van Boxtel shouted suddenly. 'What ish thish?'

'Er, it's a C,' Frankie explained.

'Well, it might well be a shee, but I can hardly *shee* it at all. You musht **EMBRASHE** each letter! Do it **BIGGER**, yesh?'

'How big?' Frankie asked.

It was already *pretty* big as it was – about the size of Frankie's head.

'For me,' she said, 'alwaysh in life, it ish besht to aim ash high ash you can posshibly reach – yesh?' and she stood on the tips of her toes and stretched her hand into the air.

So Frankie faced the wall again. This time, he reached up as high as he could, then he pressed down on the button.

'THAT ISH IT!' shouted Mrs Van Boxtel. '**BIG! BIG! BIG!**'

With a long, wide sweep of his arm, Frankie sprayed the top half of a C on the wall. Next, he got down on his knees and sprayed the bottom half, the curve stretching all the way down to the ground. He stood up and took a step backwards to admire his handiwork.

The C was even taller than him!

'Thish ish exshellent!' said Mrs Van Boxtel, taking the spray can from him. 'Now which one of you would like to paint the **H**?'

'Me!' said Harry, thrusting his hand in the air.

Mrs Van Boxtel handed the can to him and Harry pushed his glasses up on his nose with his finger. He was about to start the letter when he heard a voice say:

'What in the name of GOD are you doing?'

It was Mr Maskell, the principal.

'I am teaching,' Mrs Van Boxtel replied. 'And you, Mishter Mashkell, are interrupting my clash.'

'Teaching what?' Mr Maskell said. 'How to daub graffiti all over school property? I'll not stand for this!'

Harry fished out his asthma inhaler and took two nervous blasts from it.

'Mishter Mashkell,' Mrs Van Boxtel said, 'you knew when I first came to thish shchool that my teaching methodsh were – how to shay? – a little bit different, yesh?'

'Yes,' Mr Maskell replied, 'but I will not stand idly by while you encourage students to deface school property!'

'It ish jusht a wall, Mishter Mashkell. You know, human beingsh shtarted off writing on wallsh – for

60

hundredsh of thoushandsh of yearsh, that ish how our language developed.'

'Yes, but then we invented paper. And we have lots of it here in the school.'

'*Thish* ish how *I* teach, Mishter Mashkell. Now, can you pleashe leave me to do my job?'

The principal shook his head in exasperation.

'I'm going to speak to Maintenance,' he said, his jowls wobbling, 'and demand that they paint over it the instant this class is finished!'

Then he stormed off.

'Now, Harry,' said Mrs Van Boxtel, 'do the **H** – and make shure you do it nishe and big!'

Harry put away his asthma inhaler, aimed the spray can at the wall and painted an enormous **H**.

Edward Moss did the **E**.

Luke Lynn did the the **L**.

Stephanie Ryan did the **S**.

Emeka Wright did the **E**.

And, fittingly, Aldrin did the **A** at the end.

When the class finished, Aldrin walked back indoors with Harry, Frankie and Sisely.

'That was the best English class **EVER!**' Harry declared happily.

But Sisely disagreed.

'We should be learning about the rules of grammar and punctuation,' she huffed, 'not defacing school property.'

It was at that moment that Frankie suddenly remembered something.

'Here,' he said. 'I had a nightmare last night, Aldrin – and you were in it!'

'OK, that's weird,' Aldrin replied, 'because *you* were in *my* nightmare as well!'

'Was I?'

'Yeah, I dreamt that you were stuck up a really, really high tree.'

Frankie stopped. He stared at Aldrin, his mouth forming a perfect **O**.

'You didn't,' he said.

'I did,' Aldrin told him. 'And I climbed up the tree to save you. But then this really high wind started blowing and shaking the tree. And the branch was about to snap. But then – and this is the best bit – we just jumped. But instead of falling, we suddenly found ourselves in a –'

'– hot-air balloon!'

'Yeah! How did you know that?'

'Because I dreamt exactly the same thing!'

Sisely whirled round.

'That's impossible,' she said.

'It's not impossible,' Frankie insisted. 'I have that nightmare all the time. Except the bit with the hot-air balloon. That was new.'

'What colour was the balloon in your dream?' Aldrin asked.

'Let me think,' Frankie said. 'Yeah, it was sort of stripy. It was red and yellow!'

'Red and yellow! Same as mine!'

'I'm sorry,' Sisely said, 'but there is absolutely **NO WAY** in the **WORLD** that two people could have exactly the same dream on exactly the same night. What you're saying just isn't credible.'

'Then how would *you* explain it?' Harry asked.

'Easy,' Sisely said. 'Frankie's telling lies – again!'

'I ain't lying!' Frankie said. 'How come I knew about the balloon then? I even knew the colour!'

'You guessed,' Sisely told him.

'No, I didn't! I'm telling the truth, Aldrin! I swear!'

Aldrin didn't know what to think. Did they, by some fantastical, fifty-gazillion-to-one coincidence, just happen to dream the same thing on exactly the same night?

No, Sisely was right. It seemed too far-fetched to be believable.

So Frankie *was* lying. He guessed that there was a hot-air balloon involved – *and* he guessed the colour.

Unless, Aldrin thought, *there is a third explanation.*

8

A MAD IDEA

PL**IN**K ... PL**O**NK ... PL**III**N**N**K ... P**L**O**N**K ...
P**L**O**O**O**N**NN**K** ... P**L**I**N**K ...

It was nine o'clock that night, and Aldrin was playing
the piano, with Silas sitting on top of his head.

Silas was a plump green American bullfrog, with
giant, bulbous eyes, a wide mouth that
turned upwards at each end to form
a smile, and a round lump in his
throat that bobbed up and down
and made it look like he was
permanently trying to swallow
a tennis ball.

And the top of Aldrin's head
was *his* happy place.

Aldrin had finished his homework and helped Doug to clean the shop and wrap all the cheeses for the night. And now he and Silas were enjoying a moment to themselves – creating their own unique brand of music.

PLINK . . . PLINK . . . PLINK . . . PLINK . . . PLUUUNNNK . . . PLUNK . . . PLUUUNK . . .

While Aldrin jabbed randomly at the keys, Silas accompanied him on vocals:

RRRIBBIT . . . RRRIBBIT . . . RRRIBBIT . . .

Aldrin enjoyed playing the piano, even if *playing* was too generous a word for what he actually did to it. It would be fair to say that he was far from naturally gifted. When his last piano teacher, Miss Bennett, quit, she told Doug: 'Your son has no ear for rhythm, melody, harmony, form or timbre! He is the most musically deaf child I have ever met in forty years of teaching the piano.'

And yet Aldrin still loved to sit in front of it and tinkle those ivories – especially when he was trying to figure something out.

PLIINNNK . . . PLUNK . . . PLUUUNK . . . PLINK . . .

RRRIBBIT . . . RRRIBBIT . . . RRRIBBIT . . .

Whenever Doug heard the sound of Aldrin murdering

a tune on the piano, he knew there was something on his mind. Suddenly, he was standing in the doorway of the living room.

'Is that "*Für Elise*",' he asked, 'by Beethoven?'

'No, it's "Love Me Like You Do",' Aldrin told him, 'by Ellie Goulding.'

pLu**NK** . . . P**L**i**I**in**K** . . . Pl**O**nk . . .

*RRRI*bb*It* . . . *rrribbit* . . . *RRRibbIt* . . .

'Oh, yes,' Doug said weakly. 'I thought I recognized it. You seemed miles away just then. You're not still worried about that letter from the bank, are you?'

Aldrin stopped hitting the keys.

'No,' he said. 'It's not that.'

'What's on your mind then?'

'Dad, do you think it's possible for two people to have exactly the same dream at exactly the same time?'

'The *same* dream? I would have thought it was highly unlikely, Aldrin.'

'That's what Sisely said.'

'Who's Sisely?'

'Oh, she's a girl in my class. She's really clever.'

'Why are you asking about dreams anyway?'

'Well, the thing is, you see, I had this sort of nightmare last night.'

'I know what your mother would say,' Doug told him. 'She'd say it was my fault for letting you eat that Gouda before you went to sleep.'

'It wasn't *that* bad a nightmare, Dad,' Aldrin assured him. 'It's just that, well, this friend of mine, who was *in* my nightmare, he said he dreamt exactly the same thing as I did.'

'This friend of yours – it wouldn't happen to be Frankie Fidderer, would it?'

'It *was* Frankie, yeah.'

'Didn't he tell you once that he played football for Real Madrid?'

'No, it was Barcelona.'

'Barcelona! That was it! And Lionel Messi said he was the best player he'd ever played with. He does tell a lot of whoppers, Aldrin.'

'I suppose he does.'

Doug yawned.

RRRIBBIT! RRRIBBIT! RRRIBBIT!

'No,' Aldrin told Silas. 'I think we've kept Dad awake long enough with our racket.'

Aldrin noticed the dark circles under his dad's eyes. The poor man hadn't had a proper night's sleep since Cynthia died.

'Yeah, I think I'm going to bed,' Doug announced.

'Me too,' Aldrin replied, removing Silas from the top of his head and standing up.

'***Sweet dreams –***' Doug said.

'**– are made of cheese,**' Aldrin smiled.

'***Who am I –***'

'**– to diss a Brie?**'

'Night, son.'

'Night, Dad.'

Aldrin had been asleep for about an hour when he was awoken by the sound of shouting coming through the wall. Doug was having a nightmare of his own.

'HELP ME!' he was calling out. **'HELP ME! HELP ME!'**

'I wonder . . .' Aldrin said to himself.

An idea had been forming in his head ever since his conversation with Frankie that morning. On the face of it, it seemed like a really mad idea – so much so that he didn't dare say it out loud, not to his friends, and certainly not to his dad.

Even so, he couldn't get it out of his mind.

The idea was this: what if, by some magical means that he didn't quite understand yet, Aldrin had somehow managed to stumble into his friend's dream?

Yes, it seemed insane. But it was Frankie who first mentioned the hot-air balloon, not him – *and* he knew the colour. So maybe he *was* telling the truth.

And if Sisely was right – that two people having exactly the same dream on exactly the same night was too big a coincidence to be believed – then Aldrin had to consider a third possible explanation . . .

That something strange had happened – maybe even something . . . supernatural?

But if he did somehow access his friend's dream, then how did he do it? he wondered.

In his mind, he retraced the events of last night. The only thing he'd done that was out of the ordinary was eat cheese just before he fell asleep.

So was that *it?* he thought.

Could it really have been the Gouda? And if that was the secret key that allowed him to enter Frankie's nightmare, could he use it to help his dad?

One way or the other, Aldrin decided, he had to know the truth.

He threw back his duvet, climbed out of bed and stepped into his slippers. As softly and as quietly as he could, he tiptoed across the landing and down the stairs. He turned the key and pushed the heavy steel door that opened out into the shop. A cold blast of air hit him immediately and sent a shiver through his body.

He took the piece of Gouda that was shaped like a slice of birthday cake down from the wooden shelf and brought it over to the cutting block. He removed the shrink-wrap, then brought the wire down on it, cutting himself off three very generous slices.

He shivered again. It was very chilly standing in the shop in just his pyjamas.

He rewrapped what was left of the cheese and returned it to the shelf. Then he took the three slices and returned to his bedroom.

Through the wall, he could still hear his dad calling out: **'HELP! HELP! HELP ME!'**

Aldrin slipped under the covers again. Then he did exactly what he'd done the night before. He bit into the cheese, except this time, as he ate it, he thought about his dad. He pictured him in his mind's eye – his kindly face, his rosy cheeks and his giant walrus moustache that sometimes had crumbs of Emmental, or Pecorino, or Grana Padano in it.

He chewed the Gouda until it was just a honey-tasting ball of mush in his mouth.

And *very quickly* . . .

without even realizing . . .

that it was happening . . .

his eyes **started to feel** . . .

very,

very

heavy . . .

And then . . .

he was suddenly . . .

out

for

the . . .

9

A BIG, SHARP MEAT CLEAVER

Aldrin found himself in the kitchen of a restaurant. There was a lot of noise and a lot of smells and a lot of steam. Men and women wearing chef's uniforms were running around and bumping into each other and shouting in French accents:

'What do you mean, ze sauce is not ready? Why **ISN'T** ze sauce ready?'

And:

'You 'ave burned ze steak, you **IDIOT!**'

In the midst of this racket, he couldn't hear his father's voice at all.

A waitress walked into the kitchen and said, 'I need three chicken, two duck and one risotto for table five!'

This dream felt less real than last night's nightmare.

The colours, he noticed, were less vibrant, the sound more muffled. Then, slowly, he became aware that he was watching the scene through a pane of glass. He looked all around him. He seemed to be standing in some kind of fish tank with no water in it.

And that was when he heard a croak behind him:

RRRIBBIT . . .

He spun round. There was a giant frog standing there. And he recognized his face immediately.

'Silas?' he tried to say.

But it came out of his mouth as, **'RRRIBBIT . . .'**

'OK,' Aldrin said. 'This is *all* very weird.'

But it was about to get a whole lot weirder.

It was then that Aldrin looked down – and noticed that his arms were green!

His hands looked strange as well. He held them up in front of his face. He had only four fingers on each one. And there was webbing in between them. It was almost as if . . .

Hold on, Aldrin thought. *Am I a –?*

But he didn't get the chance to finish his thought.

A waiter stuck his head round the door of the kitchen and shouted, 'Ze frog legs. Table eight, *s'il vous plaît!*'

Aldrin stared through the glass in horror as a chef came walking towards the tank – holding the biggest, sharpest meat cleaver he had ever seen.

Aldrin turned round and looked at Silas. The poor frog was terrified.

RRRIBBIT…RRRIBBIT…RRRIBBIT…

Suddenly, the ceiling disappeared from above them and a large hand reached into the tank. It felt around the base for a few seconds. Aldrin heard a long croak . . .

RRRRRRIIIBBBBBBBBBIIIIIIIITTTTTTT . . .

. . . then he watched Silas spring into the air and over the edge of the tank.

The chef let out a scream.

'AAARGGHHH!!!'

Without even thinking about it, Aldrin leaped over the edge of the tank as well.

The chef let out a second scream.

'AAARGGHHH!!!'

Aldrin landed on a large wooden table. He could see Silas just in front of him, leaping off it and on to the tiled floor. He decided to follow his green amphibian friend.

There was now a loud commotion in the kitchen. People were screaming and shouting: **'ZERE ARE TWO FROGS LOOSE IN ZE KITCHEN! ZERE ARE TWO FROGS LOOSE!'**

And that was when Aldrin became **VERY** scared – because heavy feet started to hit the floor beside him, behind him and in front of him. The kitchen staff . . . were trying to **STAMP** on them!

Aldrin watched as Silas, with a sudden explosion of energy . . .

RRRRRRIIIBBBBBBBBBBBIIIIIIIITTTTTTT . . .

. . . sprang from the floor and sailed through the air, out through an open window.

But while Aldrin paused to witness his friend's heroic leap to freedom, a giant hand suddenly surrounded him, its fingers squeezing his little body tightly. He felt himself being lifted from the floor, then he was slammed down hard, on his back, on to a wooden chopping board.

A chef held him down with one hand. In the other

hand, Aldrin noticed, was that meat cleaver! Aldrin gulped. The chef grinned at him and said:

'Ze frog legs – table eight?'

Aldrin started kicking his legs wildly, trying his best to break free. But it was no use. The chef was too strong. He lifted the cleaver. The sharp metal edge glinted above Aldrin like the blade of a guillotine.

Aldrin closed his eyes as the chef brought the cleaver down hard.

Aldrin screamed.
'AAARRRGGGHHH!!!'

But, when he opened his eyes again, he was relieved to discover that he was back in his bedroom.

His head ached and his pyjamas were drenched in sweat. His heart was beating fast and his breathing was ragged, like he'd just been running.

He lay there for several minutes, staring at his vintage *Fromages de France* poster, in a state of complete and utter bewilderment, until two things became clear to him . . .

He had to stop eating cheese before he went to sleep at night. And he was an **IDIOT** to believe he had some kind of supernatural power.

10

A WORLD OF MAGIC

'Today,' said Mrs Van Boxtel, 'we are going to shtart working on a project that you will enjoy **VERY** much!'

'Are we going to be spray-painting the names of our favourite football teams on the school wall again?' Frankie asked.

'No. I think that Mishter Mashkell wash not sho happy with me after the lasht time. Perhapsh we will wait a few weeksh before we do thish again, yesh?'

Everyone laughed.

'So what *is* this project?' asked Harry.

'Each of you,' she said, 'ish going to write a short shtory – then, in a few weeksh, we will publish them all in a book!'

A book! That *was* exciting, Aldrin thought –

79

even though it was her next line that really grabbed everyone's interest.

'Alsho,' she said, 'there will be a prizhe of fifty poundsh for the besht shtory.'

You could hear the excitement ripple through the whole class.

'Fifty quid?' Frankie said. 'Did she really just say fifty quid?'

'What kind of stories should they be?' Aldrin asked.

'That,' Mrs Van Boxtel replied, 'ish entirely up to you. All I want ish for you to engage your imagination.'

'Could it be a *true* story,' Frankie asked, 'about my double life as a spy, for instance – parachuting behind enemy lines, that sort of thing?'

'Yesh,' said Mrs Van Boxtel. 'True shtoriesh are often the mosht thrilling shtoriesh!'

'You're telling me!' Frankie replied. 'I've seen a few things in me time. Although I'll obviously have to get permission from MI5 if I want to write about them – Official Secrets Act and all that.'

'Could the story be a comic strip?' Harry asked, at the same time pushing his glasses up on his nose. 'With drawings?'

'Ash long ash there are alsho lotsh of words in it,'

said Mrs Van Boxtel, 'made up of all the beautiful, beautiful lettersh we have practised – then absholutely, Harry, yesh!'

Everyone was excited about the prospect of winning the fifty-pound prize – everyone, that is, except Sisely.

'This is such a waste of time,' she said to Aldrin, in a voice loud enough for Mrs Van Boxtel to hear. 'We come to school to learn, not to write silly stories and paint graffiti on the walls.'

'I am eshpeshially looking forward to *your* shtory,' the teacher said.

When the class was finished, all the children stood up and headed for the door. As he was passing Mrs Van Boxtel's desk, Aldrin couldn't help but notice a paper bag with a familiar logo on the side.

'*C'est Cheese!*' he said out loud.

'I'm shorry?' said Mrs Van Boxtel.

He stopped.

'I just noticed your lunch on the desk there,' he said. 'That's actually my dad's cheese shop.'

Sisely was standing behind him.

'*C'est Cheese* is a pun,' she told the teacher, 'meaning a joke that plays on the different possible meanings of words. In French, *C'est Cheese* means

"It's cheese". But in English, **Say cheese!** is a popular command to draw a smile from someone who's having their photograph taken.'

'Yesh, I wash aware of that, Shishely,' said Mrs Van Boxtel with an amused look on her face.

She looked at Aldrin then.

'Sho your father ish the cheeshemonger man, yesh?' she asked. 'He ish very knowledgeable about cheeshe – and alsho very helpful.'

'He absolutely loves his job,' he said.

'Hish asshisshtant ish not sho helpful, I think.'

'Belinda? No, she's not helpful at all.'

'I shay to her, "I think I would like shome cheeshe – perhapsh you can recommend shome for me?" And she shaysh to me, "Jusht pick one yourshelf – I'm reading my flipping magashine here!"'

'That sounds like our Belinda,' he chuckled. 'She's not what you would call a people person. So what did my dad recommend?'

'Aldrin, we're going to be late for our next class,' Sisely said impatiently.

'Well,' the teacher said, 'I *wash* looking for shome Camembert, but your father shaid that it ish imposshible to get theshe daysh.'

'That's true,' Aldrin told her. 'No one knows why. So what did he recommend instead?'

She opened the bag and Aldrin peered inside.

'Robiolo Bosina!' he said, instantly recognizing the white, papery rind, as well as the delicious doughy smell. 'That's actually one of my favourite Bries! I especially love its springy consistency.'

'You alsho know a lot about cheeshe,' Mrs Van Boxtel said.

'I want to be a cheesemonger when I grow up – just like my dad!'

'Perhapsh if you like cheeshe sho much,' she suggested, 'you could write your shtory about the legend of Luuk van den Hoogenband.'

'Who's Luuk van den Hoogenband?' Aldrin wondered aloud.

Dutch names, he was quickly discovering, were so much fun to say out loud!

'Luuk van den Hoogenband wash a shimple farm boy,' Mrs Van Boxtel explained with a distant look in her eyes, 'who grew up in a village near Utrecht in the Netherlandsh more than one thoushand yearsh ago. When he wash jusht a little baby, he wash taken away by the fairiesh.'

'The fairies?' Sisely asked, sounding more than a little doubtful.

'Yesh,' Mrs Van Boxtel told her, 'and he wash brought to live with a goddessh named Moorah. She fed thish little boy on nothing but cheeshe until he wash eleven yearsh old.'

'Did she have any idea what an unhealthy diet that was for a child?'

'Cheeshe wash the food of the godsh. And Moorah believed that it would give him immortality – that he would live forever!'

'With the increased risk of heart disease, as well as high cholesterol and blood pressure, I would say that was highly unlikely.'

'Hang on, Sisely,' Aldrin said. 'I want to hear what Mrs Van Boxtel has to say.'

'Then, when Luuk wash eleven yearsh old,' the teacher continued, 'he wash shent back to hish village again. But now, he dishcovered, shomething had changed – he had very, **VERY** shpecial powersh –'

'I'm sorry,' Sisely said, holding up her hands, 'I can't listen to any more of this absolute rubbish!'

'Every word of what I am shaying to you ish true,' the teacher said.

'There's no such thing as fairies, Mrs Van Boxtel. Or a goddess named Moorah. And there was never any farm boy called Luuk van den Hoogenband.'

Mrs Van Boxtel opened her desk drawer. She reached into it and took out a thick book bound in green leather. She placed it on the desk.

'Here,' she said, pushing it across to Aldrin. 'You can borrow thish book and read all about him.'

Aldrin picked it up. On the cover, in gold embossed letters, it said *Myths and Legends of the Netherlands*.

He flicked through it. It smelled of damp and all the pages were stained with mildew and frayed at the edges.

'*Myths and Legends of the Netherlands*?' Sisely said, irritation in her voice. 'I can't believe I'm wasting my time even talking about this.'

'It ish a mosht intereshting book,' Mrs Van Boxtel said. 'There ish a whole chapter about Luuk van den Hoogenband.'

'Myths and legends are words for stories that aren't true!' Sisely said. 'They're folk tales. They didn't actually happen.'

Mrs Van Boxtel smiled patiently at her.

'Shishely,' she said, 'you have a very logical mind.

And a logical mind ish a very usheful thing to have. But there are shome thingsh that cannot be exshplained logically. There ish a whole world of myshtery and magic out there, Shishely, that defiesh rational exshplanation – one that even you, with all your brainsh, would shtruggle to undershtand.'

'Thank you for the book,' Aldrin said.

Mrs Van Boxtel winked at him.

'I will shee you both tomorrow,' she said.

11

WHERE THE ODDBALLS SIT

'How are we **EVER** going to learn **ANYTHING** from that woman?' Sisely fumed. 'You know everyone is calling her Mrs Van Bonkers?'

Aldrin laughed.

'I have to say, she's really growing on me.'

It was lunchtime. They were sitting in the cafeteria at the table where they'd sat all week – the one with the wobbly leg, next to the cupboard where they kept the mops and buckets.

'I can't believe I have a teacher who LITERALLY believes in fairies,' Sisely said.

'I don't know,' Harry said, taking a bite from his sandwich. 'I think it's good to keep an open mind. Agent Cunning always says there are millions of things in the universe that are unknowable to the human mind.'

'Who's Agent Cunning?' Sisely asked.

'He's a superhero. From a comic book called *The Defenders*.'

'Yeah, this is the real world,' Sisely huffed. 'And in the real world there is a logical explanation for absolutely **EVERYTHING**.'

She went back to writing in her exercise book.

'I wonder what her story is,' Frankie said, taking a bite from an apple. 'I'm talking about Mrs Van Boxtel. Like, where did she come from?'

'The Netherlands,' Aldrin said. 'Where they make Edam. And Gouda. And Roomano.'

'No, I mean, how come she ended up here, in this school?' Frankie asked. 'And I wonder, does she have a family – like a husband and kids?'

'I'm wondering why she has that collar on her neck,' Harry said. 'She must have been in a car accident or something.'

'Well, unlike you lot,' Sisely said, looking up from her work, 'I don't find her fascinating. I just think she's a crazy person.'

'She lent me this book,' Aldrin said, holding up *Myths and Legends of the Netherlands*.

'Why?' Frankie wondered.

'She thinks I should write my story about the legend of Luuk van den Hoogenband,' Aldrin explained.

'Who's Luuk van den Hoogenband?' Harry asked. 'Luuk van den Hoogenband. Oh my God, his name is so much fun to say. Luuk van den Hoogenband.'

'I know!'

'So who is he? This Luuk van den Hoogenband?'

Aldrin recounted the story that the teacher told him.

'He was a farm boy from the Netherlands,' he said. 'When he was a baby, he was taken away by the fairies and he was raised by a goddess named, er –'

'Moorah,' Sisely reminded him, without looking up from her work. 'Even though the story is obviously a lot of nonsense.'

'Anyway,' Aldrin continued, recalling his favourite part of the story, 'while he was living with this Moorah, he ate nothing but cheese . . . for eleven years.'

'That's a bit like you, Aldrin,' Frankie laughed.

Aldrin laughed too. 'How dare you,' he said. 'I had muesli for my breakfast this morning – well, one day last week.'

It was at that moment that he lifted the lid of his lunch box, releasing the most **hideous** smell into the air. Harry and Frankie were forced to turn away from the table. Sisely covered her mouth and nose.

'What *is* that?' she asked.

'It's just a little bit of Époisses de Bourgogne,' Aldrin explained. 'It was Napoleon's favourite cheese.'

'That's one of the most **DISGUSTING** things I've ever smelled,' Harry said.

He wasn't wrong about the whiff. It is difficult to describe in words the very distinctive aroma of Époisses de Bourgogne. But imagine you went away on a round-the-world trip for a whole year. And, before you set off, you accidentally forgot to clear out the fridge and left a bag of fish guts, a head of cauliflower and a couple of dozen sprouts in there. Then you returned home, suntanned and fully rested – only to open the fridge door . . .

That's kind of what Époisses de Bourgogne smells like.

Which explains why it is forbidden to eat it on public transport in France.

'Aldrin,' Sisely told him, 'you're going to have to close that box.'

'Fine,' he said, replacing the lid. 'I'll eat it later on, over by the window.'

Harry had an idea then.

'Here, do you want to come over to my house tonight?' he asked. 'We could all work on our stories together.'

'I'd love to,' Aldrin said, 'if it's OK with your mum and dad, that is.'

'Well, it's actually just my mum,' Harry told him. 'My parents are separated.'

'Oh, I'm sorry to hear that,' Aldrin said.

Harry put his sandwich down and took a blast from his asthma inhaler.

'It's fine,' he said. 'I get to spend weekends at my dad's place. It means I've got *two* bedrooms filled with comics!'

'I'd love to come,' Frankie said, 'but I've got, er, *other* work to do.' Then he tapped the side of his nose twice with his index finger to indicate that his plans for the evening were officially classified and knowable only to those with the appropriate security clearance.

He'd probably tell them everything he got up to tomorrow anyway.

'What about you, Sisely?' Harry asked. 'Would you like to come to my house?'

'No,' she said, 'because I'm not writing a story. It's a complete waste of time. Aldrin, can you please stop wobbling the table?'

'Sorry,' Aldrin apologized. 'It's just that one leg is shorter than all the others. What's that you're writing anyway, Sisely?'

'It's my maths homework,' Sisely told him.

'Maths homework?' Aldrin repeated. 'I didn't know we had maths homework.'

'It's not for this school,' she explained. 'I have special classes in Advanced Mathematics at the university.'

'What? You go to university?' Aldrin asked.

'On Thursday evenings and Saturday mornings.'

Aldrin watched her pen move across the page at high speed. It wasn't any kind of maths he recognized. Numbers, he understood. But this involved letters and lines and shapes and symbols.

It looked incredibly complicated.

'Sisely can do any sum in the world in her head,' Frankie said.

'Is that true?' Harry asked.

Sisely shrugged like it wasn't a big deal.

'OK then,' Harry said, 'what's **707.995** plus **2.359** plus **112.575** plus **22.001** plus **757**?'

Sisely didn't even pause to think.

'It's **845.687**,' she said.

'**Wow!**' Harry exclaimed in amazement. 'That's

presuming you're right, of course.'

'She's always right,' said Frankie, who had seen her perform the trick many times for the kids on their road. 'At least ask her a difficult one – with subtraction and multiplication and division.'

'I've got one,' said Aldrin.

'Hold on,' Harry said, reaching into his schoolbag and pulling out his calculator. 'At least let me check it. OK, ready when you are, Aldrin.'

'Right,' said Aldrin. 'What's **78** times **350** divided by **11** minus **501** times **37** plus **62**?'

'It's **73,352**,' Sisely said, before Harry had managed to key the entire sum into the calculator. 'That's rounding down to the nearest decimal point.'

Five seconds later, Harry looked up.

'She's absolutely right!' he said. 'That's the most **amazing** thing I've ever seen!'

It was at that exact moment that a shadow fell across their table – and every conversation in the cafeteria seemed to stop at once.

'So,' a posh voice said, 'this is where the oddballs hang out together, is it?'

Aldrin, Harry, Frankie and Sisely all looked up. It was the boy with the blond, floppy hair who had sniggered about Mrs Van Boxtel in assembly. He was with his two friends, who, Aldrin could see now, were identical twins. They were identically tall, with identical red hair and identical underbites that made their faces look identically mean. Even the pattern of their acne seemed to match, spot for spot.

'Oddballs?' Aldrin said, repeating the word.

'You *are* oddballs,' the boy pointed out. '*He's* got no hair. *He's* got glasses and asthma. *She's* some sort of brainiac freak. And *you're* **fat**.'

The twins laughed nastily. The boy then turned his attention to Harry.

'You were supposed to meet me this morning,' he said. 'Where were you?'

'Oh, I, um, forgot,' Harry stuttered.

'What do you mean, you forgot?' the boy asked.

Aldrin stood up and stepped between them.

'I'm sorry,' he said, 'but who *are* you exactly?'

The boy laughed:

'**BA-HA-HA-HA-HA-HA-HA-HA-HA-HA-HA-HA-HA-HA!**'

Then he looked at each of his two friends in turn, like he couldn't believe Aldrin's nerve in asking such a question.

'I'm Sebastian Rees-Lane,' he said. 'I'm the school bully. And this is Hercy and that's Algernon.'

'No, *I'm* Hercy,' said Hercy, 'and *he's* Algernon.'

'Well, we're having a private conversation here,' Aldrin told them, 'so would you mind leaving us alone?'

Sebastian's eyes widened in surprise. No one EVER stood up to him like this.

'Who do you think you are?' Sebastian started to rail, but then a look of confusion suddenly passed over his face and his nose started to twitch. 'What the **DEVIL** is that smell?'

'That's my lunch,' Aldrin said.

'What are you having? A roadkill hedgehog or something?'

'I'm having cheese.'

'How can you eat something that smells like that?'

'Very easily. It tastes delicious. Now, like I said, would you mind getting lost, please?'

Aldrin watched Sebastian's face harden.

'Is there some kind of problem here?' a man's voice suddenly said.

It was Mr Maskell, doing his rounds of the cafeteria.

'No,' said Sebastian, staring at Aldrin. 'Nothing that I can't deal with . . . later.'

'Good Lord!' Mr Maskell suddenly exclaimed. 'Is someone here eating a dead animal for their lunch?'

12

FRIENDS

Aldrin had never seen a bedroom like Harry's before. It reminded him of the comic-book shop in the precinct. He had shelf upon shelf of superhero and supervillain figurines: Batman, Spider-Man, Ironman, Catwoman, Batgirl, Captain America, Harley Quinn, the Joker, Thor, Aquaman, Flash, Lex Luthor, the Incredible Hulk, the Green Lantern, the Black Widow, Hawkeye, Antman, the Thing . . .

There were almost two hundred of them, covering three entire walls of the room, from floor to ceiling.

Then there were the comic books. Aldrin counted thirty boxes of them, with all sorts of exciting titles: *The Amazing Spider-Man*, *Spawn*, *Wolverine*, *Ultimate Fallout*, *Venom*, *The New Mutants*, *Daredevil*, *The*

Savage She-Hulk, *Young Avengers*, *Black Panther*, *Mrs Marvel* . . .

'**Wow!**' Aldrin said, spinning around in wide-eyed wonder. 'You are *so* lucky to have a bedroom like this!'

'Thanks,' Harry said. 'Dad has kind of spoiled me ever since, you know, he and Mum got separated. They're getting divorced soon.'

'I'm really sorry, Harry. That must be hard.'

'It was at first,' Harry admitted. 'I suppose I've got used to it now.'

Aldrin continued staring at the figurines. He recognized the Green Arrow and Deadpool and the Penguin. And then, on the very top shelf . . .

'Agent Cunning!' Aldrin said.

He recognized him from the sketch that Harry had drawn for him.

'That's right,' Harry said. 'By day, he's just a mild-mannered gentleman's tailor – by night, he's Agent Cunning –'

They both said the next line at the same time:

'**Fearless Protector of the City and its People!**'

'He's not scared of anything!' Harry added.

Aldrin smiled.

'Harry,' he said, 'can I ask you a question?'

'Yeah, of course,' Harry said.

'Why was it that Sebastian wanted to meet you before school today?'

Harry looked away, embarrassed.

'He told me I have to meet him every morning,' Harry said, 'to hand over my lunch money.'

'Your lunch money?'

'Yeah, I bring a packed lunch,' he explained, 'but my mum gives me one pound a day for a treat – crisps, chocolate or a fizzy drink, if I want it. Sebastian says I have to give it to him. He said if I don't, there'll be consequences for me. He said he'll shove my head down the toilet.'

'Harry, you have to stand up to bullies like Sebastian. If you give him what he wants today, he'll come back tomorrow, looking for more.'

'The way you stood up to him, Aldrin – weren't you scared at all?'

'I was a bit scared,' Aldrin admitted. 'My mum told me once that the hero and the coward feel exactly the same fear – it's only what they *do* that makes them different from one another.'

'Your mum sounds **amazing**.'

'She was.'

'*Was?*'

'Yeah, she died. Last year.'

'Oh. I'm so sorry, Aldrin.'

'It's OK. It's just me and my dad now.'

'Didn't you mind that Sebastian called you fat?'

Aldrin laughed.

'I *am* fat,' he pointed out. 'Which is down to all the cheese I eat. But I'm happy with who I am. It's just a name anyway.'

'I suppose that it's no worse than me being called Harry Stiles.'

'Yes, that *is* an unfortunate combination of names you've got there.'

'I have to explain it to people about twenty times a day. No, I'm not *that* Harry Stiles. I spell my name with an **I** and he spells his with a **Y**.'

'Is your mum going to go back to her old name again – you know, after the divorce?'

'Yes, she's already changed it back.'

'So can't you use her name instead?'

'No, because it's worse.'

'It couldn't be any worse than Stiles.'

'Yes, it could.'

'Tell me.'

'You'll laugh.'

'I promise I won't.'

'It's Potter!'

'Potter? What's wrong with –?'

'*Harry Potter*, Aldrin!'

The penny dropped. Aldrin burst out **laughing**.

'Sorry,' he said. 'I promised I wouldn't, but you're right, that name definitely *is* worse.'

There was a knock on the bedroom door. It opened and Harry's mum was standing there. She was a short woman with red hair scraped back into a ponytail, large glasses and narrow lips. She wore a trouser suit, high-heeled shoes and a permanently ticked-off expression.

'I hear a lot of laughter coming from this room,' she said crossly, 'and no sound of homework being done.'

'Sorry, Mum,' Harry said. 'We were just, um, taking a quick break.'

'Well, it's after eight o'clock,' she pointed out. 'It's probably time your friend was going home anyway. Say goodnight to him.'

She left then.

'Sorry about that,' Harry said.

'Is your mum strict?' Aldrin asked.

'She can be,' Harry told him, 'but just when it comes

to my schoolwork. She wants me to be an architect like her when I grow up.'

'Is that what *you* want?' Aldrin asked.

Without saying anything, Harry led Aldrin over to a drawing table in the corner of the room. On it was a large cartoon illustration of a young boy wearing green camouflage trousers, army boots and a white vest – and he was wrestling with a fearsome-looking crocodile.

'What's this?' Aldrin asked.

'This is the story I'm doing for Mrs Van Boxtel's book,' Harry explained. 'It's about a boy who hunts crocodiles in the swamps of Florida.'

'Whoa!' Aldrin said. 'This is like something you'd see in an actual comic.'

'Well, this is what I want to do,' Harry told him. 'I want to start my own superhero comic book.'

Aldrin stared closely at the drawing of the boy who hunts crocodiles. He noticed his pudding-bowl haircut and his glasses that resembled swimming googles. And tucked into the waistband of his camouflage trousers was an asthma inhaler.

'It's you!' Aldrin exclaimed. 'The boy who hunts crocodiles is you!'

'It's probably stupid,' Harry said.

'Why is it stupid?'

'Who's going to believe that a superhero looks like that?' Harry asked.

'Not all superheroes have big muscles and square jaws,' Aldrin reminded him.

'I suppose they do come in all shapes and sizes.'

'Hey, do you remember today when Sebastian called us oddballs?'

'He's such a mean person,' Harry said.

'No,' Aldrin insisted, 'I actually liked it.'

'Really?'

'I like being different. I don't want to be like everyone else. I'm actually proud to be an oddball.'

'For what it's worth, most superheroes are oddballs.'

'I rest my case! Anyway, I'd better go. I'll see you in school tomorrow.'

'You will. Hey, Aldrin?'

'Yeah?'

'I'm glad we're friends.'

Aldrin smiled.

'Yeah,' he said. 'I am too.'

13

THREE MORE SLICES OF GOUDA

Aldrin was sitting up in bed, unable to sleep. His dad was having another nightmare. He could hear him through the wall, crying out:

'HELP! HELP! HELP!'

Twice, Aldrin had gone next door and woken him up to stop him crying out.

'Dad, you were having a bad dream,' he'd told him.

'Oh, sorry, son,' Doug had said. 'Thank you for waking me.'

But then, within minutes of Doug falling back asleep, it started up again:

'HELP! HELP!'

Aldrin tried to distract himself from the sound of his father's distress. He picked up the book that Mrs

Van Boxtel had lent him – *Myths and Legends of the Netherlands* – and he took it into bed with him.

He opened it. It smelled of mildew and many of the pages were stuck together. He flicked backwards through it until he found the chapter about Luuk van den Hoogenband.

There was a drawing of a man with broad shoulders, arms like tree trunks and golden shoulder-length hair. He was wearing a white shirt, open to the belly button, showing off his chiselled torso; wide black trousers that exposed his ankles; and sandals on his feet.

The chapter was thirty pages long, and Aldrin knew he'd be asleep long before he finished it. So he decided to read just the first few pages. Much of what they contained he had already heard from Mrs Van Boxtel. Luuk was born in 1017 in a tiny village named Spor, near Utrecht, in what is now the Netherlands. His father was a dairy farmer. When Luuk was a baby, he disappeared from his crib – apparently into thin air. Then, eleven years later, he returned, as a boy, claiming that he'd been taken away by the fairies to live in heaven with the gods. He was raised by a goddess named Moorah, who fed him on a strict diet of cheese. In time, it said, Luuk discovered that he possessed a very, **VERY** special power . . .

Aldrin's jaw suddenly fell open. He couldn't believe what it said next – so much so that, once he'd read it, he couldn't read another word.

> *By eating cheese just before he went to sleep, Luuk van den Hoogenband had the ability to enter into other people's dreams.*

Aldrin started to remember what Mrs Van Boxtel had said about the world of magic and things that defied rational explanation.

Maybe he *did* have power – just like Luuk.

But, *if* he did, what had gone wrong the previous night? Why had he ended up dreaming that he was a frog and his legs were an entrée item on the menu of a posh French restaurant?

Did he eat too much Gouda? Or too little? Did he eat it too quickly? Should he switch to a similar cheese but with a lower fat content – perhaps some Edam?

The questions swam around in his head for more than an hour until he finally started to feel sleepy.

RRRIBBIT . . . RRRIBBIT . . . RRRIBBIT . . .

Silas was in his tank, ready to go to sleep too.

106

'Yeah, goodnight, pal,' Aldrin told him.

'HELP!' He could hear Doug shouting again. **'HELP!'**

'You're lucky frogs don't have nightmares,' Aldrin told his little friend, then he closed *Myths and Legends of the Netherlands* and returned it to his bedside table. He switched off his bedside light and lay back on his pillow.

Ten seconds later, he sat up and switched on the light again.

A thought had suddenly struck him. What if frogs really *did* have dreams? What if his nightmare about a chef attempting to chop off his legs with a meat cleaver hadn't actually been *his* nightmare at all?

He replayed last night's events in his mind. He'd got into bed. He'd eaten three slices of Gouda. He'd pictured his dad – his smiley face, his rosy cheeks and his enormous walrus moustache. And then he'd started to feel tired.

But just suppose, he speculated, that in the seconds before he fell asleep, Silas croaked, just like he did a moment ago, distracting him at the vital moment. And instead of entering his father's dream, he'd entered – crazy as it sounded – his pet frog's nightmare.

Was that believable?

One way or another, he decided, he would know the truth tonight.

He threw back his duvet. Moments later, he was downstairs again, shivering in the cold of the shop, cutting himself three more slices of Gouda.

Then he returned to the warmth of his bed.

'OK, Silas,' he said, 'I'm going to need you to stay very, very quiet.'

Through the wall, he could still hear his dad, calling out:

'HELP!!'

One by one, Aldrin popped the slices of Gouda into his mouth and felt them melt on the heat of his tongue. And he thought very, very hard about his dad – his smiley face, his rosy cheeks, his enormous walrus moustache.

He chewed the cheese until it was a salty, slightly nutty-tasting ball of mush in his mouth.

And *very quickly* . . .

without even realizing . . .

that it was happening . . .

his eyes started to feel . . .

very,

very

heavy . . .

And then . . .

he was suddenly . . .

out

for

the . . .

14

DOUG'S NIGHTMARE

Aldrin found himself in a tiny rowing boat in the middle
of the sea. A furious wind was stirring up the water
around him and ten-foot-high waves were throwing his
little wooden vessel around like it was a toy.

He was convinced that the boat was going to capsize.

Suddenly, over the howl of the wind, he could
hear the faint sound of his father's voice calling out,
'HELP! HELP!'

Aldrin looked around. He could see two oars
jammed into their locks. He grabbed one in each
hand and started to row in the direction the voice was
coming from.

It was **heavy, back-breaking work**. Doug's voice
grew louder as Aldrin pulled and pulled on the oars

with all his might. But every time he felt like he was making progress, an enormous wave would crash down on him and beat him back.

Soon his arms were numb from the effort, and the saltwater spray stung his eyes.

But then, at last, he spotted Doug. He was in the water, submerged up to his neck, waving his arms frantically.

Aldrin watched in horror as the sea pulled his dad under. But then, a few seconds later, he resurfaced, gasping for breath and shouting: **'HELP! HELP! HELP!'**

That was the spur that Aldrin needed. All at once, he forgot about his pain. He started pulling on the oars with a superhuman strength he didn't know he possessed.

'DAD!' he shouted. **'HOLD ON, DAD! I'M COMING!'**

Doug turned his head, the shock of seeing his son written all over his face.

'ALDRIN?' he yelled, through gasping breaths. **'WHAT . . . ARE YOU . . . DOING HERE?'**

'I'VE COME TO RESCUE YOU,' Aldrin **shouted**, closing the distance between them with three huge tugs on the oars. **'HERE, GRAB THE END OF THIS!'**

Aldrin finally reached Doug. He stood up in the boat

and held out one of the oars at arm's length. But just as his dad attempted to grab it, a wave shook the boat and Aldrin fell backwards. As he did, he watched his dad get sucked under the water again.

'NO!' Aldrin shouted. 'NOOOOOO!!!!!!'

He struggled to his feet, picked up the oar again and stared at the churning sea.

'DAD!' he shouted. 'DAAAAAAD!!!!!!'

He listened, but he couldn't hear anything over the angry roar of the waves.

But then something broke the surface of the water just behind him. He heard it. He spun round. It was Doug. The current had dragged him to the other side of the boat. Aldrin could see his head, just above the water.

His mouth was open and pointing at the sky. He was trying to breathe in as much air as he could.

Aldrin held out the oar again.

'**TAKE IT, DAD!**' he shouted. '**QUICKLY!**'

This time, Doug managed to grab it. Aldrin pulled his dad towards him. Then he leaned into the water, took a firm grip of Doug's shirt and, summoning up all the strength that was left in him, pulled him into the safe sanctuary of the boat.

'**YOU . . . SAVED . . . MY LIFE!**' Doug said.

'**JUST GRAB AN OAR, DAD!**' Aldrin told him. '**AND START ROWING!**'

They rowed and rowed in silence until the wind quietened down and the sea grew still.

And then . . .

Aldrin opened his eyes. He was back in his bedroom. He was sweating profusely, yet his teeth were **chattering** with the cold. His head **throbbed** and his throat was dry.

He needed a drink of water.

He got out of bed. He opened the door of his bedroom and took a step backwards in fright. Doug was standing outside on the landing.

'I'm sorry, son,' he said, 'I didn't mean to frighten you like that.'

'I was, um, thirsty,' Aldrin told him. 'I was just going to get a drink of water.'

'Funny, I was too,' Doug said. 'Come on then.'

Aldrin followed him down to the kitchen, where Doug poured them each a glass of water from the tap. Aldrin took a long drink while he stared at his dad. The man looked like there was something on his mind.

'Is everything OK?' Aldrin asked.

'Yes, fine,' Doug replied. 'I just had another nightmare, that's all.'

'Oh, right,' said Aldrin.

If there was anything unusual about it, Doug didn't mention it. He drank his water and left the empty glass on the draining board.

'*Sweet dreams –*' he said.

'**– are made of cheese,**' Aldrin replied.

'*Who am I –*'

'**– to diss a Brie?**'

'Night, son.'

'Night, Dad.'

Then Doug walked past Aldrin and headed back to his own bedroom.

A second or two later, however, he reappeared at the door of the kitchen, looking like a man with something to get off his chest.

'It was the strangest thing,' he said.

'What?' asked Aldrin.

'*You* were *in* it.'

Aldrin felt a sudden shock – like someone had thrown a bucket of ice-cold water over him.

'Was I?' he asked.

'I've never told you this before,' Doug said, 'but I've been having this nightmare ever since your mum died, where I'm drowning in the sea.'

'That's . . . awful,' Aldrin said.

'Except this time – I don't know why – you showed up in a little rowing boat, then you pulled me out of the water and you rowed us both to safety.'

'And that's never happened before?'

'No, usually I just drown. And then I wake up. Anyway – night, son.'

'Night, Dad.'

Doug returned to his bedroom, while Aldrin stood motionless in the kitchen, still struggling to take it in.

But it was real.

Just like Luuk van den Hoogenband, Aldrin Adams possessed a very special power. But how he'd managed to come by it, and what he was supposed to do with it, he had absolutely no idea.

15

'I KNOW WHO HE IS'

Habeas Grusselvart watched as the little boy dragged Doug Adams into the safety of a rowing boat. He felt his mouth twitch into an angry grimace.

'BEDDY BYES!' he called out. **'BEDDY BYYYEEESSS!'**

Seconds later, Beddy Byes came running.

'You called?' he said, out of breath.

'Our little *friend* has returned,' Habeas said, through gritted teeth.

Beddy Byes sensed the anger gathering in his boss, and he swallowed hard. He'd just had the place fixed up after his last display of temper.

'Please, Oh Wise and Statuesque One,' he said soothingly, 'try not to throw anything this time.'

'He's just saved Doug Adams from drowning.'

'Can't we make the waves bigger?'

'I *did* make the waves bigger. But the boy wasn't frightened – not . . . one . . . bit.'

They watched in silent wonder as the two figures in the boat each picked up an oar.

'I know who he is,' Habeas said in a clear and even voice.

'Really?' Beddy Byes said.

'His name is Aldrin . . . Aldrin Adams.'

'Adams? You don't mean he's –?'

'Why haven't we been keeping an eye on him?'

Beddy Byes was slow to answer. Habeas repeated the question, this time in an **angry growl**.

'I said, why haven't we been keeping an eye on him?'

'He . . . He . . . He's just a boy. We've never seen this kind of power in one so young. Not since –'

'Well, look at him now! **JUST LOOK AT HIM!**'

'I am looking.'

'This boy could bring down everything we've worked so hard to achieve.'

Habeas stood up from his desk and walked towards the Wall of Torment.

'Do you think he knows yet *why* he has the power?' Beddy Byes asked.

'He has no idea,' Habeas told him. 'But he must be stopped – before he finds out.'

'Yes, Your Highness-ness-ness.'

Habeas watched the boy and his dad row their boat away from the centre of the storm, towards calm and tranquil waters. He moved his face closer to the TV screen until his nose was almost touching the glass. And, at the top of his voice, he roared:

'I'M COMING FOR YOU, ALDRIN ADAMS!'

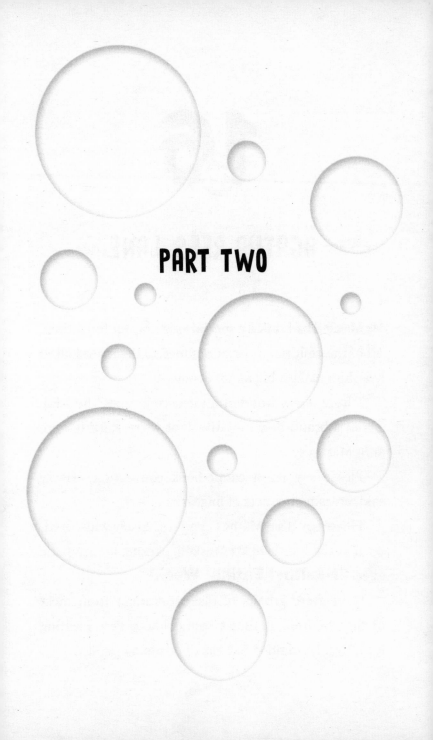

PART TWO

16

AGATHA REES-LANE

Mr Maskell had called a special assembly for lunchtime. All of the children were summoned to the main hall to hear him make a big announcement.

'I have some wonderfully exciting news,' he said, 'about a brand-new initiative that we're starting here at St Martin's . . .'

'Please say it's a comic-book convention,' Harry said, crossing two sets of fingers.

'Please say it's a Maths Olympics,' Sisely whispered.

'It's called . . .' said Mr Maskell, pausing for dramatic effect, **'Healthy! Eating! Week!'**

There were groans of disappointment from most of the children. It didn't sound like a very exciting initiative. It sounded like the opposite.

'And here to tell you all about it,' he said, 'we are privileged indeed to have the nutritionist and healthy-eating campaigner Agatha . . . Rees . . . Lane!'

A woman stepped up on to the stage. She was as tall and thin as a bus stop, with blonde hair that went all the way down to her waist, lots of make-up and a pinched face that made it look like she was sucking hard on a boiled sweet, even though she wasn't. Because, as it was about to become clear, Agatha Rees-Lane never allowed **ANYTHING** that wasn't one hundred per cent nutritious and wholesome to pass her blood-red lips.

'Thank you, thank you, thank you for that wonderful applause,' she said, even though no one clapped. 'I am Agatha! Rees!

Lane! And as Mr Maskell said, I am here today to talk to you about **Healthy! Eating! Week!** It's an exciting new initiative that I'm planning to introduce to **All! Local! Schools!**'

She smiled at the children, revealing two rows of brilliantly white teeth.

'Now,' she said, 'let's start off with a fun game. Can anybody name some **UN! HEALTHY!** foods for me? Anyone? Hands up, please!'

'Chocolate?' someone called out.

'Excellent answer! Chocolate is **VERY** bad for us! **DIS! GUSTING!** Anything else?'

'Fizzy drinks?' someone else suggested.

'Yes!' Agatha agreed. 'Fizzy drinks are FULL of sugar and E-numbers and are absolutely **RE! VOLTING!** What else? Anyone?'

Aldrin wasn't listening. He was going over what had happened last night. He was tempted to think of this *thing* he'd discovered as a superpower, but he had no idea yet what he was supposed to do with it. It wasn't like superhuman strength, or the ability to spin webs, or the power to change into an animal, where there was an obvious, practical use for it in fighting the enemy.

And did he even *have* an enemy?

'What about doughnuts?' someone else shouted.

'Doughnuts!' Agatha said. 'Frightful things! **RE! PUL! SIVE!**'

Aldrin had considered telling his dad the truth over breakfast. But Doug had been in such a great mood when he got up, he didn't want to worry him by telling him that his only son possessed strange, supernatural capabilities. It wasn't the kind of thing anyone needed to hear first thing in the morning.

He felt awful. His head hurt and he felt weak all over, like he was coming down with the flu. His mum used to host wine and cheese-tasting evenings once a month in *C'est Cheese*. Sometimes, she would have a little bit too much to drink and the following morning she would end up with a hangover. The symptoms she always complained of seemed very similar to what Aldrin was feeling now.

This Agatha woman was still droning on:

'I hope that the good habits we learn during **Healthy! Eating! Week!** will become part of our routine forever more when the week is over. Now, when we talk about **HEALTHY** eating, what kind of foods are we talking about?'

'Broccoli,' someone suggested.

'Yes,' she said. 'All green vegetables, in fact, are **very**, **VERY** good for us. They are **WHOLE! SOME!** as well as **NU! TRITIOUS!** Anything else?'

'Brown rice,' Sebastian shouted, 'served with broiled white fish!'

'Excellent!' she said, flashing her perfect teeth at him. 'We're having that for dinner tonight – your favourite, darling!'

Darling?

There were quite a few titters in the hall. Sebastian silenced them with an icy stare.

Hold on, Aldrin thought. *Did Mr Maskell say her name was Agatha Rees-Lane? In which case, she must be . . . Sebastian's mum!*

'Now,' she said, 'what do all healthy foods have in common? Anyone?'

'They're flipping boring!' Frankie shouted.

There was an explosion of laughter throughout the school hall.

'I don't know what you find so funny,' Agatha said, 'because the boy is absolutely correct! All healthy food is **BOR! ING!** If you're ever wondering whether a particular food is good for you or not, just ask yourself one question – does it taste nice? If the answer is yes, then it is undoubtedly **BAD** for you and quite likely taking years off your life. But if it has no taste whatsoever . . . and it's so dull that you can barely bring yourself to chew it up into pieces small enough to swallow . . . then you can rest assured that it's almost certainly **VERY** healthy and **WHOLE! SOME!**'

'Ahem,' Mr Maskell said, clearing his throat as a way of bringing Agatha's presentation to an end. 'Thank you very much for that. Now, Mrs Rees-Lane will be popping into the school during the course of **Healthy! Eating! Week!** to carry out spot checks on your lunch boxes to make sure they contain lots and lots of healthy food items.'

The special assembly ended and the boys and girls spilled out of the hall.

'You're probably all wondering why I'm limping,' Frankie said.

Nobody was wondering why Frankie was limping.

'Injured meself, didn't I?' he explained. 'I was skiing down the side of a mountain last night, with all these Russian agents shooting at me from a snowmobile – oh, just on account of some top-secret plans that I stole from the Kremlin.'

'You weren't limping this morning,' Sisely pointed out.

'Yeah, the, er, pain comes, um, and goes,' Frankie tried to explain.

'And you weren't skiing down the side of a mountain last night,' she said, 'because I looked out of my window and I saw you taking the washing off the line with your mum.'

'No, you never.'

'Yes, I did. Why are you always telling lies?'

Aldrin tried to save Frankie from embarrassment.

'I don't think of them as lies,' he said. 'I just think of them as really exciting stories.'

'What?' Sisely asked. 'Like the other day, when he said he had the same dream as you?'

'I *did* have the same dream as him!' Frankie insisted.

He looked at Aldrin pleadingly. And Aldrin wanted so much to tell him that he believed him. He knew he wasn't fibbing – about this at least.

All morning, he'd thought about confiding in Frankie. Aldrin **had** been in his dream, and Frankie surely had a right to know that. But then Aldrin wanted to keep it quiet – at least until he found out where the power came from and what it was for. Could Frankie be trusted to keep such a secret to himself? Probably not, Aldrin figured. He couldn't stop talking about his spying activities – and he wasn't even a spy!

No, Aldrin was sure that, within an hour of telling Frankie about his special ability, the news would be all over the school.

And yet, at the same time, he was itching to tell *someone* about it. He thought if he didn't hear himself say it out loud, he would go mad. He then considered telling Harry. If anyone understood the world of misfit characters with special capabilities, then it was him. Plus, he thought he could probably rely on Harry's discretion. A comic-book fanatic would appreciate the importance of maintaining the veil of secrecy around a superhero's true identity.

But would Harry be able to explain to him *why* he was able to access other people's dreams?

No, that might take someone who was a little more grounded. Which meant Sisely. She'd said it herself: there is a logical explanation for absolutely everything. And, with her brains, she was the likeliest of all of his friends to figure out where this strange ability of his had come from.

Yes, the more he thought about it, the more convinced he was that she was the one who would help him get to the bottom of the mystery.

'Sisely,' he said, 'can I talk to you about something?'

He slowed up and allowed Harry and Frankie to walk on ahead.

'What's wrong?' she asked, looking at her watch. 'And bear in mind we have Geography in exactly four minutes and fifty-eight seconds.'

'So, when Frankie claimed that me and him had the same nightmare,' Aldrin began, 'well, what if I told you that we *didn't* have the same nightmare?'

'I know you didn't. I said it was impossible.'

'What if I told you that it was Frankie who had the nightmare. And that I . . .'

Aldrin paused to try to find the right form of words.

'What?' Sisely asked impatiently.

'I entered his dream state,' Aldrin told her.

Sisely screwed her face up into a look of scepticism.

'You . . . entered his dream state?' she said.

'Yes,' Aldrin confirmed.

'How?'

'I don't know – by some kind of magic.'

'You've lost your mind, Aldrin.'

'I know that's how it sounds, Sisely. But I was reading about Luuk van den Hoogenband – and he had exactly the same power.'

'There *is* no Luuk van den Hoogenband! He's a mythological figure – which means he never existed! Why am I even listening to you?'

'Sisely,' he tried to persuade her, 'I was in my dad's nightmare last night. He was drowning in the sea and I saved him by holding out an oar and then pulling him into a rowing boat.'

'You're going to make me late for Geography.'

'When he woke up, he told me that he dreamt he was drowning in the sea – then I came along in a boat and saved his life. That can't be a coincidence as well.'

'No, it can't,' Sisely agreed.

'Then how do you explain it?' Aldrin asked.

'You're making it up.'

'I'm not making it up, Sisely!'

'You are! You're an even **bigger** fibber than Frankie!'

Sisely turned her back on him and walked away.

Aldrin was hurt, but at the same time he understood her doubts about his story. Sisely believed only in things that could be proven.

So there was only one thing for him to do.

17

A CHANGED MAN

There was something different about Doug. Aldrin noticed it that night while he was sweeping the floor of the shop. There was none of the sadness that he could usually detect beneath his dad's cheery outward demeanour. Doug was humming to himself as he checked the temperature gauge.

Aldrin stopped pushing the broom around the floor.

'You seem happy,' he commented.

'That's because I *am* happy,' Doug told him. 'That, er, dream that I had last night . . .'

'What about it?' said Aldrin.

'Well, I'm beginning to think it wasn't just an ordinary nightmare.'

'What?' Aldrin asked worriedly. 'Really?'

'Yes, I'm beginning to think there was actually a message in it for me.'

'A message?'

'Well, they say all of our dreams mean something, don't they? I think this one meant that sometimes you can be so sad and full of despair that it feels like you're drowning. But there are people out there, people who love you, who are always ready to hold out an oar to pull you in and save you.'

Doug smiled at Aldrin.

'Thanks, son,' he said. 'For helping me.'

'I, um, didn't actually *do* anything,' Aldrin reminded him. 'It was just a dream you had, remember?'

'Yes, of course!' Doug chuckled. 'It did feel strangely real, though. Anyway, you'll be happy to hear I've come up with a plan to pay back the bank!'

'How?'

'It's a little thing called marketing! All will be revealed tomorrow! Have you finished sweeping that floor?'

'All done.'

'Then we're finished for the night. By the way, I've got some nice Cashel Blue here. Would you like some?'

'Cashel Blue?'

Aldrin thought for a moment. He had a plan for the evening. He was going to enter Sisely's dream and prove to her that what he was saying was true. But he didn't know if it was just Gouda that gave him the power, or whether other cheeses worked just as well.

He thought he should find out.

As it happened, Cashel Blue was another one of his absolute favourites. It was a margarine-coloured cheese, mottled with blue-green mould, and it tasted sharp and salty.

'I'd **love** some,' he said.

Doug brought the cheese wire down on the cheese and Aldrin watched as two thick slices crumbled on to the wooden block.

'Actually, can you wrap it up for me?' Aldrin asked. 'I'll, um, eat it in bed.'

'You're making a habit of that,' Doug said, wrapping the two slices of cheese in some wax paper. 'As long as it doesn't give you funny dreams.'

'It won't,' Aldrin assured him.

Later that evening, they were watching TV, with Silas sleeping on top of Aldrin's head, when Aldrin announced that he was turning in for the night.

'It's a Friday night,' Doug reminded him. 'You're allowed to stay up a bit later.'

'I'm just pooped,' Aldrin explained, yawning theatrically. 'I think Silas is too.'

'Well,' Doug said, 'you're going to need a really good night's sleep, son. Because the shop is going to be **VERY** busy tomorrow.'

'I'm looking forward to seeing this marketing plan of yours. Anyway, *sweet dreams –*'

'**– are made of cheese!** Hey, that's my line!'

'Night, Dad!'

'Night, son.'

Two minutes later, Aldrin was in his pyjamas and lying under the covers. He took out the little package that Doug had given him and unwrapped it carefully.

With trembling fingers, he broke the sticky blue cheese into smaller pieces. One by one, he popped them into his mouth and chewed them. He thought very, very hard about Sisely while he chewed and chewed until the cheese was just a salty ball of mush in his mouth . . .

And *very quickly* . . .

without even realizing . . .

that it was happening . . .

his eyes **started to feel** . . .

very,

very

heavy . . .

And then . . .

he was suddenly . . .

out

for

the . . .

18

SISELY'S NIGHTMARE

Aldrin found himself in a **large**, cavernous hall, filled with thousands and thousands of desks and chairs, laid out in rows, stretching off as far as the eye could see. Each desk had a single piece of paper on it.

It looked like some kind of examination hall.

Aldrin was almost disappointed. After the drama of his last three nightmares, this one already felt like a definite anticlimax. But then it didn't exactly come as a shock to discover that Sisely dreamt about sitting exams.

From somewhere behind him came the sound of a bell, then a crowd of children rushed into the room like a flood of water. Looking nervous, they made their way quietly to their assigned desks and sat down. Within seconds, every single seat in the hall was filled.

Aldrin spotted Sisely sitting right in the middle of the sea of desks. He made his way over to her. Her head was down, her nose buried in her paper.

'Ta-dah!' he said, like a magician completing a magic trick.

Sisely looked up from her paper.

'Oh, it's you,' she said – she didn't seem the slightest bit surprised to see him.

Aldrin looked around.

'So what kind of a dream *is* this?' he asked.

'It's not a dream,' Sisely revealed. 'It's a nightmare.'

'A nightmare? But nightmares usually involve falling, or drowning, or being chased by something scary. I would have thought you *enjoyed* exams.'

'I do. This is a nightmare I sometimes have when I'm anxious. I'm about to sit an exam and then I remember that I haven't studied for it, and I don't know any of the answers.'

'You don't seem that upset – for someone having a nightmare, I mean.'

'That's because I know it's not real. The first question on the paper is going to be *What is the capital of Kenya?* And I'm going to write *Timbuktu.*'

'And is that the right answer?'

'Of course it's not. The capital of Kenya is Nairobi. That's why it's such a horrible nightmare for me – because I hate to get things wrong.'

'Well, haven't you noticed anything different about your nightmare this time?'

'No.'

'Sisely, I'm in it!' he declared. 'I told you I could gain access to people's dreams and you didn't believe me! **But look! Here I am!**'

'You're not *in* my dream,' Sisely said dismissively. 'I'm just dreaming you.'

What did he have to do to persuade her?

'Sisely, it's **ME!**' Aldrin insisted. 'Do you remember we had that conversation in school today? It was after that Agatha woman told us about **Healthy! Eating! Week!** I told you about saving my dad from drowning. You got upset because you thought I was lying.'

'You *were* lying. And lies make me anxious. That's why I'm having a nightmare right now.'

'Sisely, you have to believe me! You're the only person I know who can help me figure out how I got this power – and why?'

Sisely picked up her pink pencil. On her exam paper, in answer to question one, she wrote, in neat capital letters:

TIMBUKTU

And as soon as she finished writing the word, Aldrin awoke with a sudden start and found himself lying in the darkness. The room was spinning. His head hurt so badly that he was forced to close his eyes again, and a cold sweat covered his body like the morning dew on a lawn.

19.

A BIG MOUSE

Aldrin eventually fell back to sleep. When he woke again, it was morning. His head was still pounding. As his mind adjusted to his surroundings, he became aware of a noise outside on the street. Someone was shouting, but he couldn't quite make out the words. The voice sounded muffled and tinny – as if it was coming from . . .

A megaphone?

He listened more closely. Slowly, the noise resolved itself into words he could understand:

'CHEESE HAS A GREAT MANY PROVEN HEALTH BENEFITS, ENSURING THAT YOU GROW UP BIG AND STRONG! I MEAN, I'M A MOUSE – AND JUST LOOK AT THE SIZE OF ME!'

Whose voice *was* that? It sounded like . . .

'**Dad?**' he said aloud.

He jumped out of bed and rushed over to the window. He pushed it open and stuck his head out. He couldn't believe the scene that was unfolding on the pavement below.

Doug was standing in front of the shop – although he wouldn't have been instantly recognizable to anyone. Because the man was dressed . . . as a **MOUSE!**

Aldrin has no idea where he'd got his hands on the costume. It was a sort of hooded grey, furry onesie, with a white patch on the belly and large, pink, round ears on top of the hood. On his face, with a black felt-tip pen, Doug had drawn a little triangular nose – and even a set of whiskers!

He was talking into a megaphone, telling passers-by about the health benefits of eating cheese, and peppering these facts with his own little jokes, which were, if Aldrin was being honest, a little bit cheesy:

'OK, HERE'S ONE FOR YOU NOW. WHAT CHEESE WOULD YOU USE TO HIDE A SMALL HORSE? . . . MASCARPONE! DO YOU GET IT? MASK-A-PONY! THIS IS ALL ORIGINAL MATERIAL YOU'RE HEARING, LADIES AND GENTLEMEN! ALL ORIGINAL MATERIAL!'

Aldrin laughed. He couldn't help himself.

'What are you DOING?' he shouted out of the window.

Doug looked up.

'OH, HELLO THERE, SON!' he said – still talking into the megaphone. Aldrin winced and hurriedly covered his ears.

'Sorry,' said Doug, taking the megaphone away from his mouth. 'So, what do you think?'

'I don't know WHAT to think!' Aldrin laughed. 'My dad is dressed as a giant mouse! Where did you get that costume?'

'What, this little thing?' Doug said, giving him a twirl. 'I picked it up in that fancy-dress shop in the precinct.'

It even had a tail!

'This is my marketing strategy,' Doug revealed. 'Too many people seem to have forgotten that cheese is very, very good for them. So I'm just giving them a little reminder!'

He put the megaphone to his mouth again:

'CHEESE IS AN EXCELLENT SOURCE OF PROTEIN, WHICH IS GOOD FOR OUR MUSCLES AND OUR DIGESTIVE SYSTEM! IT CONTAINS CALCIUM, WHICH GIVES US HEALTHY BONES AND HEALTHY TEETH! ANSWER ME THIS – WHEN WAS THE LAST TIME YOU SAW A MOUSE SITTING IN A DENTIST'S WAITING ROOM?'

Aldrin noticed that passers-by were laughing and telling Doug that he was hilarious. And not only that – some of them were taking a detour into *C'est Cheese*.

Doug looked up at Aldrin again.

'YOU'D BETTER GET DOWN HERE!' he said

through the megaphone. 'BELINDA IS GOING TO NEED YOUR HELP TODAY!'

Aldrin got dressed as quickly as he could, then he ran downstairs. The shop was already packed with customers, all waiting to be served, and Belinda was struggling to cope.

'I haven't got time for questions!' she snapped at one man. 'I've got a queue out the door, in case you haven't noticed! Just say what you want and I'll give it to you – then you can sling your hook.'

Aldrin hadn't seen the shop this busy since his mum had been alive.

'Are you just going to stand there gawping?' Belinda asked. 'Or are you going to help?'

Aldrin took his apron off the peg. He put it on over his head and tied the strings at the back.

'I've got an idea,' he said to Belinda. 'Why don't *I* serve the customers while *you* work the till. Deal?'

'Saturday mornings are never this busy,' she said. 'I've got five celebrity gossip magazines in my bag. If it keeps up like this, I'll not get to read any of them.'

She moved to the till and Aldrin started serving the customers, doing his best impersonation of his father:

'Hello, Mrs Ojulah! How can I help you? Cheddar?

OK, let me ask you, do you want something smooth, springy, dense, crumbly?'

Or it was:

'Hello, Mr Welsby! A soft cheese? Well, I can't say enough good things about the Taleggio. Would you like to sample some? No, ignore the smell – it actually *tastes* like pizza crust. What would I pair it with? Well, I find that dried apricots really enhance the flavour, but it also goes great with celery.'

Outside, Aldrin could still hear his dad rounding up customers:

'WHAT KIND OF MUSIC DOES CHEESE LIKE TO LISTEN TO? R 'N' BRIE! COME ON, THIS IS PRIME CONTENT I'M GIVING AWAY HERE!'

And:

'WHAT CHEESE LIKES TO HANG OUT WITH CELEBRITIES AND SPEND HER DAD'S MONEY? . . . PARIS STILTON! DO YOU GET IT? PARIS STILTON! OK, MY JOKES MIGHT NOT BE GREAT, BUT MY CHEESE MOST DEFINITELY IS! WHAT WAS THAT? HAVE WE GOT GOAT'S CHEESE? WE'VE GOT A HUNDRED TYPES OF GOAT'S CHEESE! STEP INSIDE – YOU CAN SAMPLE ANY CHEESE YOU WANT!'

The shop was packed all day. People came from miles around. There were familiar faces from the past, who hadn't been into the shop since Cynthia died. And then there were lots of new customers, enticed inside by Doug's funny patter. They told him they hadn't had cheese for ages and had totally forgotten how much they loved it.

It was so busy that Aldrin didn't notice his cheese hangover lifting. And he didn't feel the hours pass until it was six o'clock and it was time to shut the shop for the night.

Doug was still fizzing with excitement as he turned the sign from **'OPEN'** to **'CLOSED'**.

'We had more customers today than we've had in the past six months put together!' he said, climbing out of the mouse costume. 'A few more days like that and all our debts will be cleared.'

'You were hilarious!' Aldrin told him.

'Was I?'

'I mean, your jokes were terrible – but they were so bad, they were good. Although I suspect it's going to take Belinda a long time to recover.'

Doug looked over the counter and saw her lying on the floor, fast asleep, using a wheel of Parmigiano

Reggiano as a pillow and a copy of *Hello!* magazine to cover her face.

'Maybe I'll give her a day off next week.' Doug chuckled. 'Just to make up for overextending her today!'

Suddenly, there was a knock on the door of the shop. Outside, Doug and Aldrin heard a woman's voice say, 'Am I too late?'

Technically, the shop was closed, but Doug could never resist the temptation to serve one more customer, so he opened the door again.

Aldrin was surprised to see that it was Sisely and that she was with her mum.

'Oh, hi,' Aldrin said. 'Dad, this is Sisely – she's in my class at school.'

'Oh, yes,' Doug said. 'You're the child genius he's been telling me all about.'

Mrs Musa laughed.

'Well, I don't know about child genius! Hello, I'm Gloria – the proud mum.'

'I'm Doug,' said Doug. 'And this is my son, Aldrin. So what can I do for you?'

'I passed by earlier and I saw you standing outside dressed as a mouse –'

'Just a little bit of marketing!'

'– and I said to Sisely, it's been ages since we've had some nice cheese.'

'Well,' said Doug, 'let's find out what kind of cheese you like, shall we?' and he led Mrs Musa to the counter, leaving Aldrin and Sisely alone.

'OK, why are you looking at me like that?' Sisely asked, turning to Aldrin.

She didn't seem at all curious about Aldrin's cameo in her nightmare last night.

'So,' Aldrin said, 'was I in your dream last night?'

'No,' Sisely said in a testy voice, 'you weren't *in* my dream. But I had a dream *about* you. There's a difference.'

'You were in a big hall,' Aldrin recalled. 'You were about to sit an exam – and you didn't know any of the answers.'

'That was a guess.'

'If it was, it was a pretty good guess – wouldn't you say so?'

'Not really,' Sisely replied. 'Exam nightmares are actually one of the most common kind.'

'You were wearing a red jumper.'

'I always wear that. It's my school jumper.'

'You were writing with your pink pencil.'

'You *know* that's my favourite pencil.'

Sisely turned her back on Aldrin again.

'Mum,' she said, 'I'm going to wait outside for you, all right?'

'OK,' said Mrs Musa.

How could he get her to believe him? And then, suddenly, the answer came to him.

'The capital of Kenya is Nairobi,' he said. 'It's not Timbuktu.'

Sisely turned slowly round and stared at him, her mouth **hanging** open, like she was seeing a ghost.

For the first time in her life, smart, logical Sisely Musa was forced to accept that there really might be mysteries in the world that defied rational explanation.

'Sisely,' Aldrin said in a pleading voice, 'you're the smartest person I know. I need you to help me understand what's going on.'

'Go and get me the book that Mrs Van Boxtel gave you,' Sisely replied. 'I want to read about this Luuk van den Hoogenband.'

20

THE STINKING BISHOP

It was Monday lunchtime. Aldrin and Harry were standing in a queue outside the cafeteria.

'What's the hold-up?' Aldrin asked.

'It's that Agatha Rees-Lane,' Harry said. 'Remember she said she was going to be carrying out spot checks on our lunch boxes?'

'I can't believe she's actually doing that!' said Aldrin, shaking his head. 'So how was your weekend?'

'It was brilliant,' Harry said. 'I went to my dad's and we read comic books all day on Saturday. And then, on Sunday, I worked on my story for Mrs Van Boxtel.'

'What, *The Boy Who Hunts Crocodiles*?'

'Yeah, I got two full pages done!'

'I can't wait to see it when it's finished.'

'So what did you do?' Harry asked.

'I worked in my dad's shop,' Aldrin said.

'Oh,' Harry said, disappointed for him.

'No, I loved it,' Aldrin said. 'It's my absolute favourite thing in the world to do. And we had a great day on Saturday. We had over a hundred customers. Dad had been really worried because business has been terribly slow. But he dressed up as a mouse –'

'My mum said she saw a man dressed up as a mouse telling jokes through a megaphone,' Harry interrupted.

'That was him!' Aldrin said.

'She said she nearly crashed the car into a lamp-post when she saw him.' Harry laughed.

'**NEXT!**' a shrill voice called.

They were now at the top of the queue and Agatha was beckoning them forward.

'**Quickly!**' she snapped. 'We have a LOT of lunches to inspect!'

Aldrin noticed that Sebastian and the twins were helping Agatha conduct the inspection. Algernon – or was it Hercy? – was holding a cardboard box that was spilling over with all the chocolate bars, packets of crisps and fizzy drinks that they'd confiscated from the other children.

'You heard my mother,' Sebastian said, clicking his fingers. 'Hand them over, oddballs.'

Hercy – or was it Algernon? – snatched Harry and Aldrin's lunch boxes from them and handed them to Agatha. She peeled off the lid of Harry's first. She looked inside and performed a quick inventory of what he had to eat.

'An apple,' she said, 'and a sandwich with – what's that in it?'

'Chicken,' Harry told her.

'Is it lean?'

'Yes, it's lean.'

'And a low-fat natural yogurt. Yes, that all seems to be in order. Well done!'

She replaced the lid and handed it back to Harry.

Next, she opened Aldrin's lunch box – and the smell almost knocked her clean off her feet!

'What in the name of –' she exclaimed, falling back against the wall.

Harry was forced to hold his breath. Sebastian and his two friends covered their noses and mouths. All the other children in the queue turned away, their faces screwed up.

Agatha started retching:

'Bleeeuuuggghhh!!! Bleeeuuuggghhh!!! Bleeeuuuggghhh!!!'

It was only when she replaced the lid that she regained the power of speech.

'What *is* this odious filth?' she asked.

Aldrin shrugged. 'It's just some Stinking Bishop.'

'Some what?'

'It's a type of cheese.'

'Cheese? Were you not at the special assembly on Friday? Did you not hear me say that you were only permitted to eat food that is **GOOD** for you during **Healthy! Eating! Week!?**'

'Cheese *is* good for you,' Aldrin tried to argue.

'Cheese? Good for you? Cheese is one of the worst things you can eat! It's **DIS! GUSTING!** It's **LOATHE! SOME!** It's **AB! HORRENT!** I'm sorry, I'm afraid I'm going to have to confiscate this.'

'You can't do that!' Aldrin protested. 'That's all I have to eat!'

'Then you'll remember to bring something else tomorrow – something that *isn't* cheese! I shall have to keep the lunch box, get it disinfected. I'll be SICK if I have to smell it again. Stinking Bishop indeed! **NEXT!**'

Aldrin realized that there was no point in arguing with the woman. Mr Maskell had given Agatha the power to do whatever she wanted.

Aldrin and Harry began to make their way to their usual table.

'Your lunch was very healthy today,' Aldrin said. 'I thought your mum usually gave you money for a packet of crisps or a bar of chocolate?'

'Er, yeah,' Harry said nervously, 'but it's, um, supposed to be **Healthy! Eating! Week!** Remember?'

'Harry,' Aldrin said, 'Sebastian isn't still demanding money from you, is he?'

'Just leave it, Aldrin.'

'Harry, you can't keep giving in to him like that.'

Suddenly, Sisely was standing in front of them.

'I need to talk to you,' she told Aldrin. 'In private.'

'Er, OK,' Aldrin said. 'Harry, I'll see you at the oddballs' table, OK?'

'What's wrong?' Aldrin asked Sisely after Harry got up and walked away.

'Explain it to me again,' she said. 'How *exactly* do you do it?'

'I eat cheese,' Aldrin explained, 'just before I go to sleep. Then, as I'm chewing it, I just think about someone.'

'And that's *all* you do?'

'I concentrate really hard. I think that's the thing that sends me off to sleep.'

'And, what? You just appear in their dream?'

'Yes.'

'And then what happens?'

'Anything I want to happen. With Frankie, I made a hot-air balloon appear out of nowhere. With Dad, I pulled him into a rowing boat and saved him from drowning. With Silas –'

'Who's Silas?'

'He's my pet frog.'

'You got into your frog's nightmare?'

'Yes – and it was awful!'

'Aldrin, you need to stop doing it. You need to stop going into people's dreams.'

'Why?'

'Because,' she said, 'you don't know why you have this ability yet.'

'It's a superpower,' Aldrin corrected her. 'And it's

obviously for helping people.'

'You don't know that.'

'Sisely, pretty much every night since my mum died, my dad has had the same nightmare, where he is drowning in the sea. I went into his dream state, and I rescued him. Then he woke up the next morning a new man. You saw how happy he was on Saturday.'

'Did you read the chapter about Luuk van den Hoogenband?' Sisely asked in a grave voice.

'Er, some of it,' Aldrin told her. 'Just up to the bit where it said he had the same power as me.'

'Well, *I* read it all,' Sisely said. 'Including the part where he was stripped of his powers.'

'What? Why?'

'I can't believe you didn't bother to read the whole chapter of that book.'

'Sisely, please. Tell me.'

Sisely huffed.

'According to the book,' she said, 'Luuk entered the dream state of a princess named Femke van den Bos. He was in love with her, and he wanted to give her what her heart most desired.'

'OK,' Aldrin said. 'And what was it that her heart most desired?'

'The ability to fly!'

'To fly? OK, I get that.'

'So Luuk entered her dreams and persuaded her that she *could* fly. The following morning, she jumped from the top of the castle tower – to her death.'

'Oh.' Aldrin gulped.

'The gods were furious with him,' Sisely told him. 'They took away his ability to enter people's dreams – and also his immortality. The following day, he died of a broken heart.'

'Yeah,' Aldrin tried to argue, 'I'm not going to do something that stupid. What? Persuade someone that they can fly?'

'Aldrin,' Sisely said, 'you shouldn't mess around with things you don't understand.'

'You're the one who doesn't understand, Sisely. I have the power to make people happy.'

'So did Luuk van den Hoogenband.'

'Yeah, last week, you didn't even believe he existed.'

'You asked for my advice,' Sisely said, 'and I'm advising you to stay out of other people's dreams – at least until I've found out why you have this power.'

21

A GIFT IS A GIFT

It was late that night and Aldrin was playing the piano like only he could – which is to say very, very badly.

PLi**N**K . . . pLO**NK** . . . PLIiiN**N**N**K** . . . pLO**NK**. . . pLooOn**N**nk . . . PLi**N**k . . .

As a matter of fact, his playing was even worse than it normally was, so bad that even Silas was struggling to stay in key:

rrribBIT . . . *rrrIBBIT* . . . *rrRIbbIT* . . .

Aldrin was thinking about Sisely's warning – about staying out of people's dreams.

PLu**N**K. . .pLun**K**. . .pLO**N**nn**K**. . .PLi**N**k. . . pLooOn**N**nk . . . pLO**NK** . . .

But what was the point of having a superpower if he wasn't allowed to use it? It would be like telling

Agent Cunning to stick to men's tailoring and forget that he had the powers of telepathy, psychokinesis and teleportation. He'd say that was crazy talk.

pLONK... PLiNK... plInnNk... pLUnK... PLUunNNK... pLink-PLONK...

For some unknown reason, Aldrin had been given the power to change the outcome of people's dreams. He'd helped his dad. And Frankie. How could that be considered misusing his powers?

PLiNk... pLANK... PLANnNk... pLUnK... plAAANnNk... PLaNK-PLaNK...

At that exact moment, Doug stuck his head round the living-room door.

'Is that, um, one of Ed Sheeran's?' he asked.

'No,' Aldrin replied. 'It's *"Für Elise"* – by Beethoven.'

rrribBIT... rrrIBBIT... rrRIbbIT...

'Of course it is!' Doug nodded. 'I recognize it now! Another great day today, Aldrin. If it keeps going like this, I'll have those arrears paid off in a matter of weeks, I reckon.'

'That's, er, great news, Dad.'

pLONK... pLoNK... PLOnnNK... PLiNk- pLONK...

'I was just about to pack your lunch box for

tomorrow,' Doug said. 'I've got some delicious Caerphilly downstairs. It's got a lovely buttery crumble to it. I was thinking it might go well with some digestive biscuits and maybe a fruit chutney of some kind.'

'No, I'm not allowed to bring cheese to school,' Aldrin told him.

'Who says?'

'We're doing this **Healthy! Eating! Week!**'

'Well, they do say that a balanced diet is important. You can't eat cheese for every meal – much as you'd like to. Why don't I give you some hummus?'

'Er, fine,' Aldrin said, with as much enthusiam as he could muster – which wasn't much.

'And some carrot and celery sticks?' Doug said.

'Yeah, why not? Really push the boat out!'

PLINK ... PLINK ... PLINK ...

'Is that why you're playing the piano?' Doug asked.

'No,' Aldrin said. 'It's nothing to do with that.'

'Do you want to talk about it?' Doug asked.

'There's this, um, *boy* at my school,' Aldrin told him. 'And he's got this, well, pretty amazing ability.'

'This isn't another one of Frankie Fidderer's stories, is it? Didn't he tell you once that he jumped the Grand Canyon on a motorcycle?'

'Yes, but this is a different boy.'

'OK.'

'He has this ability – it's a gift, really – but he isn't sure if he should use it.'

'Does using this ability make other people unhappy?'

'The exact opposite, Dad! It makes people happy! Really happy!'

Like you! he wanted to tell him.

'Does using this ability of his mean that somebody else gets hurt?' Doug wanted to know.

'No,' Aldrin assured him. 'Nobody gets hurt – ever!'

'Then this friend of yours,' Doug said, 'should use that gift of his.'

'Thanks, Dad,' Aldrin smiled. 'I'll, um, pass that advice on to him.'

'Here,' Doug said. 'I brought you some cheese – one of your favourites!'

It was St Tola Ash, a type of goat's cheese that's rolled in black ash to help preserve it. It smelled like fresh flowers and it tasted like honey.

'Thanks, Dad,' Aldrin said, taking it from him.

'Anyway,' Doug told him, 'it's about time you were in bed. **Sweet dreams –**'

'**– *are made of cheese*,**' Aldrin added.

162

'Who am I –'
'– *to diss a Brie?*'

Aldrin headed for his room. He put Silas into his tank and he climbed into bed. His mind was made up now. He had this power for a reason – and despite what Sisely said, it was clearly to bring happiness to the lives of others.

What harm could there possibly be in that?

He put his head back on his pillow and he stared at the ceiling, wondering whose dream he would enter tonight.

What about Belinda? he thought.

Even though she always seemed so miserable, he really, **REALLY** liked her. Perhaps if he gained access to her dreams, he might discover some clue as to the source of her unhappiness.

He bit into the St Tola Ash and felt it melt, cold and creamy, on his tongue.

He thought about Belinda – this stoutish woman, with her brown hair and her pretty face, and her sunglasses perched permanently on top of her head.

He chewed and chewed the cheese until it was just a smooth, honeyish ball of mush in his mouth . . .

And *very quickly* . . .

without even realizing . . .

that it was happening . . .

his eyes **started to feel** . . .

very,

very

heavy . . .

And then . . .

he was suddenly . . .

out

for

the . . .

22

BELINDA'S NIGHTMARE

Aldrin was standing backstage at some sort of concert venue. The atmosphere was tense. Men and women wearing ear mics and carrying clipboards were running around and shouting frantically:

'We don't know where she is! We're trying to locate her right now!'

Suddenly, a deafening crackle of applause came through the wall like a thousand fireworks going off at the same time. The floor shook.

Then he heard a woman shout:

'She's locked herself in her dressing room. She says she's not coming out.'

'She *has* to come out!' a man's voice replied. **'She's supposed to be singing next!'**

165

Where was he? Aldrin had no idea. Until he saw the logo on the wall that said:

BRITAIN'S GOT TALENT!

So *this* was Belinda's dream? To appear on a TV talent show?

Aldrin wandered down a long corridor until he came to a door. On it, there was a sign that said:

Belinda Orpen

He knocked three times.

'I'm not going on. You'll have to tell them I'm poorly. Or me nan died.'

'Belinda,' Aldrin said. 'It's me.'

'Aldrin?' he heard her say through the door. 'What are you doing here?'

'Can you open the door, please?'

Aldrin listened carefully. After a few seconds, he heard a key turn in the lock. The door opened. Belinda was standing in front of him, wearing a very sparkly dress and a lot of make-up.

'Is this your dream?' Aldrin asked.

'No,' she said, 'it's me flipping nightmare.'

'What, to sing in front of a huge audience, with half the country watching on TV?'

'*That* bit – yes, *that's* my dream. But how it ends – that's the nightmare.'

'How *does* it end?'

'You don't want to know, Aldrin.'

'Tell me. I might be able to help you.'

'They **bang** on the door a few more times. Eventually, I agree to come out and sing. But when I walk out on to the stage, all the folk in the audience start laughing – and that's when I look down and I realize –'

'What?'

'I'm standing there in just me underwear!'

Aldrin couldn't help but laugh.

'It's stage fright,' she explained. 'I've suffered from it all me life. I should have been a singer, see. When I were younger, I wanted to be the next Shirley Bassey.'

'Who's Shirley Bassey?' Aldrin wondered.

'She were a really famous singer – from years ago. And I wanted to be just like her. But any time I went to do an audition or a competition, I just fell to pieces. My life would have been totally different today if I could have just conquered me nerves.'

'But you can,' Aldrin told her. 'I'll help you.'

'How?' Belinda asked.

'I'll walk with you to the stage. I'll stand in the wings while you audition. Then you won't have to be nervous. And you won't feel like, you know –'

'Like I'm standing there in me whatsits.'

'Exactly.'

There was another urgent knock on the dressing-room door.

'All right, all right!' Belinda shouted. **'Keep your hair on – I'm coming.'**

Belinda threw open the door. Waiting outside was an entourage of people ready to escort her to the stage. They set off. Aldrin followed closely behind, offering her encouragement every step of the way.

'You're going to absolutely smash it!' he assured her. 'And don't worry – you *do* have clothes on!'

Moments later, Aldrin was standing in the wings, watching his dad's assistant walk on to the stage. There was a smattering of applause – the audience didn't seem too convinced by her.

He heard one judge say:

'What's your name and what do you do?'

'My name is Belinda,' she answered, 'and I work in a cheesemonger's.'

The audience laughed. Aldrin had no idea what was funny about working in a cheesemonger's. It was his dream job.

'And what are you going to do for us tonight?' she was asked by a judge.

'I'm going to sing "Diamonds Are Forever" by Shirley Bassey,' Belinda announced confidently.

The audience laughed again. What was wrong with these people?

'OK,' one of the judges said. 'The stage is yours.'

There followed a moment of silence that seemed to go on forever.

Belinda looked tense. Aldrin whispered her name as loudly as he dared:

'Belinda! Belinda!'

She turned her head and saw Aldrin standing silently in the wings.

'You can do this!' he told her. 'Now blow their blooming socks off!'

She smiled and nodded. Then the music started. Belinda closed her eyes, preparing herself.

Aldrin checked – yes, she still had her dress on.

And then she sang the opening line, '**DIAMONDS ARE FOREVEEERRR!!!**'

The audience gasped as one. Then they started jumping to their feet and **clapping** – not even five seconds into the song!

Aldrin joined in the applause. Because one thing was immediately clear after just the opening line . . . Belinda had a voice so strong and powerful that it seemed to shake the foundations of the building. The positive feedback seemed to do something to her. Aldrin watched her suddenly grow in confidence. She started swinging her hips and pursing her lips and winking at the audience, which made them cheer even louder.

She finished the song, hitting the high note at the end and holding it for twenty seconds before taking a bow. The audience roared its approval. Belinda had tears streaming down her face.

She turned and looked at Aldrin, still standing in the wings.

'Thank you!' she mouthed to him. **'Thank you!'**

And then he woke up. His head throbbed and his mouth was so dry that he could barely swallow. But it had been worth it to see what a happy Belinda looked like – even for just those few minutes.

23

'THE BOY MUST BE STOPPED!'

Habeas Grusselvart was a vain man. At least once a night, he liked to walk round what he called his 'kingdom', admiring the evil empire that he had built for himself.

He operated out of a large factory in the market town of Todmorden in West Yorkshire. The signs outside suggested that it was a building where fish were packaged for sale in supermarkets. But the Codfather Packing Company was, in fact, a front for Habeas Grusselvart's real business, which was imagining, writing, rehearsing and directing nightmares for millions and millions of people each night.

When he walked, he had the habit of putting his hands behind his back, just as he did on this particular day, as he strolled round the facility, with Beddy Byes in tow, admiring each and every aspect of his operation.

They walked down a long corridor. Off it, in a series of acting studios, a collection of bogeymen, monsters, ghosts, clowns, vampires, and other characters who populate nightmares, practised their routines.

'Put some *feeling* into it, darling!' said Count Dramatist, the Head of Casting. He had sharp fangs, dark, greased-back hair and a long black cloak with red lining. 'That so-called *evil* cackle of yours wouldn't frighten a two-year-old! It's not "Ha ha ha ha ha!" It's "$_M$WAAAHAHAHAHAHAHA!!!!!" Now try it again – from the top!'

Habeas stopped. To his left, there was a very large window. Through it, he could look down on his favourite part of the entire Todmorden nightmare-generating enterprise. It was a giant warehouse, the size of two football pitches laid end to end, and the equivalent of four storeys high.

And it was filled to the roof . . . with cheese!

There were millions of tons of the stuff, in every variety – Cheddar, Gouda, Gruyère, Brie, Emmental, Edam, feta, Roquefort – piled high to form a towering, foul-smelling, decomposing mountain of sludge.

The room was sealed airtight to prevent the stench from leaking out – for one sniff of that rotting slurry would be enough to knock you out cold. Indeed, it stank so badly that the warehouse workers who shovelled more and more cheese on to the pile each day were forced to wear hazmat suits and breathe with the aid of oxygen masks.

Habeas sighed.

'Will I ever own it all?' he asked.

'I believe you will,' Beddy Byes said. 'You already own almost all of the Camembert in the world.'

'Do I?'

'Oh, yes. It's become so rare now that it's actually considered a delicacy.'

Habeas smiled. But, whatever joy that thought gave him, it quickly faded.

'I can't enjoy anything at the moment,' he complained. 'Our friend has been at it again.'

'The Adams boy?' Beddy Byes asked.

'He was in Belinda Orpen's nightmare last night.'

'Belinda . . . ?'

'Works for his father. She has this anxiety dream where she's about to sing in front of an audience, but then she discovers –'

'She's standing there in her underwear!'

'The very one.'

'That's one of my absolute favourites, Oh Great and Belevolent One.'

'Except our little friend convinced her last night that she has absolutely nothing to fear from performing in public. And that's not all.'

'There's more?'

'He's told someone about his power.'

'Who?'

'He showed up in young Sisely Musa's dream last Friday night. Told her everything.'

'Why her?'

'Oh, she's some kind of child genius. He probably figures she'll help him discover the secret behind his powers.'

'They're waiting for us in the boardroom,' Beddy Byes told him.

'All the heads of department?' Habeas asked.

'Yes, as you requested, Your Excellentness-ness.'

'Let's go then.'

The boardroom was filled with the excited jabber of talented creatives who loved their diabolical work. They were sitting round a long table, so preoccupied with their talk of the nightmares on which they were working that none of them noticed Habeas and Beddy Byes enter the room.

Rita Choo – Training Delivery Manager with Special Responsibility for Things that Go Bump in the Night – was telling her colleagues about a three-eyed monster, still in the developmental stage, whose speciality was hiding under children's beds.

'He's the scariest I've ever worked with,' she said. 'He even frightens me!'

Holt Hession – Training Delivery Manager with Special Responsibility for Things that Bite and Sting – said that recent research has revealed that grown-ups are far more frightened of crows than they are of bats.

'It's going to totally change our approach to adult nightmares in the fourth quarter of the financial year,' he said happily.

Habeas cleared his throat.

'You know,' he said, 'I'm accustomed to people standing up when I walk into a room.'

There was the sound of chair legs scraping on the hard wooden floor as the entire room jumped to its feet.

'An eleven-year-old boy has been entering other people's nightmares,' he said in a cold, measured voice, 'and changing the wonderful endings that we've created for them.'

There were shocked faces all round the room.

'Sit down,' Habeas said firmly. 'All of you.'

They did as they were told.

'An eleven-year-old boy?' Rita said. 'I mean, how is that even possible?'

'He eats cheese before he goes to sleep,' Habeas said, 'and he finds himself in the dream of the last person he thought about. You **KNOW** how it works.'

'But a boy of that age –' Rita said.

Habeas brought his fist down hard on the table.

'DO YOU DOUBT WHAT I'M TELLING YOU?' he thundered.

The atmosphere in the room tightened. All of the other heads of department looked down at the table, terrified to make eye contact with their boss.

'N-n-n-no,' Rita sputtered.

'GOOD!' Habeas continued to rage. **'BECAUSE HE'S DISCOVERED HIS POWERS AND HE'S SHARED HIS SECRET WITH SOMEONE ELSE! SO WE'RE ALREADY PLAYING CATCH-UP HERE! THE BOY MUST BE STOPPED! WHAT I WANT**

FROM YOU ARE IDEAS AS TO HOW WE'RE GOING TO DO IT!'

'Erm, wh-wh-wh-wh-what if we were to give him the same t-t-t-terrifying nightmare every time he eats ch-ch-ch-cheese,' stuttered Don Decadent, Training Delivery Manager with Special Responsibility for Scary Clowns. 'It might put him off eating the stuff. I could give you Arno, my best clown.'

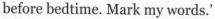

'Or,' Holt Hession piped up, 'I could give you something equally scary that has a clearer association with cheese. Maybe a plague of mice. Or rats, perhaps. Throw them into his dreams every night and there'll be no more cheese before bedtime. Mark my words.'

'Unfortunately,' Beddy Byes said, 'the boy doesn't frighten easily.'

'He's not scared of **ANYTHING!**' Habeas confirmed.

'Sir,' said Beddy Byes.

'If I might make so bold as to suggest something . . .'

'Go ahead,' Habeas said. 'None of these have managed to come up with anything. Frankly, I don't know why I pay them.'

They all looked at each other worriedly.

'Well,' said Beddy Byes, 'it seems to me that we're approaching this problem from the wrong angle. We don't have to frighten him away from eating cheese – we just have to cut off his source of it.'

'I'm listening, Beddy Byes.'

'What we have to do is find a way to close down his father's cheesemonger's.'

'And do you have any ideas as to how we might go about that?'

'As a matter of fact,' Beddy Byes said, a smile illuminating his face, 'I do!'

A STRANGE CRAVING

Agatha Rees-Lane was fast asleep and dreaming a happy dream. She was running on a treadmill, which might not be everyone's idea of a happy dream, but Agatha simply **LOVED** to run. Along with eating nothing except green vegetables, white fish and lean meat, running was what gave her the wonderfully thin figure that drew so many admiring glances – even if she said so herself.

She reached out a bony finger and pressed the button to increase the steepness of the climb. But at that very moment, for no apparent reason, Agatha started to think . . .

. . . about cheese.

Which was very unlike her. It had been years since she'd eaten the stuff. She had once been rather partial to a bit of Wensleydale, or even some Lincolnshire Poacher, but she gave it up when she dedicated herself to becoming fit and healthy.

So why was she suddenly dreaming about it?

Strangely, she wasn't dreaming about the sort of hard cheeses that she once enjoyed. She was dreaming about something soft, and creamy, and pale yellow in colour with a pinky, orangey rind – and, yes, it was disgustingly, nauseatingly, stomach-churningly . . .

. . . STINKY!

Agatha woke up with a sudden start. She was staring at the ceiling and breathing hard. She'd never had a dream so vivid before – a dream in which she could smell *and* taste things.

And now she had only one thing on her mind.

She got out of bed.

'Is everything OK?' her husband, Harvey, asked.

'Feeling a bit peckish,' she said. 'I think I'll go and have some, um, broccoli.'

Agatha went downstairs to the kitchen. She pulled open the fridge door. She knew exactly what she wanted – and it wasn't broccoli.

Aldrin's lunch box sat on the bottom shelf. Sebastian and those two wonderful friends of his had very thoughtfully offered to dispose of all the chocolate bars, and crisps and fizzy drinks that they'd confiscated. He was such a kind and considerate boy! But Agatha had said that she would hold on to the cheese and, when bin day arrived, throw it into the back of the refuse lorry herself.

You couldn't take any chances with something that ponged like that.

She took the lunch box out of the fridge and sat down at the kitchen table with it. She took a deep breath, then popped the lid. She was surprised to discover that the smell wasn't nearly as bad as she remembered it.

Her fingers were shaking and her mouth salivating as she tore open the wax paper that said *C'est Cheese*, pulled off a piece and popped it into her mouth.

She chewed it for a few seconds and – oh my word! It was the most delicious thing she had EVER tasted!

What had she been eating all these years? Food that tasted of absolutely nothing. She might as well have been sucking on her own slippers for all the pleasure she'd got from it. Now, her entire body was trembling with the adrenaline rush of gobbling down something that actually had flavour!

She ate the Stinking Bishop in eight greedy mouthfuls. And when she was finished, she licked the lunch box clean!

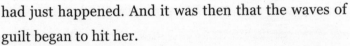

She went back to bed and lay awake for an hour, thinking about what had just happened. And it was then that the waves of guilt began to hit her.

How could *she* lecture schoolchildren about their unhealthy eating habits, then get up in the middle of the night to devour half a pound of cheese all by herself?

'Agatha,' she told herself, 'you MUST exercise more self-control!'

But that didn't alter the fact that it *was* delicious. Perhaps, she thought, it *was* possible to enjoy cheese from time to time *and* remain healthy. Yes, she thought, maybe it *was* just a question of enjoying things in moderation.

But then she fell asleep – and proceeded to have a nightmare that almost **TERRIFIED** the life out of her!

25

HUNDREDS OF TINY PIECES

Aldrin absolutely HATED hummus. His mum used to say that, while hummus was spelled **H, U, M, M, U, S**, it was actually pronounced '**BORING!**'

And even though she was joking, Aldrin thought that she had a point.

Hummus was tasteless, colourless, odourless and completely lacking in texture – especially compared to cheese. What he wouldn't give right now for some complex Gubbeen, or some oniony Challerhocker, or some sticky Moses Sleeper.

Harry saw Aldrin staring at his lunch with a look of dismay on his face and he laughed.

'Do you want to share mine?' he asked.

'Really?' Aldrin said.

'Here,' Harry said, handing Aldrin half of his chicken sandwich. 'I can't keep looking at your sad face staring at those little celery sticks and whatever's in that tub.'

'It's hummus,' Aldrin said.

'Eugh!' Harry agreed. 'Well, at least you know it's good for you – what with it being **BORING! BORING! BORING!**'

Aldrin and Frankie laughed at Harry's impersonation of Agatha Rees-Lane.

'Where is she anyway?' Aldrin wondered, because there had been no spot checks on their lunch boxes at the cafeteria today.

'Someone said she was sick,' Frankie said.

'Are you sure you don't mind sharing this sandwich with me?' Aldrin asked.

Harry shrugged. 'Of course not. You're my friend.'

Aldrin smiled, then he took a bite. It tasted . . . well, if Aldrin was being honest, it tasted just OK. It wasn't spicy Queso Ibores, or crayony Pavé du Nord, or fruity Isle of Mull. But the fact that Harry had said that thing about him being his friend made it taste all the nicer.

Sisely arrived at the table then. She put Mrs Van Boxtel's book, *Myths and Legends of the Netherlands*, on the table in front of Aldrin.

'If you're not going to listen to my advice,' she said, 'you might as well take this back.'

Harry and Frankie looked at her curiously.

'Oh,' Aldrin said, trying to think fast. 'Sisely doesn't think I should write my story about Luuk van den Hoogenband. She's thinks it's, er, too far-fetched.'

'No,' Sisely corrected him, 'I think he's a man with a ridiculous superhero complex who should have stayed out of other people's business.'

'So,' Aldrin said, quickly changing the subject, 'how's your story coming along, Harry?'

'Good,' Harry said. 'Do you want to see it?'

'I'd love to!' Aldrin told him.

'Me too!' said Frankie.

Harry reached into his schoolbag and pulled out a handful of pages.

'It's not finished yet,' he said, 'but this is what I've done so far.'

Aldrin took the pages from him.

'Wow!' he said.

Frankie looked at them over Aldrin's shoulder.

'You drew this?' he asked in wonder. 'Harry, it's like something you'd see in a proper comic.'

'It's **AMAZING!**' Aldrin agreed.

'*The Boy Who Hunts Crocodiles*,' Frankie read. 'I've had one or two close shaves with crocs meself over the years.'

Suddenly, the pages were rudely snatched from Aldrin's hands.

'What's this?' a voice asked.

They all looked up. It was Sebastian. And with him were his trusty lieutenants, Hercy and Algernon.

Aldrin leaped to his feet.

'**Give it back!**' he demanded, making a grab for the pages. 'Give it back to me now!'

But Algernon – or was it Hercy? – pushed him away.

'*The Boy Who Hunts Crocodiles*?' Sebastian said in a mocking voice, looking Harry's story over. 'Did you draw this?'

'Yes,' said Harry, 'and I want it back.'

'Why has he got glasses?' Sebastian asked. 'And an asthma inhaler?'

'Because superheroes don't always have square jaws and muscles.' Aldrin pointed out.

'They don't have bad eyesight and asthma either,' Sebastian said. 'And they're definitely not fat like you are, Adams.'

He laughed:

'BA-HA-HA-HA-HA-HA-HA-HA-HA-HA-HA-HA-HA-HA!'

Aldrin noticed that Hercy – or was it Algernon? – was holding a cardboard box filled with chocolate bars, crisps, biscuits, cakes and fizzy drinks they'd confiscated from the other children.

'My mum's not here today,' Sebastian said, 'so we're carrying out the spot checks for her. What have you got for us, oddballs?'

'Nothing,' Aldrin said. 'Give Harry his comic strip back and get lost.'

Silence fell upon the cafeteria. Suddenly, everyone was focused on the boy who was daring to stand up to the notorious Sebastian Rees-Lane.

Sebastian stared down his nose at Aldrin and smiled.

'Why aren't you frightened of me?' he asked.

'Because you're just a bully,' Aldrin told him. 'And, deep down, you're like all bullies – a coward.'

'A coward?' Sebastian laughed. 'You know I could snap you like a twig if I wanted to.'

'That's nothing to brag about,' Aldrin said calmly. 'You're a lot bigger than me. But the thought of it doesn't frighten me – not in the least. You see, you think being a bully makes you strong. I think it makes you weak.'

Aldrin could suddenly see something in Sebastian's eyes – it was uncertainty.

Sebastian glowered at Harry.

'Where's your lunch money?' he said.

'I, um, t-t-turned up to meet you b-b-before school,' Harry stuttered, 'but you didn't sh-sh-show up.'

'Well, I'm here now, aren't I? So hand over my quid.'

'Don't give it to him,' Aldrin told his friend. 'Give him back his comic strip, Sebastian.'

'Give me the money,' Sebastian told Harry, 'or I'll rip it to pieces.'

Harry reached for his pocket.

'He's bluffing,' Aldrin said. 'Don't give it to him.'

Harry withdrew his hand from his pocket – there was no money in it.

'Have it your way,' Sebastian said, then he held up Harry's comic strip in front of his face.

'No, please don't!' Harry pleaded.

Aldrin rushed forward, but Hercy and Algernon pushed him back.

Sebastian tore the pages in half, then in half again, then in half again, until Harry's comic strip had been reduced to hundreds of tiny pieces.

All that work – destroyed in an instant. Harry burst into tears. Sebastian dropped the pieces of paper on to the floor. Then he smiled.

'You shouldn't have listened to your fat friend,' he said gloatingly.

AN OLD WIVES' TALE

Doug was standing outside the cheesemonger's, dressed in his mouse costume, when Aldrin returned home from school.

'Aldrin!' he said to his son in an urgent whisper. 'There's something you need to see!'

'What is it?' Aldrin asked.

'It's Belinda,' Doug answered. 'It's probably best you see for yourself.'

Doug opened the door of the shop. And Aldrin found himself staring open-mouthed at the scene.

Belinda was being polite to the customers!

More than that, she was being . . . helpful!

'You can't go wrong with Mont d'Or,' she was telling Mrs Jancker in a cheerful voice. 'It's made with milk from cows that live in the Alps. Probably why it tastes so . . . Alpsy.'

'She's been like this since she came in this morning,' Doug explained. 'It's like she's had some sort of personality transplant.'

'Pleasure to serve you, Mrs Jancker!' she said. 'And don't forget to bake it in the oven – best way to eat it.'

As Mrs Jancker left the shop, Belinda noticed that Doug and Aldrin were standing in the doorway, staring at her with their mouths open.

'What's up with you two?' she asked.

'Oh, nothing,' Doug replied. 'It's just you seem in an unusually good mood today.'

They stepped into the shop, then closed the door behind them.

'That's right,' Aldrin agreed. 'We're saying we really like it.'

'Well, it doesn't hurt to be nice to folk,' Belinda said. 'I'm sorry if I've been a bit of a Moaning Minnie sometimes in here. See, there's days I get frustrated with how me life turned out. I never thought I'd wind up working in a cheesemonger's. No offence, Doug.'

'Er, none taken,' Doug said uncertainly.

'I had a dream,' she explained. 'When I were younger, I wanted to be a famous singer.'

'I didn't know you could sing!' Doug said.

'Oh, aye,' she said. 'I can sing all right. I mean, I haven't in years.'

Aldrin smiled a secret smile. She had the most incredible voice he had ever heard.

'I wanted to be the next Shirley Bassey,' Belinda told them wistfully.

'She's a singer, Dad,' Aldrin explained, 'from the olden days.'

'How do *you* know about Shirley Bassey?' Belinda asked.

'Oh,' Aldrin stuttered. 'I just, um, saw her name once on the, um, internet.'

'Well, my voice were often compared to hers.'

'So what happened?' Doug asked.

'I'd put me name down for auditions and competitions, then I'd just not show up.'

'Why not?'

'Because of me nerves. I were always afraid of making a fool of meself, see?'

'But if you have a talent, Belinda, that's a terrible shame.'

'Well, don't worry, because I'm doing something about it. There's a talent contest in the community centre tonight and I've put me name down for that.'

'Really?' Aldrin asked delightedly.

'I've decided to be brave,' she said. 'I know now that I'm more than capable of standing up there on a stage and blowing folk away with my voice.'

'We'll come along tonight to support you,' Doug said. 'Won't we, Aldrin?'

'That's right,' Aldrin agreed. 'We'll be like your fan club, Belinda!'

Belinda smiled.

'Anyway,' she said, 'much as I've enjoyed working here, Doug, I think it only fair to tell you that I see tonight as my first step on the showbusiness ladder.'

It was at that moment that the door of the shop opened with a **DING!** Aldrin's mouth fell open when he saw who was standing in the doorway.

It was Agatha Rees-Lane.

'Come in,' Doug said. 'You're very welcome to *C'est Cheese*. What are you looking for today?'

'I'm not here to buy cheese!' Agatha said coolly.

Aldrin was standing behind the counter, just out of her line of vision.

'What can I do for you then?' Doug asked.

'I am *here*,' she said, 'to make a complaint.'

'A complaint?' Doug repeated.

'About one of your cheeses,' Agatha said, 'that I, um, *accidentally* ate last night,' she added sheepishly.

'You *accidentally* ate one of my cheeses?'

'That's right. And it gave me **NIGHT! MARES!** As a matter of fact, the worst **NIGHT! MARES!** that I have **EVER** had in my entire **LIFE!**'

'The thing is,' Doug explained, as delicately as he could, 'cheese doesn't actually *cause* nightmares. That's an old wives' tale, I'm afraid.'

'An old wives' tale?' said Agatha. 'How DARE you! I'm forty-four – and many people think I have the figure of a woman half that age!'

'What I mean by an old wives' tale is that it's a common myth that has no basis in fact.'

'*Here* are the facts, Mr Cheesemonger person. I never, **EVER** have nightmares. And I never, **EVER** eat cheese. But last night – like I said, *accidentally* – I ate some cheese that came from this very shop . . . and had a nightmare **SO** terrible, I can't even bring myself to describe it to you.'

'Look, Mrs um . . .'

'Rees-Lane.'

'Mrs Rees-Lane, we do have an excellent returns policy if you're not satisfied. Do you have the cheese with you now?'

'No, I don't. I ate it.'

'What, all of it?'

'Accidentally, yes.'

'You *accidentally* ate all of the cheese?'

'That's right. I wouldn't eat it on purpose. **DIS! GUSTING!** stuff. And me with my figure to think about and everything.'

'Can I ask you what kind of cheese it was?'

'It was called the Pongy Priest. Or the Whiffy Cardinal. Something of that order.'

'Was it the Stinking Bishop?'

'That was it! Awful stuff!'

Aldrin couldn't believe what he was hearing. And he couldn't stay silent for a second longer.

'THAT WAS MY LUNCH!' he blurted out.

Agatha noticed him for the first time.

'YOU!!!' she said, pointing an accusing finger at him and trembling with anger.

'YOU!!!' said Aldrin, pointing right back.

'What's all the shouting about?' Doug asked.

'She didn't even buy that cheese!' Aldrin told him. 'She stole it from me!'

'She did what?' Doug asked.

'She's in charge of **Healthy! Eating! Week!** She confiscates our lunches if she thinks they're not healthy enough! That's why I had to bring hummus and carrot sticks today!'

Doug shook his head in disappointment.

'I can't believe you would try to get a refund,' he said to Agatha, 'for cheese that you didn't even pay for!'

'I didn't come here for a refund,' Agatha snapped. 'I came here to tell you that you are selling a product, namely cheese, that is not only unhealthy for our bodies, it's also bad for our minds.'

Belinda had heard enough.

'Why don't you sling your hook,' she said, 'you busy old so-and-so.'

'Belinda's right,' Doug said. 'I'm going to have to ask you to leave this shop.'

'Oh, I'm going,' Agatha snapped back. 'But I can promise you this – you haven't heard the last of me!'

27

QUITE A SHOCK

Sisely's mum opened the door.

'Oh, hello,' she said, sounding pleasantly surprised. 'You're, um, the cheesemonger's boy.'

'Aldrin,' he reminded her.

'That's right! Will you tell your dad that the halloumi he recommended was every bit as good as he said it would be. Delicious.'

'It's made from a mixture of sheep's milk, goat's milk *and* cow's milk, that one.'

'Well, I grilled it, tossed it in some lemon juice, olive oil and mixed herbs and served it with a mango salad and some crusty bread.'

'Sounds delicious. Is, um, Sisely home?'

'Sisely!' Mrs Musa called over her shoulder. 'Your

friend is here to see you!'

Sisely emerged from her bedroom and came halfway down the stairs.

'Aldrin?' she said. 'What are you doing here?'

'There's a talent contest at the community centre tonight,' he told her. 'I wondered if you wanted to come with me. There's one act especially that I really would like you to see.'

'I'm reading my maths book,' she said.

'Your maths book will still be there in the morning,' her mum said. 'It might be nice to spend some time with your friend.'

Sisely sighed.

'Fine,' she said. 'I'll get my coat.'

Minutes later, Aldrin and Sisely were walking the short distance to the community centre.

'So what *is* this act that you're so keen for me to see?' Sisely asked.

'Well, you know Belinda,' Aldrin said, 'who works with my dad in the shop? She's going to be singing tonight – and she has *the* most amazing voice EVER!'

'*That's* why you're dragging me away from my maths book?'

'The thing is, she's always wanted to be a famous

singer. But she had this recurring nightmare, where she was standing onstage at an audition, or a talent show, and just as she opened her mouth to sing she realized that she was standing there in her, um, *smalls*.'

'That's a common anxiety nightmare.'

'Well, let's just say that, after her dream the other night, she'll never be worried about going onstage again.'

Sisely stopped walking.

'What did you do?' she asked worriedly.

'I helped her!' Aldrin tried to explain. 'The fear of performing in public was stopping her from following her dreams, Sisely. All I did was show her what would happen if she conquered that fear.'

'I told you not to mess around with this thing until I find out more about it.'

'I've been given the power to make people happy, Sisely. It would be wrong not to use it.'

They started walking again. Soon, they arrived at the community centre. There was a **bu**z**z** of anticipation outside. This year's contest promised to be the best ever. Aldrin and Sisely joined the queue of people waiting to get in.

'Everything is going to change for Belinda after tonight!' Aldrin predicted.

'It looks like it already has,' Sisely pointed out.

Because it was at that exact moment that they noticed Belinda, in a sparkly dress, climbing out of the back of a long black limousine. It seemed a little bit excessive – especially as she only lived half a mile away from the community centre.

Aldrin could hear other people in the queue saying:

'Here, isn't that *her* from the cheesemonger's? The rude one? What's happened to her?'

Belinda started waving to the crowd, the same way the Queen waves – hand raised, with just the slightest twist of the wrist.

'Who does she think she is?' Aldrin heard people muttering.

The queue started moving. Fifteen minutes later, they were inside. Aldrin found Doug, who was sitting in the front row, saving them a couple of seats.

'Hello, Sisely!' Doug said. 'Exciting, isn't it?'

'We just saw Belinda arrive,' Aldrin told his dad, 'in a stretch limo.'

'Yes, she decided to treat herself. It's always been her dream to sit in the back of –'

Suddenly, Doug felt a tap on the shoulder. He turned round. It was Mr Gaskin, the local postman.

'I want a word with you,' he said.

'Is something the matter?' Doug asked.

'Oh, something's the matter all right,' he said. 'We had some of your cheese after supper last night. Bit of blue, wasn't it, love?'

Mrs Gaskin was sitting beside him.

'Stilton,' she confirmed. 'With charcoal crackers.'

'Because I were passing by,' said Mr Gaskin, 'and I liked your joke about Paris Stilton. And I thought, *We've not had cheese in ages.* I used to really love a bit of Stilton, me.'

'Are you saying that there was something wrong with it?' Doug asked.

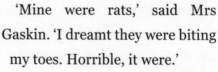

'Oh, there were something wrong with it all right. Give me nightmares, it did. Both of us, matter of fact. I were being chased by a pack of dogs and Barbara here –'

'Mine were rats,' said Mrs Gaskin. 'I dreamt they were biting my toes. Horrible, it were.'

'I'm very sorry to hear that,' Doug told them, 'but I can assure you that eating cheese had nothing to do with, well, whatever you dreamt.'

'Well, we're not the only ones,' said Mrs Gaskin. 'There's other folk around here are saying it as well. Mrs Banerjee from number 45 – same thing happened to her.'

'What did she have?' Mr Gaskin asked.

'Half a pound of ricotta salata.'

'No, I mean what were her nightmare?'

'Oh, she were attacked by seagulls. And then there's her kiddies. They had the same cheese and they *all* had nightmares – ghosts and witches and all sorts.'

'That's just a coincidence,' Doug said confidently.

'Coincidence, my eye,' said Mr Gaskin. 'I were talking to that lovely Mrs Dabrowski this morning. Her sister cleans for that Agatha Rees-whatsit, who's got a list of **FIFTY** people who've had cheese out of your shop – **AND** had nightmares after eating it.'

'But that's . . . impossible,' Doug assured him.

'I'm only telling you what I've heard.'

Aldrin looked at Sisely and she stared back at him.

'Fifty people?' she whispered. 'That's very strange.'

'Like Dad said,' Aldrin replied, 'it's probably just a coincidence.'

'No,' she insisted. 'Something weird is going on. And I wouldn't be surprised if it's somehow connected to your power.'

They didn't have time to discuss it further because the show was about to begin.

Belinda was scheduled to go on third, after a man who could recite entire passages from the works of William Shakespeare backwards and a woman with a dancing sheepdog named Colin. Both acts brought the crowd to its feet, the first with his 'Question the is that – be to not or, be to' finale, the second with their six-legged Charleston.

And then it was Belinda's turn.

'Ladies and gentlemen,' the compère announced, 'I'm very excited to introduce our next act, who some of you may know from the cheesemonger's on Burnett Road. Performing for the very first time in public – singing the Shirley Bassey hit "Diamonds Are Forever" – she is our very own Songstress of Swiss, our Chanteuse of Cheddar: let me hear some applause for Belinda Orpen!'

Everyone in the community centre clapped as Belinda sashayed out on to the stage, smiling and taking bows, even before she'd sung a note. There was definitely nothing wrong with her confidence now, Aldrin thought.

The applause died, then the music started up and Belinda closed her eyes.

'Wait until you hear her voice,' Aldrin whispered to Sisely. 'It's spectacular!'

Belinda opened her mouth. And that's when a sound came out that was quite unlike the voice that Aldrin had heard in her dream.

'Diamonds **are** forev-**aaahhh**,' she sang.

'Oh, dear!' Doug mumbled.

'Oh, no!' Aldrin groaned.

Because one thing was instantly clear . . .

Belinda had an absolutely terrible voice – even Silas was a better singer!

Suddenly, all around him, people were laughing.

'This is a wind-up!' someone said. 'She has to be putting it on!'

But she wasn't putting it on.

'Diamonds **are** forev-aaahhh . . .'

The laughter grew and grew until it drowned out Belinda's voice. And that was no bad thing, because she really **WAS terrible!**

Aldrin felt awful.

'I hate to say I told you so,' Sisely said out of the corner of her mouth, 'but I did.'

'Get off!' someone shouted.

Then the boos started to rain down on her. Belinda stopped singing. Aldrin watched her eyes fill slowly up with tears.

'Put Colin back on,' someone shouted. 'He'd make a better job of that song than you!'

Belinda fixed Aldrin with a look and screamed at him, **'This is all YOUR fault, Aldrin Adams!'** before she ran off the stage in tears.

28

'CHEDDAR! CHEDDAR! CHEDDAR!'

Aldrin didn't sleep well that night – he was so consumed by guilt. He had put into motion the events that had led to Belinda's humiliation at the community centre, and now video footage of her performance was already circulating on social media.

By eight o'clock the following morning, hundreds of thousands of people, all over the world, had watched it. Many of them had posted comments, few of which were complimentary.

Doug still couldn't understand it.

'Who on earth encouraged her to think she could sing in the first place?' he asked while they were eating breakfast on Monday morning.

They were having grilled cheese waffles. Aldrin was

having his without the waffles.

'I, um, don't know,' he told his dad. 'It's a genuine mystery to me.'

'It wasn't you, was it?' Doug asked.

'Me?'

'You heard what she said before she ran off the stage. She said: "This is all **YOUR** fault, Aldrin Adams!"'

'Um, maybe she meant that I should have persuaded her not to enter the contest.'

'But you'd never heard her sing before, had you?'

'No.'

Well, not like that anyway, Aldrin thought.

Doug had called round to see Belinda immediately after the contest, just to make sure she was all right, but she'd refused to open the door. Through an upstairs window, she'd told him that she wouldn't be back at work tomorrow. As a matter of fact, she'd said, she was never leaving the house again!

'And there's this *other* mystery,' Doug said.

'What other mystery?' Aldrin wondered.

'All these people saying that our cheese is giving them nightmares.'

'It's just a coincidence, Dad.'

'It's a pretty big coincidence, Aldrin. Agatha, Mr

and Mrs Gaskin, Mrs Dabrowski, Mrs Banerjee and her children.'

Aldrin was wondering whether Sisely was right. Was it somehow connected to his power?

'You haven't had any funny dreams lately, have you?' Doug asked anxiously.

Aldrin wanted to tell him everything. He wanted to tell him all about his strange superpower. But he was worried that he wouldn't believe him – or, worse, that he would believe him and cut off his supply of cheese.

'No,' Aldrin insisted. 'No strange dreams at all.'

'Then I'm probably worrying about absolutely nothing,' Doug said. 'I mean, no one eats more cheese from the shop than *you* do!'

Aldrin looked at the clock.

'I'd better go,' he said, 'or I'll be late for school.'

Aldrin pulled on his school blazer while Doug stepped into his mouse costume.

'I don't know *how* I'm going to manage without Belinda today,' Doug said as he walked Aldrin downstairs, 'drumming up business *and* working behind the counter.'

But that, it turned out, was the least of Doug's worries. Because a nasty surprise was awaiting him

when he opened the door.

Agatha was standing outside the shop. And with her was a group of about thirty people. Aldrin spotted Mr and Mrs Gaskin, and Mrs Dabrowski, and Mrs Banerjee with her three kids.

But these weren't the friendly-faced customers that Doug and Aldrin knew. They were angry, and they were holding placards with slogans on them, like:

CHEESE – IT'S NOT GOUDA FOR YOU!

And:

YOU CAN'T BRIE SELLING THAT POISON AROUND HERE!

And:

CLOSE THIS SHOP!
IT'S FOR THE GRATER GOOD!

And when the crowd saw Doug and Aldrin, they started chanting:

**'GO TO HELLA WITH YOUR MOZZARELLA!
GO TO HELLA WITH YOUR MOZZARELLA!'**

'What are you doing?' Doug asked Agatha. 'You'll scare away all my customers!'

'That's the idea of a picket!' Agatha replied coldly.

'You're going to put us out of business,' Aldrin said.

'And what business *is* that?' Agatha asked. 'The business of frightening people out of their wits?'

'I'll call the police,' Doug threatened.

'Yes, do that,' Agatha urged him. 'I think they'd be very interested to learn about the mind-altering substances that you're selling in this so-called shop.'

'For the last time,' Doug told the crowd, 'my cheese is NOT responsible for your nightmares!'

'Then how do you explain it?' asked Mrs Banerjee. 'For three nights in a row, I dreamt that a pack of wolves was trying to get into my house – and that was after eating your ricotta. My children had it as well. They woke up screaming

– seeing three-eyed monsters and all sorts of awful things.'

'But we've run this shop for years,' Doug tried to explain. 'And no one has **EVER** complained about our cheese giving them nightmares before.'

'I now have reports,' Agatha told him, 'from more than one hundred people who, in the past week, have eaten cheese from this shop and experienced disturbing dreams. We are not *all* liars, Mr Adams.'

'My dad isn't saying you're liars,' Aldrin told her. 'He's saying there must be some other explanation for what's been happening.'

'What *other* explanation?' she demanded.

'I don't know. But it's obvious that something very strange is going on.'

It was at that exact moment that Aldrin noticed a stranger watching them from the shadow of the bus shelter on the other side of Burnett Road. He was a tall, powerfully built man, with a pale complexion, a wild mane of black, curly hair, hooded eyes, a crooked nose and dark sideburns that ran down to his chin. He wore a long black coat, buttoned right up to his neck, and, most noticeable of all, a horrible smirk on his face.

'I've heard just about enough of this!' Agatha declared. 'We intend to stand here all day, every day,

Mr Adams, until we've turned away every last one of your customers and closed this ghastly shop down.'

'Please!' Doug begged her. 'This shop is our lives! Don't do this to us!'

'CHEDDAR! CHEDDAR! CHEDDAR!'

Agatha **shouted**.

And the others responded with:

'OUT! OUT! OUT!'
'CHEDDAR! CHEDDAR! CHEDDAR!'
'OUT! OUT! OUT!'
'CHEDDAR!'
'OUT!'
'CHEDDAR!'
'OUT!'
'CHEDDAR! CHEDDAR! CHEDDAR!'
'OUT! OUT! OUT!'

Aldrin looked at his father's devastated face. The last time he'd seen him look so desperately sad was the day of Cynthia's funeral.

29

A FRIEND LOST

It made no sense – no sense at all.

The maths teacher, Mr Swanson, had scribbled an equation on the whiteboard and asked the class to solve it before the bell sounded.

But Aldrin wasn't working on the equation. He had Mrs Van Boxtel's book about the myths and legends of the Netherlands open on his lap and he was reading the account of how Luuk van den Hoogenband was stripped of his powers.

According to the book, Luuk had wanted to give Princess Femke what her heart most desired – just like Aldrin did with Belinda. But, while Aldrin couldn't have foreseen what would happen that night at the community centre, Luuk must have known the likely consequences of persuading the princess that she could fly. If he really was in love with her, why would he convince her to do something that would probably result in her death?

That was the bit that didn't make any sense.

And then he read a new name – one that Sisely hadn't mentioned.

When the gods stripped Luuk of his powers, they gave them to a man named Prince Pim van Almsick. But there was no explanation in the book as to who he was, or why *he* was chosen, or what became of him. The story seemed to end in mid-air.

And then Aldrin suddenly discovered there was a reason for that.

There was a page missing from the book. He could see where it had been roughly torn out. He looked at the numbers at the bottom of the pages. They went from 106 to 109.

What was on the missing page? And who had torn it out of the book?

'Aldrin Adams? Do you know the answer?'

Oh, no. Mr Swanson was staring straight at him. An old man with a long, wrinkly neck and tiny glasses with round lenses, he always reminded Aldrin of a tortoise.

'The answer?' Aldrin said, stalling for time.

'It's just you seemed to be staring down very intensely,' said Mr Swanson. 'I thought you would probably be first with the solution to our equation.'

'It's 17,385,' Sisely announced, saving Aldrin's blushes.

'Yes, that's correct,' said Mr Swanson. 'But I wasn't asking you, Sisely.'

'Well,' she said, 'I had the answer after two seconds.'

'Thanks,' Aldrin mouthed to her.

The bell sounded then and everyone stood up and started making their way to the door.

Harry was walking just ahead of Aldrin.

'Hey, Harry,' Aldrin said, 'do you want to work on our stories together after school? We could start *The Boy Who Hunts Crocodiles* again. I can remember every single thing that happened in it.'

But Harry didn't respond.

'Harry?' Aldrin said, confused. 'Harry, what's wrong? Are you OK?'

But Harry just kept on walking.

Aldrin touched him on the shoulder.

'Harry, why are you ignoring me?' he asked.

Harry spun round.

'BECAUSE I DON'T WANT TO BE YOUR FRIEND ANY MORE!' he roared.

'Why?' Aldrin asked. 'Did I do something wrong?'

'YES, YOU DID SOMETHING WRONG!' Harry said. 'YOU'RE THE REASON MY STORY GOT RIPPED UP!'

At that moment, Sisely and Frankie caught up with Aldrin and Harry.

'I was only trying to get you to stand up to Sebastian,' Aldrin argued.

'AND LOOK WHERE THAT GOT ME!' Harry shouted. 'WHY COULDN'T YOU JUST KEEP YOUR NOSE OUT OF MY BUSINESS?'

Aldrin could suddenly feel the weight of Sisely's stare on the back of his neck.

'Here,' Frankie said, trying to take the heat out of the situation, 'did I tell you about the time that I trod on a landmine?'

Harry turned his anger on Frankie then.

'When are you going to stop wasting our time with your ridiculous lies?' he spat.

Frankie looked stunned – and hurt.

'They're not lies,' he said.

'Of course they're lies!' Harry raged. 'Everything

217

that comes out of your mouth is a lie! You're not a spy! You're not a professional footballer! You can't breathe underwater and you've never jumped the Grand Canyon on a motorbike! You're just a sad person with no friends who makes things up just for attention!'

Aldrin tried to stop him from saying anything else he might later regret.

'Frankie *has* got friends,' Aldrin insisted. 'He has us for starters.'

It was then that Aldrin heard a loud peal of evil laughter. **'BA-HA-HA-HA-HA-HA-HA-HA-HA-HA-HA-HA-HA-HA!'**

He turned round to see Sebastian walking towards them, along with his two ever-reliable sidekicks.

'What's this?' he asked. 'Are the oddballs falling out?'

'Stay out of our business,' Aldrin told him.

'What,' Sebastian said, 'the same way that people are staying out of your father's business? I was talking to my mother at lunchtime. She said that shop of his hasn't had a customer all morning!'

'That's because she's put a picket on the door,' Aldrin pointed out angrily.

Sebastian turned to Harry.

'You know what?' he said. 'I've always thought you didn't quite *belong* with the oddballs.'

'Don't listen to him,' Frankie warned Harry.

'Oh, shut up,' Sebastian said, 'Frankie Fibberer.'

'It's Fidderer.'

Sebastian turned his eyes back to Harry.

'You're better than this lot,' he told him. 'How would you like to join our gang?'

'Join you?' Harry asked.

'Yes, you can even sit with us in the cafeteria.'

Aldrin knew Sebastian's game.

'Harry,' he said, 'don't listen to him. He's just using you to try to hurt me.'

'I like you,' Sebastian told Harry. 'Hercy and Algernon like you as well – don't you, chaps?'

They nodded dutifully.

'He tore up your story,' Aldrin reminded Harry. 'He made you give him your lunch money every day.'

'I can promise you,' Sebastian said, 'that if you join us, you won't have to give me anything ever again. What do you say?'

Aldrin watched as his friend weighed it up. Here was a way for him to protect himself. If he accepted Sebastian's offer of friendship, he wouldn't have to be frightened of him any more.

'Harry,' Aldrin said pleadingly, 'don't listen to him. *We're* your friends. Me and Frankie and Sisely.'

But Harry just looked straight through him.

'Excellent!' Sebastian said, sliding a snake-like arm round Harry's shoulder.

Aldrin watched Harry walk away with the school bully, and he felt that particular kind of sadness that's known to anyone who has ever lost a friend.

30

MYSTERIES TO SOLVE

'It's all *my* stupid fault,' Aldrin said to Sisely as they walked home from school. 'I should have listened to you when you told me to stay out of other people's business until you found out more.'

'Feeling sorry for yourself isn't going to help,' Sisely pointed out. 'And it's not going to solve our mystery either. We still have to figure out why you *have* this ability. We also have to find out why everyone who eats your dad's cheese is suddenly having nightmares. I still think the whole thing is connected in some way. Unless, of course . . .'

'Unless what?'

'Unless it's just poor refrigeration.'

'What do you mean by that?' Aldrin said defensively.

'Cheese is basically rotting milk, right?'

'Yeah, that's true – even though it sounds disgusting when you put it that way. It's actually the bacteria that makes it taste so good.'

'And a cheesemonger's job is to control the rate at which it rots so that it keeps its flavour. That's why it's always so cold in your dad's shop, right?'

'Yes, the temperature has to stay at between twelve and thirteen degrees Celsius. Any colder and the bacteria dies. Any warmer and it grows too quickly.'

'So what would happen if you ate cheese with too much bacteria in it?'

'You'd probably be very sick,' Aldrin said. 'What exactly are you getting at, Sisely?'

'Bacteria can cause fever,' she explained, 'and fever can trigger hallucinations.'

'But these people aren't having hallucinations,' Aldrin argued. 'They're having nightmares.'

'Are they?' Sisely asked. 'Or are they experiencing hypnagogic visions?'

'OK, I don't even know what those are.'

'I was doing some research online. Hypnagogic visions *feel* like dreams. Except they're *not* dreams. They're actually hallucinations that we can experience while we're going to sleep. I'm wondering if they can be brought on by eating cheese that's gone off.'

'There's no need to wonder, because Dad doesn't sell cheese that's gone off!'

'Maybe the shop was too hot one day.'

'The temperature is controlled by a thermostat and he checks it about twenty times a day, OK?'

'OK, fine.'

There was a long moment of silence between them. Then Aldrin remembered something.

'Sisely?' he asked. 'You didn't tear a page out of Mrs Van Boxtel's book, did you?'

'No,' she replied, 'but there *is* a page missing.'

'I noticed. It's the one about Prince Pim van, I don't know, whatever-his-name-is.'

'Prince Pim van Almsick.'

'That's it.'

'So you're finally reading the book?'

'That's what I was doing in Mr Swanson's class.'

'So, what do you think?'

'I just don't believe the story about Luuk convincing Femke that she could fly.'

'Neither do I.'

'Really?' Aldrin asked.

'Well, if he loved her,' Sisely said, 'why would he persuade her to do something so dangerous that it would lead to her death?'

'That's what I thought! And who was this Pim van –?'

'Almsick.'

'Exactly. Why did the gods give him Luuk's powers? And whatever happened to him?'

'The answers to those questions,' Sisely said, 'are all on that missing page.'

Aldrin suddenly caught a whiff of something – and it wasn't pleasant.

'Eugh!' he said. 'What's that?'

Sisely caught it too.

'I don't know,' she said. 'But it's turning my stomach.'

The closer to Aldrin's home they got, the fouler the smell grew. When they turned the corner on to Burnett Road, they both stopped dead in their tracks. Because standing there, right in front of Aldrin's dad's shop, was something that defied belief.

It was a **MOUNTAIN** of cheese!

It covered the entire path and most of the road and it was even taller than Aldrin's bedroom window.

The sun was beating down on it – and it **STANK!**

'What in the name of –!' Aldrin exclaimed.

The police, Aldrin noticed, were closing off the road to traffic. And the neighbours, unable to bear the smell, were evacuating their homes, clutching what few possessions they could carry.

Aldrin spotted his dad. He was watching two policewomen use traffic cones and yellow scene-of-crime tape to create a cordon round the enormous, vile-smelling Alp.

'Sisely, I'll see you tomorrow,' he told his friend, then he ran to Doug, shouting, 'Dad, what's going on? What's happened?'

Aldrin could see that he'd been crying.

'It started just after you left for school this morning,' Doug explained, wiping away tears with the back of his hand. 'People started bringing back their cheese – and dumping it outside the shop.'

'What?' asked Aldrin. 'Why?'

'Because it's causing nightmares,' a voice behind him said. Aldrin whirled round. It was Agatha, smiling triumphantly. 'This shop is a menace to public health. And I told you I would put you out of business.'

Aldrin fixed Doug with a look.

'Dad,' he said, 'you can't let her win.'

'I'm sorry,' Doug replied. 'It's over, Aldrin. I have no choice. I'm going to have to close *C'est Cheese* for good.'

31

'THE END OF THE BOY'

The stranger was watching this scene unfold from behind the bus shelter opposite the shop.

He watched Aldrin burst into tears and Doug attempt to comfort his son. He saw Agatha smile, savouring every moment of her triumph – he rather liked her! And he heard Doug shout at her that she had got what she wanted, and now she should go away – or words to that effect.

He watched the picketers drift away with their signs and he saw the police scratch their heads, wondering how they were going to dispose of all this cheese. Someone mentioned calling in the army.

Habeas Grusselvart couldn't help but laugh. It had all gone to plan.

A moment later, Beddy Byes appeared at his side.

'I spoke to the police,' he told his boss, 'and I offered to dispose of the cheese for them.'

'Excellent,' said Habeas. 'Have our people see to it, will you? I want every ounce of it brought to Todmorden and I want it tonight.'

'Yes, Oh Just and Mighty One.'

Habeas looked around, taking in the modest street.

'So,' he said, 'this was where the great Cynthia Adams lived, was it?'

'Yes, sir,' Beddy Byes told him.

'Grotty little place, isn't it?'

'Miserable, sir. Do you think that's the end of the boy?'

'Oh, yes. We just have to get our hands on whatever's left in that shop. Then I'm absolutely certain we'll have seen the last of Aldrin Adams.'

Beddy Byes chuckled. 'He never even knew what he had. Or why he had it.'

'Let's be thankful for that,' Habeas told him. 'You did excellent work, Beddy Byes.'

They watched the sign on the door of *C'est Cheese* change from **'OPEN'** to **'CLOSED'**.

And, instantly, the sense of unease that Habeas had been feeling of late lifted. As a matter of fact, it was the happiest he'd felt in a long, long time.

PART THREE

32

THE NEW NORMAL

The weeks trundled by.

Beddy Byes arranged the removal of the big, stinking mountain of cheese, which was blocking the path and half the road in front of what was once the best cheesemonger's for miles and miles around. In their oxygen masks and hazmat suits, Habeas Grusselvart's men laboured for fourteen hours to clean it up and transport it, in three truckloads, to his secret lair in Todmorden.

After a few days, the neighbours began to drift back to their homes and life returned to normal. For everyone, that is, except Aldrin and Doug.

Their lives had changed utterly.

Now that **C'est Cheese** was closed, Doug had no

reason to get up early in the morning. So he didn't bother. He was still in bed when Aldrin left for school most days now.

Sometimes, Aldrin would try to encourage him to make an effort. He'd pull back his curtains for him and say, 'Rise and shine, Dad! A brand-new day! Who knows what it holds!'

'Probably more misery,' Doug would reply, his face buried in a pillow. 'Close the curtains again, Aldrin, there's a good lad.'

He stopped shaving. He rarely showered. When he did manage to drag himself out of bed, he did nothing more than sit around the flat in his dressing gown, occasionally watching one of those TV programmes where members of the public are encouraged to be mean to each other for the entertainment of a studio audience and people watching at home.

With no money coming in, the bills quickly piled up. And then the letters started arriving again from the bank, threatening to take the roof from over Doug and Aldrin's heads.

At school, things had changed for Aldrin too. Harry didn't speak to him any more. He ignored him in class, and at lunchtime he sat with his new best friends –

Sebastian, Hercy and Algernon.

Aldrin made up his mind that he would never use his strange supernatural power again. Who would be so irresponsible as to give a child an ability like that and not provide instructions? If you buy a toaster, for instance, it comes with a 300-page manual, explaining in ten different languages how to plug it in. So where was his user's guide?

And while it bothered Sisely that, for once in her life, she had failed to solve a puzzle, she respected Aldrin's wish to never discuss the matter again. Unable to talk about the extraordinary secret they shared, a distance opened up between them.

Sisely read her school books in the cafeteria now, while Aldrin sat and listened to Frankie tell him how he'd jumped across the Thames on his skateboard, or climbed up the outside of the Eiffel Tower, or broken into the Pentagon by skilfully evading the photoelectric-beam sensors.

Frankie's stories were about the only exciting thing in Aldrin's life now.

One Saturday afternoon, Aldrin was sitting in front of the piano, with Silas on top of his head. He was hammering away at the keys, producing a tune that sounded something like this:

PL**O**NK-PL**O**NK...**P**L**A**NK...P**LA**AA**N**N**N**K...
PL**I**NK...PL**II**I**N**N**NK**...**P**L**I**N**K...

Silas did his best impersonation of Adele in an effort
to cheer Doug and Aldrin up.

RRRIBBIT...RRRIBBIT...RRRIBBIT...

But he wasn't sure if they noticed.

'Are you going to see your friends this weekend?'
asked Doug, who was still in his dressing gown, even
though it was almost two o'clock.

'I'm not really friends with Harry any more,' Aldrin
told his dad.

'Oh, that's sad,' Doug said.

'And Sisely does Advanced Maths at the university
on a Saturday.'

'Such a clever girl. What about Frankie?'

'He's in New York this weekend, abseiling off the top
of the Empire State Building. I know it's just a story,
but I don't want to embarrass him by calling round and
catching him out.'

'You're a very thoughtful boy,' Doug said. Then, after
a moment's silence, he added, 'I really miss Belinda,
don't you, Aldrin?'

Aldrin still felt bad about what he'd done to her. The

233

clip of her slaughtering 'Diamonds Are Forever' now had more than three million online views.

'You haven't heard from her?' Aldrin asked.

'Apparently, she's working in that big supermarket on Digges Road,' Doug said, 'giving out cheese samples. I know she could be grumpy with the customers, but she's been a good friend to me since your mum died.'

This made Aldrin feel even worse.

'Do you want some lunch?' Doug asked.

'Yeah,' Aldrin said. 'I think I'll have some hummus.'

Doug's eyes widened in surprise.

'Hummus?' he repeated.

'Yeah.'

'Not cheese?'

'No,' said Aldrin, sick of the stuff and all of its unhappy associations. 'There are *other* foods in the world, you know? Do we have any celery sticks?'

It was at that moment that they heard three sharp knocks on the front door.

Doug was expecting to receive an eviction notice any day now. He opened the window and looked out.

'Who is it?' he called down.

'Don't worry, I'm not the bailiffs!' a man said in a

polite voice. 'I wondered if I might have a word with you, if it's not too much trouble?'

'As long as you're not here to throw us out,' Doug said, 'I'll be right down.'

For some reason, Aldrin's curiosity was roused by this stranger. He followed his dad downstairs.

Doug opened the front door. Standing there was a friendly-faced man in his late forties. He was thin, like a broom handle, with dark, slicked-back hair and black horn-rimmed glasses set upon a large nose, and dressed in a dark suit complete with a red bow tie.

'Hello,' the man said, presenting his hand to Doug. 'The name is Maurice Mackle.' He pronounced it *Morr-eece*. 'I knew your late wife, Cynthia.'

There was something

about this stranger that Aldrin instantly disliked.

'Oh, yes,' said Doug. 'I met you – didn't I? On the day of the funeral?'

'A sad day,' the man said, then he turned his attention to Aldrin, standing just behind Doug. 'And you must be her son, of course?'

'Yes,' said Doug. 'This is our boy, Aldrin.'

'I can see the likeness. Cynthia and I worked together in Farlowe's. I suppose you could say we served our apprenticeship together – under Madame Lacombe.'

The name made Doug smile.

'She often talked about her,' he said. 'Everything she knew about cheese, she learned from Aline Lacombe – she always said that.'

Doug took a step backwards.

'Come in,' he said.

The stranger stepped into the shop and took an admiring look around.

'What a wonderful cheesemonger's,' he said. 'Such a shame to see another one close. Seems fewer and fewer people are eating the stuff these days.'

'So,' Doug said, 'what can I do for you, Mr Mackle?'

'Well,' the man said, 'I hope you won't think this

insensitive of me, but I heard that the shop had closed. As it happens, I'm still in the business myself – the wholesale end of things. Like I said, cheese is becoming something of a rarity. And, without meaning to be indelicate, I wondered whether you'd be interested in selling your leftover stock.'

'Selling it?' Doug asked.

'Yes,' the man said. 'You've got an awful lot of cheese here. And it's all going off – well, it's going off from the day it's made, isn't it? There's no point in you paying to refrigerate it if the shop is closed.'

Hearing him say those last four words did something to Aldrin. He realized that he wasn't ready to say goodbye to **C'est Cheese** and the happy life they shared. Getting rid of the stock would be the final act – there would be no coming back from it.

'Take it,' Doug told the stranger. 'Take it all.'

'Dad, no,' Aldrin heard himself say.

Maurice laughed nervously.

'Er, I couldn't possibly just *take* it,' he said. 'I'm willing to pay good money for it.'

'I don't want money,' Doug told him. 'I just want rid of it. You'll be doing me a favour.'

'Dad, don't do this!' Aldrin pleaded.

'If you were a friend of Cynthia's,' Doug said, 'then I can't think of anyone better to have it. Help yourself.'

Aldrin took one last sorrowful look around the shop that he loved so much.

At the white cheeses, the orange cheeses and the yellow cheeses.

At the cheeses that were covered with brilliantly coloured wax – fire-engine red, dark chocolate brown and bright tangerine.

At the cheeses filled with holes, the cheeses dusted with charcoal and the cheeses marbled with mould.

At the cheeses that crumbled when you cut them and the cheeses that oozed.

At the cheeses that smelled of fresh-cut grass and the cheeses that smelled of butterscotch ice cream and the cheeses that smelled like sweaty feet.

And, yes, even the Babybels that Cynthia loved so much and that cheese snobs said didn't belong there.

'Dad,' he said again, 'please don't do this.'

'Sorry, son,' Doug said. 'That part of our lives is over now. I'll leave the door open, Mr Mackle. Take it in your own time.'

'My boss will be absolutely thrilled,' the man said.

33

'NO ONE CAN HELP ME'

It was lunchtime. Aldrin was on his way to the cafeteria when he heard familiar mocking laughter coming from the end of the corridor:

'BA-HA-HA-HA-HA-HA-HA-HA-HA-HA-HA-HA-HA-HA!'

Sebastian Rees-Lane was just like his mother. He was only ever happy when he was making someone else's life miserable. So if he was laughing, it could mean only one thing.

It wasn't in Aldrin's nature to ignore it. So, not for the first time in his life, he walked *towards* the danger.

As he came closer, he realized that the laughter was coming from one of the science labs. As well as Sebastian's machine-gun guffaws, he could hear the snorting laughter of Hercy and Algernon. And then the **titters** of a fourth boy.

For a horrible moment, Aldrin thought that it sounded just like . . .

Harry?

Aldrin stood in the doorway of the classroom. He couldn't believe his eyes. It was Harry all right. But he almost didn't recognize him. He and his new friends were surrounding a young boy, who looked in fear of his life. Algernon and Hercy had the boy pinned to the wall with his feet off the ground, while Harry was looking through his lunch box.

'There's absolutely nothing you can eat in here,' Harry told Sebastian.

'Nothing?' Sebastian asked, clearly displeased. 'No crisps? No chocolate?'

Aldrin was furious. He remembered what his mother had told him about bullies – about them being cowards at heart – and how he should **ALWAYS** stand up to them, whatever the consequences.

'Let him go,' he said in a voice as cold as marble.

Shocked, Algernon and Hercy turned round and, in the process, released their grip on the boy.

'Well, look who it is!' Sebastian said, also turning to face Aldrin. 'How are things in the cheese business? Oh, sorry, how insensitive of me!'

'What's your name?' Aldrin asked the frightened boy cowering by the wall.

'M-M-Martin,' the boy stuttered.

'Harry,' Aldrin said, 'give Martin his lunch box.'

Harry lowered his eyes. Aldrin could see that he was ashamed. Martin snatched the box out of Harry's hands and scurried out of the classroom as fast as his feet could carry him.

Sebastian gave Aldrin a twisted smile.

'How's your father?' he asked. 'I heard he's going

round the twist. The word is he just sits around all day now, watching TV in his dressing gown.'

'I'd still prefer to have him as a dad,' Aldrin said, 'than Agatha as a mum.'

Aldrin watched Sebastian bristle at that line.

At that moment, the bell for the next lesson rang and children started to file into the lab, along with Mr Craddock, the Science teacher.

'You boys aren't in my class,' Mr Craddock declared. **'Get out at once!'**

'See you around, Fatso,' Sebastian said, pushing past Aldrin as he walked out of the lab, followed by Hercy and Algernon, then Harry, who refused to look Aldrin in the eye.

'That's not how superheroes behave,' Aldrin said as Harry went past. 'Superheroes fight bullies. They're on the side of the little guy.'

'I'm not a superhero,' Harry said, stopping and pushing his glasses up on his nose with his finger.

'This isn't you,' Aldrin told him. 'You're only acting like this because you're scared.'

Harry looked at Aldrin for the first time.

'Of course I'm scared!' he said.

'You don't have to be if you just stand up to him!'

'You don't understand! I have nightmares about him all the time!'

'About who? Sebastian?'

Harry nodded, his eyes filling with tears.

'What happens in these nightmares?' Aldrin asked. 'Maybe I could help.'

'Aldrin, you can't help me,' he said. 'No one can help me with this.'

But Aldrin knew that Harry was wrong. He *could* help him. He had a very special superpower. And even though he'd vowed never to use it again, this was an emergency. He had a friend who was clearly terrified of what the darkness brought each night.

He *could* do something! He *had* to do something!

The only problem was that he no longer had access to any cheese.

But then he had an idea where he might get some.

34

THREE LITTLE CUBES

Aldrin spotted her across the floor of the dairy section in the giant supermarket on Digges Road. She was shrugging her shoulders and rolling her eyes and sighing at a customer.

He smiled. Belinda was clearly back to her old self.

Except she was now wearing her sunglasses, not on top of her head, but on her face.

'Hi, Belinda,' he said cheerily.

She was standing behind a small table, dressed as a milkmaid.

'**Aldrin!**' she exclaimed. But then she started to behave strangely. 'I mean, um, my name . . . ees not . . . Belinda.'

For some reason, she was putting on a French accent!

'My name . . . ees . . . Mee Chelle,' she said.

'Mee Chelle?' Aldrin asked, puzzled.

'That ees correct.'

It seemed that her embarrassment about what happened at the community centre had forced her to assume a new identity – a not very convincing one either.

'I was hoping to sample some cheese, um, Mee Chelle.'

'Pity,' Belinda replied, letting the act slip for a moment. 'It's three o'clock. I were about to pack up and go home.'

If the supermarket had employed Belinda to try to arrest the slump in cheese sales, they were going to be disappointed, Aldrin thought.

'I think you'll find it's only five minutes to three,' he pointed out.

Belinda sighed, shook her head and rolled her eyes.

It really was good to see her again.

'What type of flipping cheese ees eet you are wanting,' she said, 'er, monsieur?'

'Well,' said Aldrin, 'what's your Cheese of the Day?'

'Don't know its name. That ees eet there.'

Aldrin saw it laid out in cubes on a plate in front of her. He recognized it immediately.

'Ah!' he said. 'Edam! May I?'

'Do what you flipping like,' Belinda told him. 'Sorry, I mean, yes, of course, you can have some of thees cheese.'

Aldrin helped himself to a small chunk of cheese. He pretended to pop it into his mouth, but then he slipped it into his trouser pocket.

'**Mmm!!!!**' he said, moving his jaw like he was eating something.

Belinda lifted her dark glasses.

'Aldrin, it's me,' she said in a hushed voice. 'I'm only pretending to be called Mee Chelle.'

'Whoa! You certainly had me fooled,' Aldrin lied.

'How's your dad?' she asked.

'Oh, he's fine,' Aldrin said, deciding not to tell her about him watching daytime TV in his dressing gown, or about the bills and final notices that were piling up. Doug was a proud man – or he had been until a few weeks ago. 'Look, I'm really sorry about what happened, Belinda, that night at the community centre.'

'Why are *you* sorry?'

'I don't know – you said that night, before you stormed off the stage, that it was my fault.'

'I were being stupid. I'd just had this dream that you encouraged me to forget about me nerves and just go out there and sing. How is that your fault? It's not like you can control what happens in me flipping dreams, is it?'

'That really is a lovely bit of Edam,' Aldrin said, helping himself to another cube. Again, he slipped it into his pocket.

'I see the shop has closed down,' Belinda said. 'I passed by once or twice, and I thought about calling in to see how he was – your dad, I mean.'

'He would love that,' Aldrin told her.

'Oh, we had some right laughs in that shop!'

'Did you?'

'Right laughs! See, this might come as a surprise to you, Aldrin, but I've never been a people person.'

'That, er, does surprise me, Belinda – very much.'

'Your dad is the only friend I've ever really had.'

She stared wistfully into the distance. Aldrin took a third cube between his thumb and index finger.

'Three o'clock,' she suddenly declared, pulling the plate away from him. 'That's me finished for the day.'

She tipped the remaining cubes of cheese into the bin. Aldrin had been hoping to get a few more. But three might be enough.

He said goodbye.

'*Au revoir!*' Belinda replied.

Then he left the supermarket and walked home.

He arrived back at the flat to find his dad sitting in his dressing gown and watching TV.

'You know that Sir Marmaduke Birtwistle?' Doug said, not even taking his eyes off the screen.

'Who?' Aldrin asked.

'Oh, you do know him. He lives in that big house on the other side of town. Grangewood Court. He was just on the news. He's bought the world's most expensive piece of cheese at an auction. Maraspoli Bolu, it's called. It comes from Turkey and it's made from donkey's milk.'

'Dad –'

'He paid fifty thousand pounds for four ounces of it at Sotheby's! He says he's going to eat it on his ninetieth birthday! Four ounces! That shouldn't take him very long at all!'

'Dad, how long have you been sitting there like that?' Aldrin asked.

'Not long,' Doug told him. 'A few hours.'

'Dad, you can't just sit around all day in your dressing gown.'

'You're quite right, Aldrin. I'm quite tired actually. I think I'll hit the hay for the night.'

'Dad, it's the middle of the afternoon!'

'Like I said – absolutely exhausted.'

'*Sweet dreams –*' Aldrin said.

But, for once, his dad didn't even answer him.

If Aldrin had any doubts about what he was planning to do, they evaporated in that moment. Some of the people who were closest to him were falling apart, and he might be in a position to help them. He had certain powers. He wasn't sure where they came from, or why he had them, or how to use them. But he couldn't stand by and do nothing.

A short time later, he went into his bedroom. He did his homework, then he watched TV for a few hours with Silas perched on top of his head, croaking occasionally:

RRRIBBIT . . . RRRIBBIT . . . RRRIBBIT . . .

But Aldrin wasn't in the mood for conversation. He was thinking about what he had to do.

Just after ten o'clock, he returned Silas to his tank and lay down on the bed. Then, one by one, he popped the three cubes of cheese into his mouth.

It had been weeks since he had eaten even a crumb of cheese. And, although Edam has a very mild flavour, it tasted SO good to him! He pictured Harry in his mind – short, with those strange glasses, and that funny pudding-bowl haircut he had, and the asthma inhaler forever in his pocket. He chewed and chewed until the Edam had become a ball of salty, nutty mush in his mouth . . .

And *very quickly* . . .

without even realizing . . .

that it was happening . . .

his eyes **started to feel** . . .

very,

very

heavy . . .

And then . . .

he was suddenly . . .

out

for

the . . .

35

HARRY'S NIGHTMARE

Aldrin found himself standing in a darkened room. It was deathly quiet. It took a few moments for his eyes to adjust to the inky blackness. When they did, he realized that he was in Harry's bedroom.

He looked at the walls. He could see the shelves full of superhero and supervillain figurines, the boxes of comics and the drawings on the wall.

He could see Harry's bed, but it was empty. The duvet had been thrown on the floor, like he had got up in a real hurry.

'Harry?' Aldrin whispered.

There was no response, so he said it again, except with more urgency this time.

'HARRY?'

Aldrin heard sobbing coming from behind a door on the other side of the bedroom. It might be a bathroom, he thought to himself.

'**HARRY?**' Aldrin said, rapping his knuckles against the door three times.

And through the door came a response:

'Aldrin?' Harry said. 'Aldrin, is that you?'

'Yes, it's me. Are you all right?'

'What are you doing in my nightmare?'

'I've come to help you.'

There was silence for a long moment.

'Open the door,' Aldrin said in a gentle voice. 'I won't let anything happen to you.'

'You can't stop him,' Harry said sadly. 'He's much, much too strong.'

'Who?' Aldrin asked. 'Who's too strong?'

Suddenly, behind him, Aldrin heard a familiar laugh:

'**BA-HA-HA-HA-HA-HA-HA! BA-HA-HA-HA-HA-HA-HA!**'

He spun round. There was a clown standing behind him. He was an evil-looking thing. His teeth were yellow and broken and he was bald except for two tufts of hair on either side of his head. But there was something oddly familiar about him.

'Sebastian!' Aldrin said.

But Sebastian didn't respond. It was the strangest thing. It was like Aldrin was invisible to him. Sebastian took two steps forward – and then he walked right through Aldrin!

'Why do we have to go through this every time?' he said, mouth pressed against the door. 'Come out of that bathroom!'

'No!' Harry cried. **'Please! Just go away!'**

'I can't go away. The crocodiles are hun-grrryyy!!!'

'Why can't you find them something else to eat?'

'Because they want to eat **YOU**, Harry!'

Harry didn't say anything.

Suddenly, it was like a switch had been flicked, and Sebastian's tone turned ugly.

'COME OUT HERE NOW!' he growled. **'YOU KNOW HOW THIS IS GOING TO END, HARRY . . . THE SAME AS IT ALWAYS DOES!'**

Sebastian reached for the handle of the door.

From somewhere deep inside him, Aldrin summoned up a roar loud enough to be heard:

'SSSTTTOOOPPP!!!'

Sebastian turned his head and Aldrin could suddenly

see him in all his ugliness. His make-up looked like he'd applied it himself – while standing on a moving bus. And when he smiled, his mouth looked like a bucket of broken crockery.

'What do **YOU** want?' he asked Aldrin in a mean and menacing voice.

'I'm here to stop you hurting my friend,' Aldrin told him, taking a step forward.

'Oh, are you?' Sebastian said with a grin. 'Look at me! I'm shaking in my twenty-four-inch shoes here!'

Sebastian pushed down the handle and put his shoulder to the door. It gave way without much resistence.

Aldrin tried to move his feet. But, to his shock, he discovered that they were rooted to the floor.

Sebastian disappeared into the bathroom. Aldrin heard a brief struggle inside, then Sebastian re-emerged, carrying Harry over his shoulder like a sack of potatoes.

The boy was screaming:

'NO! NO! PLEASE, NO!'

Aldrin tried to move again. But it was futile. His legs were paralysed.

Sebastian started calling out in a sinister, sing-song voice:

'Oh, croccies! Look what Sebastian's got for you!'

Harry spotted Aldrin across the room and he called out to him:

'ALDRIN, HELP ME! ALDRIN, PLEASE! DO SOMETHING!'

But Aldrin's legs were useless. Something had clearly gone wrong. Was it the Edam? Was it too mild? Or had he simply not eaten enough of it?

'ALDRIN, PLEASE!' Harry cried. **'HELP ME!'**

Sebastian carried him out of the room.

'Stop **wriggling**,' he told him. 'You know how this ends as well as I do.'

'ALDRIN!' Harry shouted. **'YOU SAID YOU'D HELP ME! YOU TOLD ME THAT YOU WOULDN'T LET ANYTHING HAPPEN TO ME!'**

Outside on the landing, Aldrin could hear Sebastian say mockingly:

'OK, who ordered the special?'

'I TRIED MY BEST!' Aldrin shouted. **'I JUST DIDN'T HAVE ENOUGH CH–'**

He didn't even get to finish the word.

He woke up. He suddenly realized that he was sitting bolt upright in the bed. He was sweating profusely, and he was breathing so hard that it felt like his heart might **burst** clean out of his chest.

36

ALL THE PROBLEMSH OF THE WORLD

Aldrin was struggling to concentrate. He was thinking about last night – about Harry's terrified screams as Sebastian carried him away to feed him to the crocodiles. Even the memory of it was enough to send a chill through Aldrin. It was no wonder Harry was so frightened of Sebastian, if that was how his nightmares played out each night.

Mrs Van Boxtel was walking through the classroom, looking over the shoulder of each student to inspect the work that they were doing.

'You are all making wonderful progressh,' she said. 'Don't forget, we will be publishing our book in jusht two weeksh. Shishely, you have not told me yet what your shtory ish about.'

'I've decided to write about Nicolaus Copernicus,' Sisely said.

'Oh?' said Mrs Van Boxtel, a smile flexing across her face. 'Sho, tell ush, who wash Nicolaush Copernicush?'

Aldrin had never heard of him.

'He was a mathematician,' Sisely told her, 'and also an astronomer. He was born more than five hundred years ago.'

'And why ish he sho intereshting to you?' the teacher asked.

'Well,' Sisely explained, 'people laughed at him because he said that the Earth and all the other planets revolved around the sun. He was actually right, but nobody wanted to believe him because they couldn't accept that the Earth wasn't the centre of the universe. And he's interesting to me because . . .'

She glanced sideways at Aldrin before continuing:

'Someone taught me recently that I should open my mind. Sometimes, I can be like one of those people who laughed at Copernicus – but I've realized now that I don't know as much about the universe as I thought I did. And lots of the things that I *thought* I knew for sure . . . well, I was completely wrong about them.'

Mrs Van Boxtel smiled at her.

'Shishely,' she said, 'you are an absholute wonder!'

Then she turned to Harry. 'Harry,' she said, 'I haven't sheen you put pen to paper shince the classh shtarted today.'

Aldrin had noticed him too, staring into the distance, his mind elsewhere.

'I'm, um, thinking,' he told Mrs Van Boxtel.

'Good,' the teacher said, 'becaushe thinking ish important. I am very much looking forward to reading thish comic shtrip of yoursh.'

In that moment, Aldrin realized something. Harry's nightmare was the inspiration for his story, *The Boy Who Fights Crocodiles*. The superhero boy with the glasses and the asthma inhaler was his attempt to imagine himself conquering his fear of Sebastian and fighting back. Aldrin could help him to do it – if only he had access to . . .

'Aldrin,' Mrs Van Boxtel asked, 'how ish your shtory coming along?'

Aldrin looked down at the page. On it, he had written:

CHEESE CHEESE CHEESE CHEESE CHEESE CHEESE CHEESE CHEESE CHEESE CHEESE CHEESE CHEESE CHEESE CHEESE CHEESE CHEESE CHEESE CHEESE

CHEESE CHEESE CHEESE CHEESE CHEESE CHEESE
CHEESE CHEESE CHEESE CHEESE CHEESE CHEESE
CHEESE CHEESE CHEESE CHEESE CHEESE CHEESE
CHEESE CHEESE CHEESE CHEESE CHEESE CHEESE
CHEESE CHEESE CHEESE CHEESE CHEESE CHEESE
CHEESE CHEESE CHEESE CHEESE CHEESE CHEESE
CHEESE CHEESE CHEESE CHEESE CHEESE CHEESE
CHEESE CHEESE CHEESE CHEESE CHEESE CHEESE
CHEESE CHEESE CHEESE CHEESE CHEESE CHEESE
CHEESE CHEESE CHEESE CHEESE CHEESE CHEESE
CHEESE CHEESE CHEESE CHEESE CHEESE CHEESE
CHEESE CHEESE CHEESE CHEESE CHEESE CHEESE
CHEESE CHEESE CHEESE CHEESE CHEESE CHEESE
CHEESE CHEESE CHEESE CHEESE CHEESE CHEESE
CHEESE CHEESE CHEESE CHEESE CHEESE CHEESE
CHEESE CHEESE CHEESE CHEESE CHEESE CHEESE
CHEESE CHEESE CHEESE CHEESE CHEESE CHEESE
CHEESE CHEESE CHEESE CHEESE CHEESE CHEESE
CHEESE CHEESE CHEESE CHEESE CHEESE CHEESE
CHEESE CHEESE CHEESE CHEESE CHEESE CHEESE
CHEESE CHEESE CHEESE CHEESE CHEESE CHEESE
CHEESE CHEESE CHEESE CHEESE CHEESE CHEESE
CHEESE CHEESE CHEESE CHEESE CHEESE CHEESE
CHEESE CHEESE CHEESE CHEESE CHEESE CHEESE
CHEESE CHEESE CHEESE CHEESE CHEESE CHEESE

CHEESE CHEESE CHEESE CHEESE CHEESE CHEESE CHEESE CHEESE CHEESE CHEESE CHEESE CHEESE CHEESE CHEESE CHEESE CHEESE CHEESE CHEESE

'Erm, fine,' Aldrin said. 'It's nearly finished.'

The bell rang to signal the end of class.

'Thank you, boysh and girlsh,' the teacher said. 'You did shome fantashtic work today. Enjoy your weekend. I will shee you all on Monday, yesh?'

As Aldrin put his copybook back into his schoolbag, Mrs Van Boxtel caught his eye.

'Can you shtay behind for a minute?' she said. 'I would like to shpeak with you.'

When the classroom emptied out, Mrs Van Boxtel sat down next to Aldrin at Sisely's desk.

'Aldrin,' she said in a gentle voice, 'you sheem a little bit shad at the moment.'

Suddenly, the whole sorry story started tumbling out of Aldrin's mouth.

'My dad closed the cheesemonger's,' he said. 'Every happy memory I have of my mum was in that shop. It was her pride and joy. And, after she died, it was what kept us going . . . But Dad just closed it down and gave all our cheese away. And now he's unemployed, and all he does all day is watch rubbish daytime TV in his dressing gown. And my best friend is having nightmares and I can't even . . .'

Aldrin was on the verge of revealing his secret to her, but he managed to stop himself just in time.

'What were you going to shay?' she asked.

'Nothing,' he said. 'It's just that I *have* to have cheese, Mrs Van Boxtel. Without it, I'm no use to anyone whatsoever.'

She smiled at him.

'I don't have all the anshersh for you,' she said. 'I'm jusht thish crazshy old Dutch lady who the boysh and girlsh call Misshish Van Bonkersh behind her back.'

'I've, um, never heard that,' Aldrin lied.

'But thish much I do know – you cannot take on all of the problemsh of the world by yourshelf. It ish OK shometimesh to shay that you too need help. And, alsho, thingsh are not alwaysh ash bad ash they shometimesh sheem. There ish alwaysh hope, Aldrin.'

37

SAVED BY THE BABYBEL

Doug was having nightmares again. Aldrin and Silas were awoken by his cries through the wall:

'HELP! HELP! HELP!'

Aldrin pulled his pillow round his ears to try to block out the sound of his dad's distress.

Silas croaked sympathetically:

*RRRIBBIT . . . RRRIBBIT . . . **RRRIBBIT** . . .*

Mrs Van Boxtel had talked about hope. But right at that moment, Aldrin couldn't see any.

Without access to cheese, he was just an ordinary boy who was worried about his dad and his friend, but was powerless to help them.

Unless . . .

Aldrin suddenly threw back his bedcovers.

Unless he could find a piece of cheese downstairs in the shop. Maybe that odd Mr Mackle character left some behind by mistake?

He pulled on his dressing gown and tiptoed out of the room. He retrieved the key from the kitchen drawer where all the clutter ended up, then he crept downstairs. He opened the door and stepped into the shop that had once been his happy place.

Everything about it was different. It was no longer cold – because it didn't have to be. The shelves that were once filled with cheeses of every variety were empty. All of the colours, the shapes, the smells that made the shop so magical were gone. Without cheese, it was a dull and humdrum place – much like the world, Aldrin thought.

He searched every shelf and drawer, every nook and cranny, every dusty corner and unswept inch of the shop, looking for even the smallest morsel of cheese that might have been left behind. But Mr Mackle had been thorough – he'd managed to clear out every ounce.

Aldrin was on the point of giving up when he realized there was one final place that he hadn't looked. He got down on his hands and knees and pressed his cheek to the tiled floor, so he could see underneath the refrigerated counter.

And that was when he spotted it.

There was a Mini Babybel under there!

He pushed his hand into the gap and felt around. He touched it with the tips of his fingers, then managed to grab it. A wave of excitement washed over him as he pulled it out.

He stood up. As quickly as his trembling fingers would allow, he tore open the wrapper. With his thumbnail, he then peeled off the red wax seal.

From the spots of green mould on the cheese, it was

clear that it had been under there for quite some time. But Aldrin figured he could pick off the bits that had gone bad. And that was when he heard a voice say:

'What on earth are you doing?'

He looked up. Doug was standing in the doorway with a look of horror on his face.

'I was hungry,' Aldrin told him.

'You're not seriously telling me you were about to eat that?' Doug said.

'There's nothing wrong with it. Blue cheese is *full* of mould.'

'It's a different kind of mould. Aldrin, you'll be sick.'

'Dad, I need cheese! I HAVE TO HAVE SOME CHEESE!'

Even as the words were slipping from his lips, Aldrin knew how crazy he sounded.

'Aldrin,' Doug said, 'what's happened to you?'

'What's happened to *you*?' Aldrin retorted, the anger rising in him.

'What do you mean?' Doug asked.

And that was when all of the frustrations of the past few weeks came spewing out of Aldrin's mouth.

'I DON'T EVEN RECOGNIZE YOU ANY MORE!' he told his dad.

'Aldrin, how dare you shout at me like that!' Doug said. 'Your mother would be ashamed of you.'

'No, she'd be ashamed of *you* – for just giving in to that horrible Agatha woman! And for closing Mum's shop down. And for sitting around all day in your dressing gown, watching stupid telly!'

Doug reached out and snatched the Mini Babybel out of Aldrin's hand.

'Upstairs to your room!' he ordered him crossly. **'Right this minute!'**

Aldrin did as he was told. But as he left the shop, he shouted something over his shoulder that shattered Doug's heart into a million pieces:

'I wish you weren't my dad!'

Aldrin went back to bed. And, when he fell asleep, something happened to him that had never, ever happened to him before . . .

He had a nightmare of his own.

38

ALDRIN'S NIGHTMARE

Aldrin was in the sea. All around him, a storm was **raging**. He was kicking his legs furiously to try to keep his head above the freezing water. But the waves were too strong. They **tossed him around** like a dog playing with a chew toy.

He held his breath as the water sucked him under. He was convinced he was going to drown.

He flailed around desperately until he somehow made his way to the surface again.

He looked up at the sky, as black as oil, and tried to fill his lungs with air.

He recognized this nightmare. It was the same one he'd rescued his dad from a few weeks ago. So he knew what was happening.

He was drowning.

He could taste the sea in his mouth. His joints were stiffening with the cold, and his body ached all over from the effort of trying to keep his head above the churning water.

He closed his eyes. He knew he couldn't keep up the effort any longer. It was too hard. The next time he went under, he decided, he wouldn't fight it any more.

He would let himself drown.

But then, out of nowhere, he heard a faint voice over the sound of the raging sea. Someone was calling out his name:

'**ALDRIN?**' the voice said as if searching for him. '**ALDRIN?**'

He opened his eyes. In the mid-distance, he saw something. It was a tiny rowing boat.

'**OVER HERE!**' he gasped. '**HELP! HELP! I'M OVER HERE! HELP! HELP!**'

He watched as the boat drew nearer and nearer to him in stops and starts.

A **GINORMOUS** wave **CRASHED** down on him and pushed him back under. But Aldrin was determined to stay alive now. He **THRASHED** around in the water and managed to get above the surface again.

He sucked in **great, greedy** lungfuls of air. The boat was almost within his reach now. He felt something hard prod him in the shoulder. It was an oar.

'Take the end of it,' said a familiar voice. 'Quickly – or you'll drown.'

And, for the first time, Aldrin saw who it was who had rowed to his rescue . . .

It was Mrs Van Boxtel.

39

THE CHEESE WHIZZES

Aldrin bobbed up and down in the water with his mouth wide open. He couldn't believe his eyes. Was he just dreaming her – or was she really *in* his nightmare?

'What?' she said. 'You think you are the only one who hash thish gift? You'd better take the oar – do what Misshish Van Bonkersh tellsh you!'

Aldrin held on to the oar with both hands, then he kicked his feet while his teacher pulled him closer to the boat. She reached into the water, and with a strength that seemed almost superhuman, especially for a frail woman of her advanced years, she pulled him into the little rowing boat.

Once he'd caught his breath, Aldrin lifted himself up on to the wooden bench opposite her. She handed him a blanket and he pulled it round his shoulders.

'**You n-n-never told me,**' he said, teeth chattering, '**that y-y-y-you could do it as w-w-well!**'

'You never told me either!' Mrs Van Boxtel replied.

A wave hit the side of the boat and it lurched hard to the left. Aldrin was convinced that it was going to be toppled over and they'd be thrown into the water.

'Take the oarsh,' said Mrs Van Boxtel, 'and shtart rowing ash hard ash you can.'

'**Wh-wh-where am I rowing t-t-t-to?**' Aldrin asked her breathlessly.

'To shafety, of courshe.'

Exhausted as he was, Aldrin did what he was told. He pulled on the oars. And, in slow, jerky movements, the boat started to move, bouncing up and down over the rolling waves.

After rowing for about a minute, his body started to warm up again. But his surprise at seeing Mrs Van Boxtel only deepened.

'I can't believe you've got the same superpower as me,' he told her.

'Shuperpower?' she repeated. 'Oh, that *ish* funny. I've never thought about it ash a shuperpower before.'

'I'm not saying it's a **great** superpower. I mean, it

doesn't come with a costume, or a cape, or any cool gadgets – or does it?' he asked hopefully.

Mrs Van Boxtel laughed. 'No, there are none of thoshe thingsh shadly.'

'Well, even a book of instructions would have been nice. I have no idea what I'm doing, Mrs Van Boxtel. I entered Belinda's dream – oh, she was the woman who served you in the shop . . .'

'She wash terribly rude.'

'Yeah, that's her. She had this dream that she wanted to be a famous singer. And I encouraged her to think she could, because she had this amazing voice in her dream. But then she entered a talent contest at the community centre – and she made a complete fool of herself. She had a voice like a **foghorn!**'

'Aldrin,' Mrs Van Boxtel explained, 'you have not been given thish power sho that you can make people'sh dreamsh come true.'

'So what am I supposed to do with it?' he asked.

'What I am doing now,' Mrs Van Boxtel told him. 'Entering people'sh nightmaresh to help them come to termsh with their fearsh and their worriesh.'

'That's it?'

'That'sh really it.'

'And there's **DEFINITELY** no gadgets?' Aldrin thought he might as well check.

Mrs Van Boxtel laughed.

'Well,' she said, 'I produshed thish boat, didn't I? Keep rowing, Aldrin. We are not out of danger yet, and I have more thingsh to tell you.'

Aldrin pulled harder on the oars.

'What things?' he asked.

Mrs Van Boxtel's expression turned grave.

'You and I are part of an ancient order,' she said in a serious voice, 'known ash the Cheeshe Whizshesh.'

'The Cheese Whizzes?' Aldrin asked.

'That'sh right. The order wash founded to fight an enemy of oursh.'

'So who is this enemy?'

'Hish name ish . . . Habeash Grusshelvart.'

'Habeas Grusselvart? He sounds like a supervillain.'

'That ish becaushe he *ish* a shupervillain. He ish the worsht of them all. Sho you have read the shtory I gave you about Luuk van den Hoogenband, yesh?'

'Yes. Well, most of it – one of the pages was ripped out.'

'The page about Pim van Almshick.'

'And how he came to inherit Luuk's power? Yeah.'

'I tore that page out.'

'You did? Why?'

'Becaushe the book hash the shtory wrong. You shee, Luuk van den Hoogenband wash not reshponsible for the death of Prinshessh Femke van den Bosh. He did not encourage her to think that she could fly.'

'I knew it!'

'Why would he do shuch a thing?'

'That's what I thought! He was in love with her!'

'Yesh – and she wash in love with him alsho. But she wash forbidden from sheeing him becaushe he wash jusht a shimple farmhand, and he did not have royal blood. Sho, each night, before he went to shleep, Luuk would eat cheeshe and think very, very hard about Femke – and they would be together in her dreamsh.'

'Wow!'

'But when Femke reached the age of eighteen, the king told her that she musht marry thish other man . . .'

'Prince Pim van Almsick?'

'Yesh, but at the time he wash just a lord. Pim wash a cruel and wicked man who wash almosht three timesh her age – and, of courshe, Femke did not wish to marry him. She wash shtill in love with Luuk. But she had no choishe and the marriage went ahead. Each night, however, she continued to meet with Luuk in her dreamsh. Which, of courshe, did not pleashe Pim. He knew that hish wife did not love him at all and the only time she ever shmiled wash when she wash ashleep. Then, one night, Pim heard Femke whishper Luuk'sh name in her shleep.'

'No!'

'She shaid, "I love you, Luuk!" Pim wash furioush and he complained to the king, who shummoned the prinshessh to him. She told her father about thish shpecial power that Luuk had to enter people'sh dreamsh. The king complained to the godsh. Ash it happened, they were angry with Luuk becaushe he wash not shupposhed to ushe his power in thish way – for hish own happinessh. Sho they agreed to take away hish ability to enter people'sh dreamsh and alsho hish immortality. Sho now Luuk could no longer meet Femke each night. When she wash told that she would never shee him again, she died – of a broken heart. And, on the very shame night, Luuk died of a broken heart too.'

'But how did Pim get Luuk's powers?'

'Ash compenshation for the death of Pim's wife, the king petitioned the godsh to give them to Pim. Perhapsh they were having a bad day, but they agreed. From the very shtart, Pim wash determined to ushe hish powersh for evil. Exshept, of courshe, he doesh not go by the name of Pim any more. He callsh himshelf –'

'Habeas Grusselvart?'

'That ish correct. Embittered by the memory of hish wife'sh happy dreamsh, he hash shpent the lasht five hundred yearsh bringing fear and mishery to people while they shleep.'

'Five hundred years? So, what, does that mean he's immortal as well?'

'Yesh – and very, very powerful. Habeash doesh not even need cheeshe to enter people'sh dreamsh. He can do it whenever he wantsh.'

'So, if Habeas didn't exist, then there'd be no more nightmares?'

'No, thish ish not true. Nightmaresh are a normal part of life, Aldrin. They are the way our mindsh try to make shenshe of our fearsh, our phobiash, our anxshietiesh. But what Habeash doesh, ish he dreamsh up waysh of making the terror of nightmaresh even worshe. Waysh of making them feel overwhelming and unbearable.'

Mrs Van Boxtel looked up at the ink-black sky.

'ISHN'T THAT CORRECT, HABEASH?' she shouted.

'Wait a minute,' Aldrin said. 'Are you saying that he can actually *hear* what we're saying?'

'Of courshe – no one entersh the nightmaresh of another pershon without Habeash knowing about it. The Cheeshe Whizshesh are the only thing he fearsh. They are the only hope for the world.'

'So how did *we* get our powers?'

'Not all of the godsh were sho happy to give Luuk'sh powersh to Pim. And when he shtarted to ushe them to shpread unhappinessh and mishery, they tried to take them from him. But he wash protected by a bad god named Fóvosh. Sho inshtead, to try to frushtrate hish work, they created thish order – of people like me and you. We were given the ability to enter people'sh nightmaresh to try to counteract hish evil work.'

'I still think it'd be cooler if it came with some kind of costume,' Aldrin told her.

Mrs Van Boxtel laughed.

'Now,' she said, 'if you jusht look over your shoulder, you will shee that we have arrived at our deshtination!'

Aldrin looked behind him and discovered that they were now just a few feet away from a white, sandy beach. He had been so engrossed in their conversation that he hadn't noticed the stormy night giving way to the most beautiful sunlit morning.

'OK,' said Mrs Van Boxtel. 'Thish ish where you get out of the boat.'

'Not yet!' Aldrin said. 'There's loads more things I want to know!'

'There will be plenty of time for queshtionsh,' she said. 'I am your teacher, remember. And I will shee you on Monday morning.'

'No, wait!' Aldrin shouted.

But at that moment he suddenly woke up.

40

'HE KNOWS ABOUT ME!'

Habeas Grusselvart let out an ear-splitting animal scream.

**'NEEEUUURRRGGGHHH!!!
NEEEUUURRRGGGHHH!!!'**

It was loud enough to have been heard all over Todmorden. It was fortunate that the walls of his factory were soundproofed.

Beddy Byes came running.

'What is it?' he asked.

Beddy Byes followed his master's line of vision to a screen right in the centre of the Wall of Torment. He saw Aldrin Adams was sitting in a rowing boat on a violent sea – opposite an elderly lady with dandelion-puffball hair and a neck brace.

'Wh-wh-wh-where did he get cheese?' Beddy Byes stuttered in shock. 'I took it – every ounce.'

'He hasn't entered into someone else's nightmare,' Habeas said. 'This is *his* nightmare.'

'Is it one of ours?'

'No, it's not. But it's almost identical to the one we created for his father.'

They watched as the old woman looked up at the sky and roared, **'ISHN'T THAT CORRECT, HABEASH?'**

'Who is she?' Beddy Byes asked.

'Nel Van Boxtel,' Habeas said.

'Nel Van Boxtel? I haven't heard that name in years.'

It's not often we see her these days. Doesn't have it in her any more. The last time she entered someone else's dream state was about three months ago. She got out of bed the next morning and fell down the stairs.'

Beddy Byes laughed.

'That's how she ended up with the neck brace,' Habeas said. 'She's told him everything, by the way. He knows about me.'

'Oh, no!' Beddy Byes said.

'**Oh, yes,**' Habeas answered. 'We have a new enemy, Beddy Byes. He's an eleven-year-old boy. And he could be the most formidable force we've ever faced.'

41

BACK IN BUSINESS

Aldrin lay there in the dark stillness of his bedroom, listening to his own ragged breathing, thinking about what had just happened and what it meant.

He was a Cheese Whizz! That thought really excited him. And he had a mission now – to stop the evil Habeas Grusselvart from spreading fear and unhappiness through people's nightmares.

But why Aldrin? That was what he'd wanted to ask Mrs Van Boxtel. Why had he, of all people, been given this responsibility?

There was no chance of him going back to sleep now. His mind was racing with it all. He couldn't believe that Mrs Van Boxtel, this frail and beautifully eccentric old lady, had the same power as him. The same *superpower* –

because he felt more than ever now that that's what it was.

He thought about all of this over and over again, as four o'clock became five, five became six, six became seven, and seven became eight.

His mind was so taken up with it that he forgot about the terrible row he'd had with his dad last night. And when he did finally remember it, he felt a horrible sinking feeling in his chest. He had never spoken to his dad like that before. He knew he should apologize.

Aldrin heard a croak. He got out of bed and removed Silas from his tank.

'Time for your morning exercise,' he said, placing the frog on the floor.

Then Aldrin made his way to the kitchen. On the table was a note. It said:

> *Morning, Aldrin!*
> *If you're looking for me, I'll be downstairs!*
> *Love,*
> *Dad*

Did he mean . . . in the shop?

Aldrin raced downstairs and pushed the heavy door – and his heart surged.

Doug was dressed, not in his dressing gown, but in his white overalls and apron with the words ***C'est***

Cheese on the front. He was wiping down the shelves and humming happily to himself.

'What are you doing?' Aldrin asked.

'Morning, Aldrin,' Doug said, without looking up. 'I'm reopening the shop.'

'Oh, Dad!' Aldrin said, tears suddenly spilling from his eyes as he looked around.

'It was what you said to me last night,' Doug told him. 'About your mum being ashamed of me.'

'I was upset,' Aldrin said. 'I'm sorry.'

'No, you were right, son. Your mum wouldn't have thrown in the towel. She wouldn't have closed the shop and given all the cheese away. ***C'est Cheese*** was her absolute world.'

'It was *our* world, Dad.'

'And it will be again. At seven o'clock this morning, I started phoning all of our suppliers, telling them we needed everything – Cheddar, Brie, Parmesan, Stilton, Camembert, Gouda, mozzarella, feta, Emmental, Gruyère, ricotta, Gorgonzola . . .'

Aldrin's mouth started watering.

'But what about Agatha?' he asked.

'If it's a war she wants,' Doug told him, 'then it's a war she's going to get.'

Aldrin couldn't hold back any more. He ran to his dad and he threw his arms round him.

'Oh, Dad,' he said, 'I'm so proud of you!'

'And I'm proud of you, Aldrin,' Doug replied. 'There's, um, something else I wanted to talk to you about actually.'

'What is it?'

'I've been grieving for your mum a long time now – and I think maybe it's time I stopped. That doesn't mean I don't still love her. I'll always love her.'

'I know you will.'

'But I've been so sad since she died. There've been times when I've felt like I was drowning in grief. Does that make sense?'

'I know exactly what you mean,' Aldrin told him.

He'd seen it. He'd experienced it himself.

'And I know your mum wouldn't want that for me,' Doug said. 'I know she'd want me to move on with my life. So that's what I'm going to do. As a first step, I'm going to gather up all of her old clothes, and I'm going to give them to the charity shop.'

'Are you sure that's what you want to do, Dad?'

'I am, Aldrin. From now on, I'm moving in only one direction – and that's forward.'

42

A NEW TEACHER

It was Monday morning, and Aldrin was bristling with excitement. He was sitting in English class, waiting for Mrs Van Boxtel to arrive.

All the boys and girls were jabbering away breathlessly about the weekend just gone. But none of them had had a weekend to match Aldrin's. And now he couldn't wait to talk to Mrs Van Boxtel and find out more about this power – this incredible superpower – they shared.

The door swung open. Aldrin smiled. But, to his surprise, it wasn't Mrs Van Boxtel who walked into the classroom. It was a short man with a flat nose and a beard as thick as a rhododendron bush. He wore a tweed jacket and tweed trousers – the kind that really itched, which may have accounted for his irritable mood.

'Settle down!' he said. 'My name is Mr Arnold. I'm a substitute teacher, and I'm going to be standing in for Mrs Van Boxtel for the foreseeable future.'

Standing in for her? Where is she?

'Today,' Mr Arnold said, 'we are going to learn about the –' he turned to the whiteboard and wrote the words as he spoke them – 'Rules. Of. Grammar. I'm talking about nouns, verbs, pronouns, adjectives, adverbs, prepositions, conjunctions and interjections.'

Aldrin put his hand in the air.

'Speaking of interjections . . .' Mr Arnold said, 'what do you want, boy?'

'Where's Mrs Van Boxtel?' Aldrin asked.

'She's in hospital,' Mr Arnold said in an offhand way.

Aldrin felt his heartbeat quicken.

Hospital?

'What's wrong with her?' he asked.

'That,' Mr Arnold replied, 'is none of your concern. Let us proceed with the class.'

He turned to the whiteboard and he wrote the word 'noun' on it.

Aldrin suddenly felt sick to his stomach. Whatever

was wrong with Mrs Van Boxtel, he was almost certain that it had something to do with her entering his nightmare on Saturday night.

'Now,' said Mr Arnold, 'does anybody in the class know what a noun is?'

Sisely raised her hand.

'A person, a place or a thing,' Sisely said. 'For instance, Nicolaus Copernicus, New York City, that piece of chalk in your hand are all examples of nouns.'

'Excellent!' Mr Arnold said, then he turned back to the whiteboard and started to write again. 'A noun . . . is a person . . . a place . . . or a thing . . .'

Aldrin tried to get Sisely's attention:

'Sisely . . . **Psssttt** . . . Sisely . . .'

Sisely looked at him.

'It's my fault,' he whispered, 'that Mrs Van Boxtel is in hospital!'

Sisely gave him a quizzical look.

'She has the same power as me!' Aldrin told her. 'She was in my nightmare – on Saturday night! *That's* why she's in hospital!'

Mr Arnold banged his hand on the whiteboard.

'I'm hearing talking,' he said, 'and I want it to **STOP AT ONCE!**'

'She told me everything,' Aldrin said. 'It turns out we're both Cheese Whizzes.'

'You're what?' Sisely asked.

'We're an order of people created centuries ago to battle against the influence of Habeas Grusselvart.'

'YOU, BOY!' Mr Arnold roared. **'STAND UP!'**

Aldrin did as he was told.

'What's your name?' the teacher asked.

'Aldrin,' Aldrin replied. 'Aldrin Adams.'

'What were you talking about, Mr Adams, that was more important than nouns, verbs, pronouns, adjectives, adverbs, prepositions, conjunctions and interjections?'

'What's wrong with Mrs Van Boxtel?'

'I already told you, that is none of your concern.'

'SHE'S MY FRIEND!' Aldrin shouted. **'I WANT YOU TO TELL ME WHAT'S WRONG WITH HER!'**

Seeing the boy so visibly upset, Mr Arnold tried to soften his tone.

'From what I've been told,' he said, 'the doctors don't know. They're still running tests.'

There were worried faces throughout the class. Murmurs of concern. Mrs Van Boxtel was eccentric –

maybe even crazy. But, like Aldrin, they had all grown to love her.

'She *is* going to live,' Aldrin asked, 'isn't she?'

'At this stage, they just don't know,' said Mr Arnold. 'Now, can we please return to our lesson on the rules of . . .'

But before he could finish his sentence, Aldrin was running for the door.

43

IT COULDN'T BE TRUE

BANG!

Aldrin ran into something. Something hard and unyielding. It turned out to be the ward sister, a short, thick-set woman with red hair and a look of scowling disapproval etched on her face.

'Where do you think you're going?' she challenged him.

'I'm looking for Mrs Van Boxtel,' Aldrin said.

'You mean Nel?' she asked. 'The Dutch lady?'

Aldrin couldn't help but smile. The name suited her.

'Who are you?' the woman asked. 'Her grandson?'

'No,' Aldrin admitted.

'Then you can't see her,' she said firmly. 'It's family only, I'm afraid.'

'Please,' Aldrin said, his eyes suddenly pooling with tears. 'She's my teacher – but she's so much more than that. She's one of the most amazing people I've ever met. And I don't know what I'll do if she doesn't recover.'

Aldrin watched the ward sister's face soften.

'End of the corridor,' the woman said, stepping aside. 'Last door on the right. You take as long as you want, love.'

'Thank you!' Aldrin said, already running down the corridor towards the ward.

Mrs Van Boxtel was lying in bed with her eyes closed. There was a tube feeding oxygen into her nostrils and a second one, in the bend of her arm, feeding fluids into her veins. A machine next to the bed beeped at one-second intervals, monitoring her heartbeat.

She looked tired and pale and she had a large purple bruise on the side of her head. Aldrin burst into tears. This was all his fault, he thought. It had happened because she tried to help him.

Aldrin took her hand in his – it was cold and limp.

'Please don't die, Mrs Van Boxtel,' he whispered. 'Please, please, please don't die.'

'Die?' she said, suddenly opening her eyes. 'Who

shaid anything about dying?'

Aldrin jumped back in surprise.

'Mrs Van Boxtel?' He laughed. 'You're . . .'

'Alive?' she said. 'Yesh, it would sheem sho. But now you can shee why I don't ushe my powersh sho much any more theshe days.'

'What happened?'

'When I woke up from your nightmare, I wash feeling dehydrated, sho I got out of bed to get a glassh of water. But then I felt dizshy . . .'

'You felt dishy? Oh, you mean *dizzy*?'

'That ish what I shaid. Dizshy – becaushe of dehydration. And then it sheemsh I fainted and banged my head on the shide of the table – thush knocking myshelf out. Luckily, my neighbour downshtairsh heard the shound of me hitting the floor and phoned for an ambulanshe.'

'I was really worried about you, Mrs Van Boxtel,' Aldrin told her.

'It ish very flattering that you care sho much,' she said, then her eyes drifted to something beyond Aldrin's left shoulder. 'It looksh like I have another vishitor. Hello, Shishely.'

'Hello, Mrs Van Boxtel,' said Sisely, stepping into

the ward. 'You're not dead.'

'Sho everybody keepsh telling me,' the teacher said drily.

'So is somebody going to tell me who Habeas Grusselvart is?' Sisely asked.

Mrs Van Boxtel looked at Aldrin.

'I, um, told Sisely about my superpower,' he explained. 'I thought she might help me figure out why it was happening to me.'

Mrs Van Boxtel smiled.

'Thish shecret wash a heavy burden for a boy of your age to carry on hish own,' she said. 'I couldn't think of shomebody better to share it with than Shishely.'

'Is *anyone* going to tell me what's going on?' Sisely asked.

Over the course of the next ten minutes, Aldrin and Mrs Van Boxtel filled her in on everything. They told her about Luuk and Femke and their forbidden love. They told her about Pim van Almsick and his anger at discovering that his princess bride was meeting Luuk each night in her dreams. They told her about Luuk being stripped of his powers and Luuk and Femke dying, lonely and heartbroken, on the same night. They told her about Pim inheriting Luuk's powers and assuming the identity of Habeas Grusselvart, who, for more than five hundred years, had dedicated his life to creating specially tailored nightmares to terrify people while they slept. And they told her about the Cheese Whizzes, a secret order of people with the power to enter other people's dreams and change the ending of the nightmares that Habeas created for them.

And, through it all, Sisely – who had once been so sceptical about the world of magic and things that defied rational explanation – just nodded, like it all made perfect sense to her.

'How many Cheese Whizzes are there?' she asked.

'Not nearly ash many ash there ushed to be,' Mrs Van Boxtel told her. 'The order ish almosht exshtinct. A hundred yearsh ago, there wash maybe one million of ush. Now, there are perhapsh only fifty.'

'Fifty?' said Aldrin. 'To cover the whole world?'

'You coming here,' said Sisely, 'wasn't actually a coincidence, was it?'

Mrs Van Boxtel yawned, then slowly closed her eyes.

'I am sho shleepy!' she said. 'Sho, sho shleepy!'

'**WAKE UP!**' Sisely shouted.

'Sisely!' Aldrin exclaimed. 'She's recovering from a very nasty fall!'

'I'm sorry, Mrs Van Boxtel,' Sisely said, 'but you are **NOT** going to sleep until you tell us **EVERYTHING**. You coming to teach at our school – it wasn't an accident, was it?'

Mrs Van Boxtel looked from Sisely to Aldrin.

'Like I shaid to you before,' she said, 'you could not have choshen a better ally than Shishely. She ish quite correct, Aldrin. It wash not an accshident that I left my home in Groningen in the Netherlandsh to move to thish town and take a teaching job in your shchool. I came looking for you.'

'Looking for me? Why?'

'Becaushe I made a promishe to shomeone that, when you were eleven yearsh old, I would find you and tell you about your powersh.'

'Who did you make the promise to?' Aldrin asked.

'To your mother,' Mrs Van Boxtel said.

A wave of shock washed through Aldrin's body.

'You knew . . . my mother?' he gasped.

'Yesh, I did,' she told him. 'The ability to enter people'sh dreamsh ish shomething that ish passhed down,' Mrs Van Boxtel explained to the two children, 'from fathersh to daughtersh – and from mothersh to shonsh.'

'You're saying my mum was a Cheese Whizz,' Aldrin said.

'Yesh, she wash.'

'So you actually *knew* her?'

'Oh, we *all* know each other,' she told him. 'We each have a lisht of the namesh of all the Cheeshe Whizshesh in the world. We ushed to meet in shecret every year during the London Feshtival of Cheeshe, which – shad to shay – ish now a feshtival of shtrawberriesh. The lasht time I shaw your mother, she told me she wash very shick.'

'It was the first time the three of us went to the festival as a family.'

'She knew it would be the lasht time ash well. She ashked me if I would watch over you – and alsho, when the time came, tell you about your powersh.'

'So you moved to England just for me?'

'I wash more than happy to do it. I do not have a shon of my own to passh my powersh on to. When I die, shadly my powersh will die with me and there will be one fewer Cheeshe Whizsh in the world.'

'OK,' a voice behind them said. It was the ward sister. 'Visiting time is over for you two, I'm afraid. Nel needs her rest.'

'Before you go,' Mrs Van Boxtel said, 'your mother had shomething very, very important that she wanted you to have.'

'What is it?' Aldrin asked.

'I have absholutely no idea. She didn't give it to me. She shaid she would hide it shomewhere in her bedroom and you would find it.'

'Thanks, Mrs Van Boxtel,' Aldrin said.

Aldrin and Sisely turned to leave. Mrs Van Boxtel

was fast asleep before they reached the door.

'And your mum never said anything to you about this?' Sisely asked as they walked out of the hospital.

'Nothing,' said Aldrin. But then he remembered her telling him once that he had a rare gift and he was going to do extraordinary things in his life.

'She always warned me *against* eating cheese before bedtime,' Aldrin recalled.

'Maybe she didn't want you finding out about your power while you were still so young,' Sisely suggested.

'That would make sense, I suppose.'

'So what do you think this *something* is that she hid in her bedroom?'

'I don't know,' Aldrin said.

And then a feeling of dread swept over him.

'Oh, no!' he said. **'Dad is clearing out Mum's clothes today!** Whatever it is, I hope he hasn't taken it to the charity shop! **Come on, Sisely, let's go!'**

44

A STAGGERING DISCOVERY

Aldrin and Sisely ran all the way to Burnett Road. They burst into the shop. Doug was standing behind the refrigerated counter.

'Dad,' Aldrin said breathlessly, 'have you been to the charity shop yet?'

'Not yet,' Doug said, much to Aldrin's relief. 'What are you two doing out of school in the middle of the morning?'

'Oh, um, Mrs Van Boxtel is in hospital,' Aldrin explained, which wasn't a lie. 'So we were told to go home and work on our stories for the book project.'

That last bit *was* a lie. But he knew he couldn't tell his dad the truth.

'Do you mind if me and Sisely go upstairs to work on

our stories together?' Aldrin asked.

'Just a minute,' Doug said.

'What's wrong?'

'Haven't you noticed anything different?' Doug asked. 'The shop!'

Aldrin felt the corners of his mouth turn into a smile.

There was cheese **EVERYWHERE!**

Aldrin stood there and breathed in the creamy, grassy, chocolatey, smelly-feety, lemony, oniony, butterscotchy, meaty, biscuity, baby-vomity air of a real cheesemonger's.

'It's just like it used to be!' Aldrin said. 'When is the grand reopening?'

'No time like the present,' Doug said, then he turned the sign on the door from **'CLOSED'** to **'OPEN'**.

'Aren't you worried,' Aldrin asked, 'that people will start having nightmares again?'

'I don't believe my cheese caused all those people to have nightmares,' Doug said. 'Mass hysteria is all it was – whipped up by that awful Agatha woman.'

Sisely had another theory. But she decided to keep it to herself for now.

'Aldrin,' she said, 'we really should go and do that, um, homework for Mrs Van Boxtel.'

'Homework,' said Aldrin. 'Yes, good idea.'

They took the stairs two at a time. Seconds later, they were in Doug's room, where all of Cynthia's clothes had been removed from the wardrobe and laid on the bed.

'It would help if we knew what we were looking for,' Sisely said.

'It's probably some kind of letter,' Aldrin guessed. 'Just explaining everything. So, if you wanted to hide a letter where someone wouldn't find it, where would you put it?'

'I'd sew it into the lining of a coat or a jacket,' she said confidently.

'Brilliant!' said Aldrin.

He started picking up his mum's clothes and squeezing the lining, while Sisely stared at a framed photograph on Doug's bedside table. It was Aldrin's favourite. It was taken at the London Festival of Cheese. Aldrin and his mum and dad were smiling and holding up cocktail sticks with little cubes of Cabot Clothbound Cheddar on the end. It was Cynthia's birthday – her last.

'Your mum was very pretty,' Sisely said.

'You sound surprised,' Aldrin replied.

'It's just that you're not attractive at all,' she told him matter-of-factly.

Aldrin laughed.

'Sisely,' he said, 'you don't have to say absolutely *everything* that comes into your head.'

'My mum says I should think before I open my mouth,' she told him.

'She's giving you good advice there.'

'Well, it doesn't matter that you're not attractive, because you're kind and you're brave – and those things are more important.'

Aldrin smiled. Sisely's accidental insults could take your breath away – but so could her compliments.

'Thanks,' he said.

Aldrin had examined the lining of all of his mother's coats and jackets but found nothing. Next, he started going through all of her pockets.

'So you really *are* a superhero then?' Sisely said.

'It, um, certainly looks that way,' Aldrin replied, trying to sound modest but not really pulling it off.

'Who are you going to help next?' she asked.

'I was thinking of Harry,' Aldrin told her.

'Harry's a bully now. He called me an oddball in the corridor last week.'

'He's not a bully, Sisely. He's just frightened of Sebastian. He has nightmares about him.'

'You saw them?'

'Yeah, I went into one the other day. Sebastian was dressed like a horror clown and he fed Harry to the crocodiles. But the weird thing was, I couldn't move. I don't know if it was because the cheese was too mild, or maybe I didn't have enough of it.'

Sisely was suddenly dancing around on one foot, making the floor squeak.

'If you need the toilet,' Aldrin said, 'it's the first door on your left out there.'

'No, listen,' Sisely ordered.

So Aldrin listened.

SQUEAK-SQUEAK . . . SQUEAK-SQUEAK . . . SQUEAK-SQUEAK . . .

'The floorboard is loose,' Sisely explained.

Aldrin dropped to his knees in the corner and started tugging at the edges of the carpet. He managed to pull it up and peel it back, exposing the floorboards underneath. He found the squeaky board, forced the tips of his fingers down the side of it and pulled it up.

He looked in.

'There's nothing there,' he said, disappointed.

'You give up **WAY** too easily,' Sisely told him, then she lay down on her side and squeezed her entire arm into the space. She felt around blindly for a few moments.

'There's something in here,' she said.

'What is it?' Aldrin asked.

A few seconds later, Sisely pulled out a large padded envelope and handed it to Aldrin.

'Here,' she said.

Aldrin looked at it. On the outside, it just said:

Aldrin

The sight of his name written in his mother's handwriting brought tears to his eyes. He realized that he was shaking.

'Are you going to open it?' Sisely asked.

With trembling fingers, Aldrin tore open the envelope and pulled out a large, tattered ledger. It was two inches thick, with scraps of paper and multicoloured Post-it notes sticking out from its pages.

'What is it?' Sisely asked.

'It looks like a diary,' Aldrin said, sitting down on the edge of the bed. Sisely sat down next to him. 'The only problem,' he added, flicking through its pages, 'is it's written in some sort of code.'

Sisely laughed.

'That's not code,' she said. 'It's French.'

'Of course!' Aldrin said. 'My mum was an apprentice cheesemonger under Madame Lacombe. They spoke French all the time. It's a pity that neither of us knows how to speak it.'

'*Je parle français,*' Sisely said.

'What?'

'*Je parle couramment le français. J'ai des cours de français tous les jeudis soir.*'

'Sisely, are you trying to tell me that you know how to speak French?'

'*Oui.*'

Aldrin smiled. Mrs Van Boxtel was right. He couldn't have chosen a better friend with whom to share his secret.

Sisely took the ledger and started studying it closely, her mouth silently forming the words as she read. She said nothing for a minute or two, then she looked up.

'*Zut alors!*' she exclaimed.

'What does that mean?' Aldrin asked. 'Is it good or bad? It *sounds* bad.'

'*Attends un moment,*' she said, holding up her hand, then she went back to reading. For twenty whole minutes, she turned the pages, reading entries at random, examining the Post-it notes and occasionally repeating her earlier exclamation, except this time dragging out the words:

'***Zuuuuuut aloooooors!***'

'Sisely,' Aldrin eventually said, 'you're going to have to tell me what's going on.'

'This is your mum's dream journal,' she explained.

'Her dream journal?'

'Aldrin, for twenty years, your mum kept a written

record of every single dream and nightmare she entered. Not only that, she wrote down what cheese – or combination of cheeses – she ate each time and how that affected her ability to change the outcome.'

'Are you serious?' Aldrin asked.

Sisely turned to the back of the book.

'There's a glossary,' she said. 'It's an A to Z of nightmares – and the cheeses that work best for each.'

'What does it say for clowns?'

Sisely flicked through the pages until she found the relevant entry.

'Limburger,' she read. 'Have you heard of it?'

'Yeah, it's made in Germany,' Aldrin explained. 'It's very smelly. And I mean almost unbearably smelly.'

'Well,' said Sisely, 'it says here, for the best results when it comes to clown nightmares, eat four slices of Limburger, each one an inch in thickness.'

It was very specific, Aldrin thought. And then it suddenly dawned on him what he had in his possession.

'Sisely,' he said, 'you know what my mum has given me here, don't you? It's an instruction manual – showing me how to use my superpower!'

45

A BIT OF LIMBURGER

Doug was as excited as Aldrin had ever seen him.

'Three customers this afternoon,' he said. 'Mrs Tyner bought some Queso Ibores. Well, you know how much she likes a spicy goat. Mrs Iwobi popped in for some Kinderhook Creek and left with a block of my Flory's Truckle. And that nice Mr Cresswell bought a block of Emmental. It's not going to make us millionaires – but the word will soon spread that we're back in business!'

Aldrin was excited too. With his mum's dream journal, he felt in full control of his power now.

'So, what do you fancy for your supper?' Doug asked.

'I was thinking maybe some Limburger,' Aldrin said.

'That's a very strong cheese,' Doug reminded him. 'Still, you always know what you want.'

Aldrin followed his dad downstairs to the shop. Doug took a large rectangular block down from the shelf and brought it over to the cutting board.

'It's five months old,' Doug said. 'Nice and springy.'

He peeled off the wrapping and the aroma filled Aldrin's nostrils.

'Whoa!' he said. 'That's most definitely Limburger all right.'

It was difficult to find words to describe its unusually distinctive smell.

Imagine if, after running a marathon, you removed your sweaty socks and put them on top of a hot radiator, then you forgot about them and returned to the room twenty-four hours later . . .

That was kind of how Limburger smelled.

And there was a very good reason for that. It was made using *Brevibacterium linens* – the bacteria responsible for foot odour!

Aldrin wondered if his dad knew that his wife had kept a dream journal.

'Dad,' he said, 'do you know if Mum ever had a diary or something like that?'

'A diary?' Doug said. 'Not as far as I know. Why do you want to know, Aldrin?'

'Oh, no reason.'

'How much Limburger do you want?'

'I was thinking maybe four slices,' Aldrin said, 'each one about an inch in thickness.'

'An inch?' Doug said. 'That's an awful lot. Make sure to eat it quickly. We don't want it stinking up the flat.'

'Actually,' Aldrin said, 'I might, um, eat it in bed. I'm tired tonight. School in the morning.'

'*Sweet dreams –*'

'– are made of cheese.'

'*Who am I –*'

'– to diss a Brie?'

'Night, son.'

'Night, Dad.'

Aldrin went upstairs to his room. He put the cheese down on top of his bedside table. Silas could smell it through the glass of his tank. He pulled a face:

RRRI*BBIT* . . . ***RRRI****BBIT* . . . ***RRRI****BBIT* . . .

'Sorry, Silas,' Aldrin told his little green friend. 'It'll be gone soon.'

He climbed into bed. He spent a few minutes looking through his mum's dream journal. Amid all the French words that he didn't recognize, he could pick out the names of cheeses that he did: Försterkäse, Wicklow Bán, Puits d'Astier, Castelrosso.

He stared at his mum's handwriting – neat and slanted with occasional fancy loops – and he thought about her writing in this book every day, painstakingly recording the details of each and every cheese nightmare she experienced, knowing that one day it would be her gift to him. It made him feel special. It made him feel loved.

He slipped it under his pillow.

'Here goes, Mum,' he said.

Fortunately, while Limburger *smelled* like foot odour, it tasted absolutely divine.

He thought really, really hard about Harry as, one by one, he folded the four slices of springy, butter-coloured cheese into his mouth. He chewed them until they became a dark, chocolatey, salty, livery mass of gloop in his mouth.

And *very quickly* . . .

without even realizing . . .

that it was happening . . .

his eyes **started to feel** . . .

very,

very

heavy . . .

And then . . .

he was suddenly . . .

out

for

the . . .

46

HARRY'S NIGHTMARE REVISITED

Weird.

Aldrin was sitting on a toilet.

He was in a small, white-tiled bathroom. There was a shower to his right.

Harry was standing with his shoulder pressed against the door. In a pleading voice, he was saying:

'No! Please! Just go away!'

'I can't go away,' said a voice on the other side of the door. It was Sebastian. 'The boys are hungry.'

'Why can't they eat something else?'

'Because they want to eat **YOU!**'

'**Harry,**' Aldrin whispered. '**It's me.**'

Harry turned his head and saw Aldrin sitting there.

'What are *you* doing here?' he asked.

'I'm here to help you,' Aldrin told him.

His mum was right when she suggested Limburger for clown nightmares. He felt stronger and clearer in his mind than when he'd eaten the Edam.

'You *can't* help me,' Harry said. 'He's going to throw me to the crocodiles.'

'He's not,' Aldrin assured him. 'Not tonight.'

On the other side of the door, Sebastian raged:

'WHO ARE YOU TALKING TO IN THERE? ARE YOU GOING TO OPEN THIS DOOR OR AM I GOING TO HAVE TO COME IN THERE TO GET YOU?'

Harry, Aldrin noticed, was trembling with fear.

'Open the door,' Aldrin told him. 'Stand up to him.'

'But he'll throw me to the crocodiles,' Harry said.

'He's going to throw you to the crocodiles one way or the other. Come on, Harry, you've had this nightmare often enough to know that it always ends the same way.'

'OPEN UP!' Sebastian **shouted**, rattling the handle of the bathroom door.

'But you can create your own ending,' Aldrin told him, 'if you just open the door.'

Harry took a deep breath. Then, in one fluid movement, he pulled down the handle and threw the door wide open.

Sebastian was standing there. Aldrin watched his horrible, lipstick-covered mouth shrink into a tiny circle of surprise.

'You ... opened ... the door,' Sebastian said haltingly, the threat of menace gone from his voice completely now.

'Roar at him,' Aldrin told Harry.

'What?' Harry asked.

'Trust me,' Aldrin said. 'Roar at him.'

So that's what Harry did.

He went:

'ROAR!'

But that wasn't what came out of his mouth. What came out of his mouth was:

'RRRRRROOOOOOAAAAAARRRRRR!!!!!!'

It was a noise so loud that it blew Sebastian's hair back and forced him to retreat five steps, like a man trying to walk into a gale-force wind.

It startled Harry as much as it did Sebastian, because the roar that came from him wasn't a human sound. It was the roar . . .

. . . of a **CROCODILE!**

'Do it again,' Aldrin urged.

Harry took a deep breath and let out another roar:

'ʀʀʀʀʀRΟΟΟΟΟΟ**AAAAAARRRRRR!!!!!!**'

This one was louder, and longer, and more
terrifying. The floor shook. The bathroom window
broke, showering Aldrin in glass splinters. And then
something happened that was scarcely believable . . .

Sebastian started to cry!

'Don't hurt me!' he implored, rivers of mascara pouring down his face. 'I'm begging you! Please!'

Sebastian started backing away, but Harry pursued him across the landing, letting loose one final . . .

'RRRRRROOOOOOAAAAAARRRRRR!!!!!!'

And suddenly Sebastian disappeared!

'Where's he gone?' Harry asked, sounding strangely disappointed. 'I was enjoying that.'

'He doesn't exist,' Aldrin told him. 'The Sebastian you're frightened of – he never existed, Harry.'

And no sooner had he spoken these words than Aldrin woke up in his bed, sweating and shivering, with his head thumping, feeling worse than he'd ever felt before in his life.

But, at the same time, he knew in his heart that Sebastian would never hold the same fear for Harry again.

A BIT OF EMMENTAL

Agatha was dreaming about cheese again.

She had no idea why, since she absolutely loathed the stuff – as she'd learned from her recent slip-up.

But there it was – front and centre in her dreams once again.

She was sitting in a restaurant – one that sold only the healthiest, most wholesome food. She had just polished off an enormous bowl of broccoli in a broccoli sauce with a side of broccoli. A waiter arrived to clear away her plate.

'Would madam care to see the cheeseboard?' he asked.

'Cheese?' she said disbelievingly. 'I would **NEVER** eat such a thing! **DIS! GUSTING!**'

'Very good, madam,' the waiter said, then he went to walk back to the kitchen.

'Although,' Agatha added, 'it wouldn't hurt to take a look, would it?'

'I shall go and fetch it, madam.'

The waiter returned a few moments later, pushing a three-tiered trolley laden with cheese of every variety – the firmest Cheddars, the softest Camemberts, the crumbliest blues, the creamiest Bries, the chewiest Goudas, and the grainiest Pecorinos.

And oh, the smell!

It was fresh, and fruity, and yeasty, and garlicky, and sweet, and perfumy, and earthy, and musty, and floral, and pungent, and sour, and funky, and ripe, and gamey, and mushroomy, and limey, and herbaceous, and milky, and meaty, and nutty, and rustic, and smoky, and peanutty, and winey – all at the same time!

The waiter talked her through the selection.

'These are our blues,' he said, 'our semi-firms, our bloomy-rinded, our firm-and-aged, our washed-rind and our fresh-and-young cheeses.'

'I'll have a bit of everything,' Agatha heard herself say.

'Everything?' the waiter asked. 'There are almost

four hundred cheeses here. I'm not sure that we have a plate big enough.'

'Then leave the trolley,' Agatha replied, her two hands grasping the handle.

'I, erm, can't do that,' he told her, grabbing the handle at the other end. 'There are other customers.'

Agatha pulled it one way. The waiter pulled it the other way. And suddenly they were locked in a tug of war for control of the divine-smelling cheese trolley.

Back and forth it went with both of them pulling with all their strength, until Agatha gave it one final, furious tug, ripping it from the waiter's grasp with such force that it tipped over on top of her, burying her beneath an avalanche of cheese.

Agatha woke up. Her mouth was dripping and her heart was beating fast. She felt confused. And yet, at the same time, she was certain of one thing – she wanted cheese like she wanted her next breath.

She threw back the duvet.

'Is everything OK?' Harvey asked.

'I thought I might check if there were any, um, carrots in the fridge,' she said, pulling her dressing gown round her. 'I shan't be long.'

Agatha went downstairs to the kitchen. She opened

the fridge and looked inside. It was a waste of time, since she knew there wasn't a crumb of cheese in the entire house.

What was happening to her? She **HATED** cheese. She **DE! SPISED!** it! But it was happening again – the dream, followed by the craving. It was almost as if . . .

. . . someone was controlling her mind.

She absolutely HAD to have cheese – right **NOW!**

But where would she get some?

Then she had an idea.

She popped next door to the Cresswells'. She pressed the doorbell once, then a second time, then she kept her finger on it so that it rang continuously.

RRRRRRIIIIIINNNNNNGGGGGG!!!!!!

Inside the house, a light came on. A moment later, Mr Cresswell answered the door.

'Agatha?' he said. 'What on earth is wrong? Is the house on fire?'

'No,' she replied, smiling. 'I just wondered if I might borrow some cheese?'

'Borrow some cheese?' Mr Cresswell said, like he thought he might be dreaming this conversation. 'You do know it's four o'clock in the morning?'

'Yes,' she said. 'I just, um, fancied some.'

'Hold on, I thought you wanted cheese banned? Didn't you organize that picket of Doug's shop?'

'A little bit of cheese never hurt anyone,' Agatha replied, 'when eaten in moderation. So, um, could I have some?'

'Wait here,' said Mr Cresswell, then he went back inside, shaking his head, and returned with a paper bag with the words *C'est Cheese* on it.

'Where did this come from?' Agatha asked.

'What, you haven't heard?' said Mr Cresswell. 'Doug reopened the cheesemonger's yesterday.'

'What's in here?' Agatha asked eagerly.

'Oh, it's just a bit of Emmental,' Mr Cresswell told her with a shrug.

Agatha pulled out a large triangular wedge of pale yellow cheese, which was full of holes. Without saying a word, she bit into it like it was a slice of chocolate cake.

'Here, I didn't say you could have all of it! That's supposed to be for my sandwiches for the week!' Mr Cresswell told her.

Agatha said something in reply, although Mr Cresswell couldn't understand a word of it, because the woman's mouth was so stuffed with cheese. It sounded something like this:

'Mthg thnad abspal thunth thootha ... mmm mmm mmm.'

Agatha didn't stop at one bite. She went at it like an animal until she had devoured the entire wedge and melted cheese was dripping down her chin and on to the Cresswells' doorstep.

She scrunched up the bag and handed it back to Mr Cresswell. Then she turned on her heel and returned to her house, then to her bedroom, then to her bed . . .

. . . where she proceeded to have yet another **TERRIFYING** nightmare.

Except this one was worse than the last one, because of the appearance in it of a man, who was thin like a broom handle, with dark, slicked-back hair and black horn-rimmed glasses set upon a large nose, wearing a dark suit with a red bow tie – and a face . . .

. . . of pure evil!

48

SEBASTIAN REES-LANE

'A shark?' Aldrin said. **'Wow!'**

It was lunchtime. He was in the cafeteria, and Frankie was filling him in on what he'd got up to the night before.

'A great white,' Frankie said. 'They're the kings of the sea, you know?'

'And you *fought* it?' Aldrin said. 'That's unbelievable!'

It was *literally* unbelievable. According to Frankie, this happened just off the coast at Morecambe.

'The thing with sharks,' Frankie said, 'is that you have to show them who's boss. I got this one in a headlock and managed to clamp his mouth shut. Then I've gone, "You, my friend, have terrorized your last swimmer off this coast! I never want to see you around here again! Now, *do* one!"'

Sisely **sighed** in a bored way. She was about to say something, but Aldrin made a silent appeal to her with his eyes and she stopped herself.

Frankie slapped his forehead.

'Oh, no,' he said, 'I've left me lunch in me locker. Back in a sec.'

He walked off, leaving Aldrin and Sisely alone.

'Thanks,' Aldrin said to her, 'for not making him feel stupid.'

'He wasn't anywhere near Morecambe last night,' she said. 'He was kicking a football against the door of our garage. You look terrible, by the way.'

This morning's cheese hangover was the worst yet.

'I went into Harry's dream last night,' Aldrin told her. 'I ate four slices of Limburger – just like Mum said in her dream journal.'

'And what happened?' Sisely asked.

'I told Harry to open the door and roar at him,' Aldrin said.

'Roar at him?'

'It was just an idea that came to me in the moment. So he did it. And I made it sound like the roar of a crocodile. And then . . .'

'What?'

327

'Sebastian just burst into –'

At that moment, Aldrin noticed Harry walk into the cafeteria. He looked over to where Sebastian was sitting, along with Hercy and Algernon, then he looked over to where Aldrin and Sisely were sitting.

Sebastian was watching him dithering in the cafeteria doorway.

'Harry!' he said. 'Over here!'

'Don't go to him, Harry,' Aldrin whispered under his breath. 'Come and sit with us.'

Harry considered the dilemma for about twenty seconds. And then – unbelievably! – he made his way across the cafeteria to where Aldrin and Sisely were sitting at the oddballs' table!

'I just wanted to say sorry,' he said to Aldrin, 'for saying I didn't want to be your friend any more.'

'It's OK, Harry,' Aldrin said. 'It's forgotten.'

'And I wanted to say sorry to you, Sisely, for calling you an oddball.'

Sisely shrugged.

'I am an oddball,' she said.

'And so are you!' Aldrin reminded him. 'Do you want to come and join us?'

Aldrin indicated the chair beside him.

'*If* that's OK?' Harry said, sitting down.

Frankie returned with his lunch box in his hand. He acted like there was nothing unusual about Harry being there.

'You've only gone and missed me story,' Frankie said. 'I was telling Aldrin and Sisely how I fought off two great whites!'

Oh, it's two now, is it? Aldrin thought.

'You know, Frankie,' Harry said, 'I absolutely love these stories that you tell us. And I was thinking, wouldn't it be really great if you could bring them to a bigger audience?'

'What do you mean?'

'I've been thinking about making my own comic book. But a comic book has to have **LOADS** of characters and I've only got one – the Boy Who Hunts Crocodiles. And you've got all these amazing stories about the **Boy Who Parachuted Behind Enemy Lines**, and the **Boy Who Played for Barcelona**, and the **Boy Who Jumped the Grand Canyon on a Motorbike**. And I was thinking, what if this comic was something that me and you could work on together?'

Frankie's face lit up.

'Seriously?' he asked.

'I thought that you could come up with the stories,' Harry suggested, 'and I could illustrate them.'

'I'd love that!' Frankie said.

It was at that precise moment that a dark shadow fell across the table.

'Why on earth are you sitting with the oddballs?' Sebastian asked.

Aldrin could tell immediately from Harry's body language that he wasn't frightened of him any more. The spell had been broken.

Harry looked Sebastian dead in the eye.

'These oddballs,' he said, 'are my friends. And this table is where I belong.'

Sebastian couldn't believe what he was hearing.

'If that's your choice,' he said, 'you can go back to handing over your lunch money every day.'

'No,' Harry told him, 'I won't be giving you anything – ever again.'

'WHO DO YOU THINK YOU ARE?' Sebastian loudly demanded.

Every single conversation in the cafeteria came to a dead halt.

'I'm someone who's not frightened of you,' Harry told him calmly.

Sebastian took a step towards him. And that was when it happened.

Harry let loose a roar.

It wasn't quite as loud as the crocodile roar that he'd produced in his nightmare last night. But it was loud enough to give Sebastian a fright.

'RRRRRROOOOOOAAAAAARRRRRR!!!!!!'

He took a step backwards. Hercy and Algernon, lurking behind Sebastian as usual, took a step backwards too. Harry suddenly had a wild look in his eyes and they didn't like it one bit.

He roared again – angry and animal-like – and he started walking towards Sebastian.

'RRRRRROOOOOOAAAAAARRRRRR!!!!!!'

Sebastian backed away.

'What are you doing?' he asked nervously. 'What's the matter with you?'

'RRRRRROOOOOOAAAAAARRRRRR!!!!!!'

'He's gone mad!' Sebastian said, a note of genuine fear in his voice now. 'Someone fetch Mr Maskell! Get him here now! Tell him Stiles has gone nuts and there's no guessing what he might do!'

But no one budged. Because they were witnessing

something they had never expected to see . . .

The bully was terrified.

Aldrin smiled. Frankie smiled. Sisely very nearly cracked a smile.

Sebastian kept backing away and Harry kept walking after him until, finally, Sebastian had his back against the wall.

'RRRRRROOOOOOAAAAAARRRRRR!!!!!!'

And Sebastian started to gibber madly.

'Not the face!' he pleaded, covering it with his hands. 'Please don't hurt my beautiful face!'

And that was the cue for the laughter to begin. It started small – just a snigger or two. Then it swept like a wave through the cafeteria until all of the children who lived in fear of Sebastian Rees-Lane were laughing hysterically.

Harry didn't lay a finger on him. He just smiled at the cowering bully, then turned on his heel and went back to his table, where Aldrin, Frankie and Sisely were looking on, impressed.

Hercy and Algernon did nothing. They just stood there, staring at Sebastian in shock, realizing something that Aldrin had suspected right from the beginning. And now it was confirmed.

Sebastian was a coward.

And no one in the school would ever fear him again.

HA!

HA!

HA!

HA!

HA!

HA!

HA!

HA!

HA!

49

'CLOSE THIS SHOP!'

'So what are you going to do next?' Sisely asked.

'I don't know,' Aldrin admitted. 'Do I just wait around for someone else to tell me that they're having nightmares? I don't know how it works.'

They were walking home from school, and Aldrin's cheese hangover was beginning to lift.

'And then there's Habeas Grusselvart,' Aldrin said.

'What about him?' Sisely asked.

'Well, Mrs Van Boxtel said that Habeas is the enemy we have to fight. Did she mean that literally? Because I'm not much of a fighter. I don't know if you've noticed, but I'm not exactly in peak physical condition. Or did she mean fight in the battle-of-wills sense?'

'I don't know.'

'I mean, I wouldn't know where to find him even if I was in fighting shape.'

'You can ask her when she comes back to school.'

'That's *if* she comes back.'

They turned the corner on to Burnett Road. And they both stopped dead in their tracks when they saw the scene outside the shop.

Because the protesters were back. They were holding placards that said:

CHEESE IS BAD!
YOU FETA BELIEVE IT'S TRUE!

And they were marching back and forth in front of the shop, chanting:

'CHEESE! OUT!'
'CHEESE! OUT!'
'CHEESE! OUT!'

Aldrin spotted Mrs Tyner, who'd been a customer of *C'est Cheese* since before he was born.

'Your dad's Queso Ibores gave me nightmares!' she told him crossly.

'Mrs Tyner, cheese doesn't cause nightmares,' Aldrin tried to persuade her. 'You've been eating it for years!'

'How do you explain it then?' she said. 'Giant spiders. Big, hairy things – fifty feet tall!'

335

'I had nightmares too,' said Mr Talese. 'I ate half a pound of Gorgonzola in the middle of the night, and I dreamt I was being chased by a scarecrow!'

'Half a pound?' Aldrin asked. 'Why did you eat half a pound of Gorgonzola in the middle of the night?'

'Because,' a voice behind him said, 'he woke up with a terrible craving.'

Aldrin and Sisely wheeled round. It was Agatha.

'You!' Aldrin said. 'I might have known you were behind this! Why can't you just leave my dad alone?'

'Because he should **NEVER** have reopened this shop,' she said. 'It's the same story as before. Everyone here who has eaten your father's cheese has had bad dreams – including me!'

'I thought you hated cheese?' Sisely said. 'Why do you keep eating it if you think it gives you nightmares?'

'Because,' Agatha told her, 'it clearly has addictive qualities, as well as mind-altering ones.'

'What a load of nonsense!' Aldrin declared.

Agatha picked up the chant again and the others joined in:

'CHEESE! OUT!'
'CHEESE! OUT!'
'CHEESE! OUT!'

Aldrin and Sisely stepped past the protesters and into the shop, which was predictably empty. Doug was standing behind the counter, seemingly unconcerned by what was happening outside on Burnett Road.

'Dad,' Aldrin said, 'you do know that Agatha's back, don't you?'

'Yes, of course,' he said, absently chomping on a piece of soft and spicy Monte Enebro. 'I haven't had a single customer all day. **Hmmm**. That's delicious. Would you like some, Sisely? It's got a sort of metallic, mushroomy taste.'

'Dad,' Aldrin said, 'they're picketing the shop again. What are you doing about it?'

'I'm waiting for the cavalry to arrive,' Doug said.

'The cavalry? What are you talking about?'

Just then, the bell above the door pinged. Aldrin looked round. And he couldn't believe who was standing in the doorway.

'Belinda!' Aldrin exclaimed. 'What are you doing back here?'

'Your dad's offered me my old job back,' Belinda said. 'Although I might as well tell you now, Doug, that I don't do sweeping or cleaning up. And I'd have to insist on taking me breaks.'

Doug laughed.

'It's great to have you back,' he said, 'because it frees up time for me to return to the important job . . . of marketing!'

Aldrin and Sisely watched as Doug stepped into the mouse costume and pulled it up round his shoulders.

'Hand me my megaphone, will you, please, Belinda?' he said. 'It's behind the counter there.'

Belinda sighed.

'I'm only just back,' she said, retrieving it for him, 'and he's already bossing me around.'

Doug zipped up the suit and took the megaphone from Belinda.

'Don't forget your whiskers!' Aldrin said, picking up a black marker pen. 'And your nose.'

Doug leaned down and Aldrin drew five whiskers on each side of his dad's face and a black triangle on the end of his nose.

'Here goes!' Doug said, then he opened the door and stepped into the crowd of protesters. He stood in the middle of the road, pressed one end of the megaphone to his lips and he said:

'WHAT DO YOU GET IF YOU CROSS AN AMERICAN POP SUPERSTAR WITH A CHEESE

THAT'S GOT HOLES IN IT? . . . TAYLOR SWISS!'

Sisely turned to Aldrin, standing in the doorway of the cheesemonger's.

'I don't get it,' she said.

She really didn't have any sense of humour.

'YOU DIDN'T LIKE THAT ONE, SISELY?' Doug said. **'A BIT CHEESY FOR YOU, WAS IT? WELL, DESPITE WHAT SOME OF YOU MAY THINK, A LITTLE BIT OF CHEESE DOES YOU NO HARM AT ALL! CHEESE CONTAINS VITAL NUTRIENTS, SUCH AS CALCIUM, ZINC AND VITAMINS A AND**

B-12. IT ALSO CONTAINS PROTEIN, WHICH CAN GIVE YOU LEANER MUSCLES AND HEALTHIER SKIN. LET ME ASK YOU THIS – WHEN WAS THE LAST TIME YOU SAW A MOUSE WITH ZITS?'

Agatha attempted to shout him down:

'YOUR EMMENTAL GAVE ME THE MOST GHASTLY NIGHTMARES!'

And suddenly a thought struck Aldrin hard.

'Sisely, it's not a coincidence,' he whispered to her.

'What do you mean?' Sisely asked.

'You said it yourself,' he reminded her. 'You said there had to be a link between me having this superpower and all my dad's customers having nightmares. This is *his* doing, Sisely.'

'Habeas Grusselvart?'

'He's trying to force Dad out of business to cut off my access to cheese.'

'That would explain it.'

'Sisely, I have to confront him – face to face.'

'How are you going to find him?'

'I have no idea,' he said with a shrug.

'Go and get me your mum's dream journal,' Sisely instructed. 'The answer must be in there.'

50

NIGHTMARE CLUSTERS

Mr Arnold was being especially boring this morning.

'A verb is an action,' he said. 'An adverb is a word that *modifies* an action. Can anyone here give me an example of an adverb?'

Aldrin turned to Sisely.

'So?' he asked. 'Did you find out?'

'I'll tell you after class,' she whispered.

'Quickly! Slowly! Sadly! Silently!' Mr Arnold said. 'These are examples of adverbs.'

But Aldrin couldn't wait.

'Tell me now,' he insisted. 'How do I meet Habeas Grusselvart?'

'ALDRIN! ADAMS!' Mr Arnold said. 'Perhaps **YOU** would be good enough to conjugate this verb for us.'

'To what?' Aldrin asked.

'I explained what the word conjugate meant not sixty seconds ago. Stand outside, you STUPID boy!'

Aldrin stood up.

But as he did, the door opened. And into the classroom walked Mrs Van Boxtel, with her dandelion-puffball hair, her cardigan, her tweed skirt, her brown fur-lined ankle boots and her surgical collar.

Aldrin's stomach somersaulted with excitement.

'What are *you* doing here?' he asked.

'I am the teacher of thish classh,' she reminded him.

'But I thought you were in hospital.'

'Ash you can clearly shee, I am not. But thank you for your conshern, Aldrin. Take your sheat, pleashe.'

Aldrin sat down.

'Adams, stand up!' Mr Arnold commanded.

Aldrin stood up.

'I am your teacher,' Mrs Van Boxtel pointed out. 'Now, pleashe take your sheat.'

This time, Aldrin thought he'd stay seated until they'd figured out who was in charge.

'I was not told that your return was imminent,' said Mr Arnold crossly.

'What ish thish on the whiteboard?' Mrs Van Boxtel asked.

'I've been attempting to teach your class the rudiments of English grammar,' Mr Arnold said, except he really rolled his Rs, so that it came out as . . . the 'rrrrrrudiments of English grrrrrrammar'.

'And I am shure they will remember you very fondly for it when you are gone!' said Mrs Van Boxtel to him. 'Goodbye, Mishter Arnold!'

He stared at her, furious, then he turned on his heel and left the room.

The children laughed and cheered loudly.

'SHILENSHE!' said Mrs Van Boxtel. 'Everybody, take out your shtoriesh!'

A ripple of excitement went through the classroom.

'You musht finish your shtoriesh before the

weekend,' Mrs Van Boxtel added, 'becaushe next week we will be shending them to the printersh ash planned – sho we can produshe our book!'

When the bell sounded at the end of class, Aldrin almost sprinted to the front of the class to talk to her.

'I'm so happy you're back,' he said.

'I am happy to be back alsho,' she replied.

'You were right about my mum leaving me something,' he said. 'It was her dream journal. She wrote down everything!'

'That wash very clever of her,' said Mrs Van Boxtel.

'Except it's all in French. Sisely's been reading it – although she still hasn't told me how to find Habeas Grusselvart.'

'You can't find him,' said Mrs Van Boxtel. 'At leasht not in the world of dreamsh.'

'That's what your mum said in her journal.' Sisely said, joining them. 'HE has to come to YOU.'

'And he will,' Mrs Van Boxtel added in a sombre voice.

'And it's NOT a coincidence that all of your dad's customers are having nightmares,' Sisely added. 'Habeas *is* doing it.'

'They're what we call Nightmare Clushtersh,' said Mrs Van Boxtel.

'That's right,' Sisely said. 'Your mum knew all about them. When he wants to put a cheesemonger's out of business, he focuses all of his nightmare-making efforts on their customer base.'

'But how does Habeas know who's buying cheese from Dad's shop? How did he know about Mrs Iwobi and her Flory's Truckle? And Mr Cresswell and his Emmental? And Mrs Tyner and her Queso Ibores?'

'Someone must be watching the shop,' Sisely suggested ominously.

'Beddy Byesh,' Mrs Van Boxtel said.

'Who *is* Beddy Byes?' Sisely asked. 'Aldrin's mum mentions him a LOT in her journal.'

'Beddy Byesh ish the right-hand man of Habeash. He doesh all hish dirty work for him. He alsho hash shupernatural powersh. He likesh to show up in people'sh nightmaresh from time to time – jusht to take pleashure in their dishtressh.'

'According to your mum,' Sisely said, 'it was Beddy Byes who came up with the plan to take control of all the cheese in the world.'

'So people like me and Mrs Van Boxtel can't gain access to other people's nightmares,' Aldrin realized. 'So what do I do now?'

'Your firsht priority,' said Mrs Van Boxtel, 'musht be to shave your father'sh shop.'

'But how do I do that?' Aldrin asked. 'Agatha's not going to just give up.'

'She might,' Sisely said, 'if you help her with her own nightmare.'

'No way!' Aldrin responded, disgusted at the thought. 'I'm not helping *her*. She tried to destroy my dad's life – she's STILL trying!'

'Being a Cheeshe Whizsh,' Mrs Van Boxtel said in a serious voice, 'ish a rare honour, Aldrin. You are one of the choshen few. But with thish power comesh great reshponshibility. You cannot chooshe jusht to help the people that you care about. Do you undershtand?'

'But *her*?' he exclaimed.

'All of ush who have thish gift,' she told him, 'have a duty to help *all* people in dishtressh – even thoshe who are not our friendsh.'

'You have to do it,' Sisely said. 'You have to go into Agatha's dream – tonight.'

51

A BALL OF MOZZARELLA

It was a day for surprises.

When **C'est Cheese** closed that evening, Belinda didn't rush out of the door. She offered to stay behind to help Doug and Aldrin wrap all of the cheeses and wipe down the shelves for the following day.

'You really don't have to,' Doug assured her.

'It's only fair,' she said. 'We've not had a customer through the door all day. You're not paying me to just sit around reading magazines.'

Doug and Aldrin smiled at each other.

'Here,' Aldrin said, handing her a sweeping brush. Belinda stared at it for a long moment – like she'd never seen one before.

'You hold it at this end,' Aldrin told her, 'and you sweep with that end.'

'I know how to use a sweeping brush!' she said. 'I'm not flipping daft! It's just I've got something to say and I were thinking about how to say it.'

'Oh?' said Doug.

'I suppose what I want to say is . . . sorry.'

'Sorry?' Doug said. 'What on earth for?'

'I've probably not been as helpful and friendly as I should have been – for someone working in a customer-facing business, I mean. Truth is, I get a bit down in the dumps sometimes – same as other folk. I thought it were because I'd never fulfilled my dreams of becoming the next Shirley Bassey. But I only found out what it was after you closed down the shop that time. I were just lonely. I don't really have anyone in my life except you two – and Mrs Adams when she were alive. You're the closest thing to a family I've got.'

'That's a lovely thing to say,' Doug beamed.

'I only realized when I were working in that supermarket how much I missed seeing you every day.'

'We missed you too,' Aldrin said.

'Well, you're going to be seeing a different me around here in future,' she told them.

'We don't want to see a different you,' Doug told her. 'We love you just the way you are.'

Belinda blushed a deep shade of pink.

'Oh, enough of your flattery,' she said.

Aldrin looked from Doug to Belinda, and a smile crept across his face.

It was at that precise moment that the telephone rang. Doug answered.

'Good evening,' he said, '*C'est Cheese*. Doug Adams speaking . . . Oh, hello there, Sisely. Aldrin, it's for you.'

Aldrin took the phone.

'Hi, Sisely,' he said.

'Mozzarella,' she told him.

'Excuse me?'

'In her dream journal, your mum says you shouldn't just jump into someone else's dream without going in first as an observer.'

'OK – and how do I go in as an observer?'

'I just told you! Mozzarella! Or three small cubes of Edam. But Mozzarella is best. According to your mum, it will allow you to see everything – but you won't be able to change the outcome'

'Right.'

'No one will be able to hear you or see you.'

'Mozzarella?'

'Mozzarella.'

'Thanks, Sisely.'

She hung up.

Doug and Belinda were chuckling away at some private joke.

'Dad,' Aldrin said, 'can I have some mozzarella for my supper.'

'Mozzarella?' Doug said. 'You don't often ask for that. Although your mother loved it.'

'Did she?'

'I think she had some every other day. Here you go.'

Doug handed Aldrin a little bag with a ball of soft cheese inside, swimming in brine.

Later that night, when his dad was asleep, and Silas was quiet in his tank, Aldrin took the bag to the bathroom. He tore it open and poured the brine down the basin. Then he reached into it with his finger and thumb and removed the moist white ball of cheese.

He took it into bed with him. Then he bit into it like he was eating an apple. And even though he didn't want to, he thought about Agatha – as tall and thin as a bus stop, with blonde hair that went all the way down to her waist, lots of make-up and a pinched face that made it look like she was sucking hard on a boiled sweet – even though she wasn't.

He ate the entire ball of mozzarella, chewing it until it was just a mass of warm, meadowy mush in his mouth . . .

And *very quickly* . . .

without even realizing . . .

that it was happening . . .

his eyes **started to feel** . . .

very,

very

heavy . . .

And then . . .

he was suddenly . . .

out

for

the . . .

AGATHA'S NIGHTMARE

The scene that greeted him was one of chaos.

Crowds of people were running past him, some of them screaming, some of them shouting warnings, like:

'It's going to blow!'

And:

'Run for your lives!'

He could hear a loud bubbling sound, growing more and more insistent.

Aldrin pushed his way through the crowds, moving against the flow of people, trying to discover the source of their panic.

He thought he could smell nacho cheese. The further he walked, the stronger the smell became, until it was almost overpowering.

The crowds began to thin out as the last few people hurriedly made their escape. Aldrin looked up. And that's when he saw it.

Standing high above him, towering over the town, was a giant bowl, resting on metal stilts. Underneath the bowl, he could see that a fire was raging.

No, Aldrin thought. *It couldn't be.*

He was standing in the shadow of a giant fondue set. And from the furious boiling sound, and the steam pouring out of the bowl, it was clear that it was about to bubble over.

Suddenly, there was a loud bang, then Aldrin watched as jets of boiling cheese were shot high into the air like lava spewing from a volcano.

It began raining down, starting to fill the streets below.

Aldrin heard a woman scream.

'AAAAAARRRRRRGGGGGGGHHHHHH!!!!!!'

He knew instantly that it was Agatha. He followed her screams until he eventually spotted her. She was trying to get into a car outside the supermarket on Digges Road. But the door wouldn't open.

'HELP ME!' she was shouting. 'SOMEONE, PLEASE HELP ME!'

Aldrin saw a raging river of hot molten cheese moving fast towards her.

'Run!' he shouted at her. 'You don't *need* your car, Agatha! Just run!'

'**AAAAAARRRRRRGGGGGGHHHHHH!!!!!!**' Agatha continued to scream.

The air was so thick with nacho cheese now that Aldrin could feel it in his lungs.

He rushed over to the car.

'Agatha,' he said, 'leave it here and just run!'

But Agatha didn't seem to hear him. Then he remembered what Sisely said. Mozzarella would only allow him to observe the dream and not affect its ending.

'**HELP!**' Agatha screamed, tugging frantically at the handle of the door. '**SOMEBODY, PLEASE HELP US!**'

Us?

And that was when Aldrin noticed a figure sitting in the front passenger seat. It was Sebastian.

'**MY SON IS TRAPPED IN THE CAR!**' Agatha screamed.

Aldrin heard laughter then – cruel, mocking laughter. He looked up and saw a man standing on the other side of the car, making no attempt to help Agatha as she struggled to open the door.

His face was familiar.

'WHY WON'T YOU HELP US?' Agatha shouted. 'WHY WON'T YOU HELP US?'

But he just laughed at her.

Aldrin heard one final scream.

'AAAAARRRRRGGGGGGHHHHHH!!!!!!'

Then he turned just in time to see a giant wave of thick mustard-coloured gloop crashing down on Agatha, submerging her, and her car, and poor Sebastian sitting inside.

Aldrin opened his eyes.

He sat bolt upright in the bed.

He knew him. The mystery man who was laughing at Agatha's attempts to save her son from drowning. It was Maurice Mackle, the man who'd served his apprenticeship alongside Aldrin's mum, the man who'd helpfully offered to clear out all of their cheese – a man who now went by another name. And that name, Aldrin somehow knew, as if it was instinct that was telling him . . .

. . . was Beddy Byes!

53

THE MARASPOLI BOLU DILEMMA

'It was horrible!' Aldrin said.

'Nacho cheese?' Sisely asked.

'Rivers of it,' Aldrin told her, 'flooding the whole town. And Sebastian was trapped in Agatha's car! It's no wonder she hates cheese so much!'

They were sitting in the computer room and their conversation was drawing more than a few curious stares from the other children in their Information Technology class.

'You should probably keep your voice down,' Sisely advised.

'The bit I haven't told you yet,' Aldrin added, 'is that I saw Beddy Byes! And I've met him before.'

'What? When?'

357

'He's the man who came to the shop to take away Dad's cheese! I need to go back in there, Sisely. Except this time I'm going to need something stronger than mozzarella.'

'There's no mention of a killer fondue set in your mum's dream journal.'

'Are you sure?'

'Well, given that I have a photographic memory and I only have to read something once to remember it forever, yes!'

'OK, I believe you. There's no mention of a killer fondue set.'

'But there *is* a reference to a volcano nightmare. People running to escape the lava flow. It's definitely the closest thing in your mum's journal to what you described.'

'Right, so what cheese do I have to eat to access a volcano dream?'

'It's called Maraspoli Bolu,' Sisely said.

'Maraspoli Bolu?' Aldrin repeated. 'OK, why is that name familiar?'

Sisely typed the name into a search engine.

'It says here it's one of the rarest cheeses in the world. It's made in Turkey. From donkey's milk.'

'That's it!'

'It says it's matured in a cave where this very unusual mould grows. Because of flooding, the cave is only accessible for two months of the year – April and September.'

'Dad was talking about it. It was on the TV. That Sir Marmaduke Birtwistle bought some at an auction. It went for fifty grand, or something.'

Sisely typed Sir Marmaduke's name into the search engine.

'You're right,' she said. 'It was fifty thousand pounds for four ounces! I presume you don't have access to that kind of money, Aldrin?'

'Unfortunately not.'

There was a long moment of silence between the two of them then.

'Sisely,' Aldrin said, a smile inching its way across his face, 'are you thinking what I'm thinking?'

'Probably not,' Sisely replied.

'Well, *I* was thinking we should bunk off school for the afternoon –'

'OK, that's definitely **NOT** what I was thinking.'

'– and we should go to this Sir Marmaduke Birtwistle's house and steal his donkey cheese.'

'Yeah, I wasn't thinking **ANY** of that.'

'Sisely, please! This is our chance to save the world!'

'Don't be melodramatic. It's our chance to stop some people from having nightmares.'

'Don't you see? It's **bigger** than that! This is my chance to confront Beddy Byes – and, who knows, he might even lead me to Habeas Grusselvart!'

'But we have Geography next.'

'Please, Sisely! You're my Linda Dale!'

'I'm your **WHAT**?'

'She's a character in this comic book that Harry told me about. She's the sidekick of Agent Cunning. He has these amazing superpowers. But Linda Dale is the brains of the outfit – he'd be nothing without her.'

Sisely sighed.

'I could tell Mr Maskell that I'm not feeling well,' she said, 'and I need to go home. But we'll have to be quick about it. It says here that Sir Marmaduke is planning to eat the cheese today.'

'What?' Aldrin asked.

'To celebrate his birthday,' Sisely said. 'He's going to do it in front of the world's press – and in exactly one hour from now.'

OBNOXIOUSLY AWFUL

Sisely and Aldrin formulated a plan as they hurried home from school.

'Maraspoli Bolu looks almost identical to Gorgonzola,' Sisely said. 'Same consistency, same greenish-blue marbling.'

'So why don't we get some Gorgonzola from my dad's shop,' Aldrin suggested, 'sneak into Grangewood Court and then, when nobody is looking –'

'Switch the two cheeses.'

'Great minds think alike.'

They turned the corner on to Burnett Road.

'I'll wait here,' Sisely said. 'But you need to hurry.'

'I'll be quick,' Aldrin said.

Agatha and the other protesters were still standing

outside *C'est Cheese*, chanting:

'CLOSE THIS SHOP!'

'CLOSE THIS SHOP!'

'CLOSE THIS SHOP!'

But Aldrin didn't hate Agatha now that he'd witnessed, first-hand, the terrifying reality of her nightmares. He even shot her a sympathetic smile.

'What are *you* grinning at?' she asked.

Aldrin walked into the shop. Belinda was serving a customer.

'Now, don't eat it straight from the fridge,' she was saying. 'Cheese always tastes best when it's eaten at room temperature.'

Doug stepped out from the back of the shop, wearing his mouse costume.

'What are you doing home?' he asked.

'I had a free period,' Aldrin said. 'And I remembered that I hadn't brought any cheese for my lunch.'

Aldrin hated fibbing to his dad. But all superheroes had to do it occasionally to protect their identity.

'What would you like?' Doug asked.

'I was thinking about some Gorgonzola,' Aldrin said.

'I've got some nice Cashel Blue just in.'

'Go nice with digestive biscuits,' Belinda suggested,

'and a spoonful of fruit chutney.'

She really *was* making an effort.

'No, definitely Gorgonzola,' Aldrin insisted.

'OK, how much would you like?' Doug asked, picking up a large quarter-wheel and laying it down on the cutting block.

'Four ounces,' Aldrin told him.

'That's not very much,' Doug said. 'You came all the way home from school for four ounces?'

'I'm, er, trying to lose a little bit of weight.'

'You know best.'

Using the cheese wire, Doug sheared precisely four ounces of Gorgonzola from the block, wrapped it in wax paper and handed it to Aldrin.

Sisely was waiting impatiently for him at the end of the street.

'We have exactly twenty-seven minutes,' she said, 'before Sir Marmaduke eats that cheese.'

'Then we'd better run,' Aldrin said.

The only drawback with that plan was that Aldrin wasn't exactly in optimum physical condition. They ran. But Aldrin soon slowed to a jog and then to a stop. He was standing with one hand against the wall of the post office, doubled over and out of breath.

'Nineteen minutes,' Sisely pointed out.

'OK,' Aldrin wheezed, 'just let me . . . catch my . . . second wind here.'

When Aldrin had almost, but not quite, regathered his breath, they set off again, haring along the hard shoulder of the road that led out of the town and into the countryside.

Grangewood Court eventually hove into view. It was an enormous stately home, with thirty-two bedrooms, all *en suite*, a swimming pool, stables and a ballroom as big as a football pitch.

'Six minutes!' Sisely shouted over her shoulder to Aldrin as they sprinted up the driveway, their feet scattering the gravel.

They reached the front door.

'So how . . . are we going . . . to get in?' Aldrin wondered in between gasps.

'The way normal people do,' Sisely said. 'By knocking on the door.'

She reached up, took the heavy knocker in her hand and banged it three times.

A moment later, the door was opened very slowly by Smythson, Sir Marmaduke's elderly and painfully short-sighted butler.

'Yeeeeeesss?' he said, looking down his nose at them.

'We're here to watch Sir Marmaduke eat the cheese,' Sisely said confidently.

'It's only for invited friends and members of the press,' Smythson told them.

'We are . . . members . . . of the press,' Aldrin said, still out of breath.

'Oh, I do beg your pardon,' said Smythson, opening the door wide for them. 'My eyesight isn't what it used to be. For a moment there, I thought you were a little boy and girl!'

'A little boy and girl,' Aldrin chuckled. 'That's . . . a good one.'

Smythson led them through a large entrance hallway that was bigger than the entire terrace on which Sisely lived.

'Sir Marmaduke,' he said, 'is receiving his guests in the drawing room.' And he pointed them to a door.

Aldrin pushed down the handle nervously. Fortunately, the room was so full of people that Aldrin and Sisely were able to slip in unnoticed.

Sir Marmaduke was a short, plump man, with a jolly smile and large muttonchop sideburns. He was a man who enjoyed nothing more than holding court – which is what he was doing at that precise moment, sunk into his favourite armchair and regaling his guests and the assembled press with the story of how the cheese came to be in his possession.

'It arrived here from Istanbul on a ship,' he said. 'I am reliably informed that twelve members of the crew left the vessel in a lifeboat because they couldn't bear the smell of it any longer. The captain ordered that it be put in an airtight cooler box for the rest of the voyage because it smelled so obnoxiously awful!'

'So how do you expect it to taste?' a member of the press asked.

'I have literally no idea. I was just intrigued when I saw that it was going under the hammer at Sotheby's. And I thought, what better way to celebrate my ninetieth birthday than by eating the world's most expensive piece of cheese – in front of you lot!'

On a side table, Aldrin noticed, there was a grey slate cheeseboard, with a selection of knives laid out right next to it.

'It's time,' he said, picking up a napkin from the table and tucking it into the top of his shirt. He pressed a button in the arm of his chair and a bell rang. A moment later, Smythson appeared at the door.

'You rang, Sir Marmaduke?' he asked.

'Yes,' Sir Marmaduke told him. 'I shall have my cheese now, Smythson. Would you mind fetching it for me? It's in a red cooler box in the pantry.'

'As you wish,' Smythson said, then he left.

Aldrin turned to Sisely.

'What are we going to do?' he asked.

'You have to get down to the pantry and switch the cheeses before he gets there,' Sisely said. 'Thankfully, I know a short cut.'

She grabbed him by the wrist and pulled him out of the room.

'How do you know a short cut?' Aldrin wondered.

'These kind of houses **ALWAYS** have a dumb waiter,' she said confidently.

'What, are we going to ask *him* to get it for us?' Aldrin asked.

'I don't mean a waiter who happens to be not very clever,' she said. 'A dumb waiter is a small lift that's used to send food from the basement kitchen to the dining room upstairs.'

Sisely led Aldrin into a large dining room. At one end of the room, there was what looked like a boarded-up window in the middle of the wall. At the bottom of it, there was a handle. Sisely pulled it upwards and the door opened, revealing what appeared to be a lift for a very, very tiny person.

Sisely pointed out the buttons on the wall. They were marked **'UP'**, **'DOWN'** and **'EMERGENCY STOP'**.

'It's very simple to operate,' Sisely told him.

Aldrin was confused.

'What exactly are you asking me to do here, Sisely?' he said nervously.

'Get in,' she told him.

Aldrin couldn't believe what he was hearing.

'What, me?' he asked. 'Get in there?'

'It'll take you straight down to the kitchen,' she said. 'The pantry should be right next to it.'

'Sisely, look at the size of me!' he pointed out. 'I can't squeeze in there. You do it – you're thinner than me!'

'I'm scared of confined spaces,' Sisely confessed matter-of-factly.

Aldrin sighed, then reluctantly, he climbed into the dumb waiter. It was a **VERY** tight squeeze.

'Bang three times on the wall when you want me to press the button to bring you back up,' Sisely said as she pulled the door closed.

She pressed the **'DOWN'** button and the motor

rumbled to life.

Ten seconds later, there was a ping and the lift stopped. Aldrin pulled up the door and got out. He was in a large kitchen. He spotted the pantry directly opposite him.

He crossed the kitchen and ducked into the pantry. The shelves were bursting with food of every variety.

He spotted the red cooler box resting on a high shelf. He found a stool, climbed up on to it and, with the tips of his fingers, managed to slide the box off the shelf and into his hands.

The stool wobbled under his weight and Aldrin thought he was going to topple off it. But he managed to correct himself just in time. He jumped down and popped open the cooler box lid.

The smell almost knocked him off his feet!

It was like something had died in the box several months earlier.

Aldrin covered his nose and mouth and peered inside. The piece of cheese was small enough to fit inside a closed fist.

How could something so tiny **STINK** so badly?

Aldrin reached into his pocket and pulled out the Gorgonzola. He made the switch, then he replaced

the lid on the cooler box, stood on the stool and returned it carefully to the top shelf.

Suddenly, he heard foosteps in the passage outside the kitchen. He jumped down off the stool, ran out of the pantry, across the kitchen floor and dived head first into the dumb waiter, pulling the door up just as Smythson walked into the kitchen.

Upstairs, Sisely heard him bang three times on the wall and she pressed the button to bring the dumb waiter back.

Stuck in that confined space with that revolting smell, Aldrin was forced to hold his breath. Sisely had to cover her nose and mouth too, as the fumes wafted their way up the lift shaft.

Just as the dumb waiter was about to reach its destination, Sisely heard a woman with a posh voice say:

'What are you doing in here?'

She pressed the button marked **'EMERGENCY STOP'**.

Sisely wheeled round to see an elderly lady with purple hair, bent over a Zimmer frame.

'I was just, um, having a look around,' Sisely explained politely.

Aldrin could hear this conversation from inside the dumb waiter. He had been holding his breath for almost sixty seconds now. He had no choice. He had to breathe out. And then in again.

'I'm Lady Melicent Birtwistle,' the woman told Sisely. 'Sir Marmaduke's wife. Are you interested in the history of the house?'

Aldrin thought, *Please say no, Sisely!*

'Yes,' said Sisely.

'Oh, good!' said Lady Melicent. 'Grangewood Court is a Jacobean house, built in 1608 by Cecil Armitage, the Seventh Earl of Rumsbury, on the grounds of a former palace. It is regarded as one of the finest examples of Jacobean architecture in the country . . .'

Aldrin, still trapped in his tiny metal prison, was convinced he was going to pass out due to the foul stench coming from his pocket.

'At least seven kings and queens have holidayed here over the centuries, including –'

Sisely watched Lady Melicent's nose twitch. The fumes from the Maraspoli Bolu had reached her nostrils.

'What *is* that ghastly smell?' she asked.

'It could be the plumbing,' Sisely suggested.

'That's exactly what it is! Again! Would you excuse me while I ask Smythson to phone that useless plumber?'

One slow step at a time, Lady Melicent moved out of the room on her Zimmer frame. When she was finally gone, Sisely hit the button marked **'UP'** and the motor woke up again. A few seconds later, there was a PING. Sisely pulled up the door and Aldrin fell out on to the floor, coughing and spluttering.

'Did you get it?' Sisely asked.

'I hope so,' Aldrin replied. 'Otherwise, I would

be **SERIOUSLY** worried about where that smell was coming from.'

They crept out of the dining room and tiptoed down the hallway. As they were passing the drawing room, Aldrin couldn't resist poking his head round the door to find out how Sir Marmaduke was enjoying his birthday present to himself.

He did *not* seem happy.

'IT TASTES JUST LIKE GORGONZOLA!' he was raging. 'FIFTY THOUSAND POUNDS? FOR FOUR OUNCES OF GORGONZOLA? SMYTHSON, GET ME SOTHEBY'S ON THE PHONE THIS INSTANT!'

55

'IT'S JUST NIGHTMARES'

It was late that night – and Aldrin was back at the piano again.

PLIIINK . . . PLIIINK . . . PLIIINNNK . . . PLOOONK . . . PLOOONK . . . PLOOONNNNK . . .

'Your playing is really coming on,' Doug commented.

Silas looked at Doug sceptically from his perch on top of Aldrin's head.

'Do you think?' Aldrin asked.

'That piano teacher didn't know what she was talking about. Musically deaf indeed! She wouldn't say it now – not if she was stood here, listening to you play . . . well, whatever tune that is you're trying to play.'

Aldrin smiled. He didn't mind that he was bad at the piano. Everyone has a gift. His just happened to be something else. Unfortunately, that something else had to remain a secret from the world.

He looked at the clock on the sideboard. It was almost time for bed.

'What *is* that smell?' Doug asked. 'It's been in the air all afternoon.'

Aldrin had hidden the Maraspoli Bolu in the window box outside his bedroom.

'Must be a problem with the sewers,' Doug answered his own question. 'I'm going to walk round the block – see if there's a manhole open.'

As soon as Doug left, Aldrin picked up the phone. He dialled Sisely's number. Her mum answered.

'Hello, Mrs Musa,' Aldrin said. 'Is Sisely there?'

'Yes, she's here. Are you getting that smell where you are?' asked Mrs Musa.

'Smell?' Aldrin said innocently.

'It's like nothing I've ever smelled before.'

Just be grateful you're not stuck in a dumb waiter with it, Aldrin thought.

'Never mind,' she said. 'Sisely, it's for you!'

A few seconds later, Sisely came on the phone.

'I just wanted to say thanks again for today,' Aldrin told her. 'I couldn't have done it without you.'

'So where is it?' she asked.

'I put it in the window box outside my bedroom.'

'Everyone in town is talking about the smell.'

'I'm going to eat it tonight.'

There was a short silence between them.

'Are you scared?' Sisely asked.

'Yes, I'm scared,' Aldrin confessed. 'But when she was sick, Mum told me this thing. She said that the hero and the coward feel exactly the same fear. It's only what they *do* that makes them different.'

'Knockdrinna Snow,' Sisely said. 'Do those words mean anything to you?'

'Knockdrinna Snow? Yeah, it's a goat's Brie made in Ireland. The flavour is surprisingly complex and it's got a bloomy white rind –'

'I'm not looking to buy some, Aldrin. According to the dream journal, "Knockdrinna Snow" is what you should say if you're in trouble.'

'I'll remember that.'

'I won't be able to sleep tonight, Aldrin. I'll be too worried about you.'

'I'll be OK. It's just nightmares – that's all.'

'Please be careful.'

'I will. I'll see you at school tomorrow.'

Doug returned home just as Aldrin was hanging up the phone.

'No open manhole covers,' he said. 'Mr Hamilton thinks it smells like pig slurry.'

'Oh, well,' said Aldrin, 'hopefully it will have gone away by the morning. I'm going to go to bed, Dad.'

'*Sweet dreams –*'

'– are made of cheese.'

'*Who am I –*'

'– to diss a Brie?'

A few minutes later, Aldrin lifted his bedroom window and felt inside the window box for Sir Marmaduke Birdwistle's foul-smelling birthday present to himself. He found it and brought it inside. His stomach lurched as the indescribably disgusting aroma of Maraspoli Bolu filled the room.

Silas would have pinched his nose if he'd had fingers and thumbs.

Aldrin got into bed. He opened the wrapping and his stomach heaved again. He would have to eat it quickly.

He braced himself, then he bit into it. It yielded easily under his front teeth and it crumbled into his mouth. He waited for the taste to register. And then it did . . .

It was the most beautiful cheese he had ever tasted!

And worth every penny of the £50,000 that Sir Marmaduke had paid for it!

As he chewed, he again thought about Agatha – as tall and thin as a bus stop, with blonde hair that went all the way down to her waist, lots of make-up and a pinched face that made it look like she was sucking hard on a boiled sweet – even though she wasn't.

He ate the cheese in three hungry bites. Then he chewed it until it was just a lump of salty, caramelly gloop in his mouth . . .

And *very quickly* . . .

without even realizing . . .

that it was happening . . .

his eyes **started to feel** . . .

very,

very

heavy . . .

And then . . .

he was suddenly . . .

out

for

the . . .

AGATHA'S NIGHTMARE REVISITED

The screams were even louder this time.

Louder and more hysterical.

'AAARRRGGGHHH!!!'

Aldrin found himself, once again, trying to make his way through an oncoming crowd. People were pulling him by the arm and telling him:

'YOU'RE GOING THE WRONG WAY!'

And:

'IT'S GOING TO BLOW!'

He shook himself free of their grabbing hands, then the crowd began to thin out.

'AAARRRGGGHHH!!!'

This time, he knew exactly where he was going.

Digges Road.

He could see the giant fondue set bearing down on the town like a robot invader from space. He heard the dreadful sound, like rolling thunder, as the cheese in the bowl reached boiling point. There was a loud explosion that shook the ground and cheese started spewing upwards, then falling, forming a steaming-hot river that flowed through the town, consuming everything in its path.

He spotted Agatha outside the supermarket, trying to pull open the door of her car.

'MY SON!' she shouted. **'MY SON IS TRAPPED!'**

Aldrin saw Beddy Byes smiling at her across the roof of the locked car.

'DON'T JUST STAND THERE!' she shouted at him. **'HELP US!'**

But Beddy Byes didn't move.

'Agatha!' Aldrin called out as he walked towards where she was standing by the car.

Agatha turned and Aldrin saw the recognition register on her face.

'You're that . . . AWFUL cheesemonger's boy!' she said rudely.

'Hey, I'm not exactly *your* number-one fan either,' Aldrin told her. 'Step back.'

He could see Sebastian inside the car, slapping the window uselessly with his palms.

Aldrin closed his eyes and thought about a key. Suddenly, he could feel one swinging between his fingers. Without hesitating, he pushed it into the lock and turned it. The button on the inside of the door popped up. Aldrin reached for the door handle. But as soon as he did, the button went down again. He turned the key a second time – again, the button popped up. But the very moment he tried to open the door it locked again.

He heard laughter – cruel, taunting laughter. He looked at Beddy Byes. He was smirking and holding up a remote key fob.

Agatha **screamed**. The river of bubbling hot processed cheese was just thirty feet away from them all now.

'Turn your head away!' Aldrin ordered Sebastian. 'I'm going to smash the glass!'

Sebastian did as he was told. Aldrin summoned up a hammer – it was quite a bit bigger than the one he imagined, but no matter. He struck the window with it. The first blow only spiderwebbed the glass. But he hit it again and it shattered into a million pieces.

He reached into the car. With two hands, he grabbed Sebastian by his jacket and pulled him out through the window and on to the road.

Agatha rushed towards him. Tears streaming down her face, she threw her arms round her son.

'My boy!' she said. **'My beautiful boy!'**

Aldrin suddenly felt himself being lifted off the ground. Beddy Byes had gripped the front of his shirt with one hand. There was rage in his eyes.

'You need to learn to stay **OUT** of other people's nightmares!' he growled at him.

All at once, Aldrin heard a dull thud. Beddy Byes dropped him and staggered forward. Agatha had taken off one of her shoes and hit him across the back of the head with the heel.

'How DARE you!' she said. 'That boy saved my son's life!'

Aldrin turned round and saw the river of hot cheese snaking its way towards them. In a matter of seconds, they would be smothered in it like hapless nachos.

'RUN!' Aldrin shouted. **'RUN FOR YOUR LIVES!'**

Agatha and Sebastian broke into a sprint.

Beddy Byes took off too, racing down Digges Road and turning right at the stationer's on to Albion Walk and out of the path of the fast-flowing yellow gloop. Aldrin followed him, past the butcher's, where the roads were clear, past the vegetable shop, the pound shop and the post office, then left on to Prince Charles Terrace, past a row of houses, past the scout hut, past the bowls club.

Aldrin wanted to talk to him. He might be able to lead him to Habeas Grusselvart!

He kept up his pursuit of Beddy Byes, walking up the hill to the top of Motherwell Road, then through the adventure playground, over the footbridge, across the football pitch, until they approached the giant metal legs of the fondue bowl.

The bowl had stopped spitting cheese, which suggested to Aldrin that Agatha had probably woken up. Yet *he* was still trapped in her nightmare.

How?

Was it Beddy Byes who was keeping him here?

But for a few yellow puddles here and there, the ground around the fondue bowl was mostly clear, the cheese having flowed down the hill, flooding Digges Road.

'**Maurice!**' Aldrin called out. '**Maurice Mackle!**'

Beddy Byes looked back over his shoulder.

'That name,' he said, 'means **NOTHING** to me now!'

'It's how you introduced yourself to my dad,' Aldrin reminded him.

Beddy Byes stopped. He turned round.

'He shouldn't have reopened that shop,' he said.

'It's finished,' Aldrin told him. 'Agatha won't be scared of that nightmare any more. And all those other people you've been terrorizing – I'll show them that they have nothing to fear from cheese either.'

'There are *other* ways of stopping you.'

'What are you talking about?'

'You'll find out. In the meantime, there's someone who's been looking forward to meeting you.'

'Who?'

Beddy Byes closed his eyes, lowered his head, then disappeared in a puff of dust. And standing in the spot where he had been was a tall, powerfully built man, with a pale complexion, a wild mane of black, curly hair, hooded eyes, a crooked nose and dark sideburns that ran down to his chin. He wore a long black coat, buttoned right up to his neck, and, most noticeable of all, a horrible smirk on his face.

Aldrin recognized him immediately. It was the man he'd seen watching Agatha's protest from the shadow of the bus shelter on the other side of Burnett Road.

'Aldrin Adams,' Habeas Grusselvart said, 'we meet at last. Allow me to introduce myself –'

'I know who you are,' Aldrin **spat**.

'Do you indeed?'

'Your real name is Pim van Almsick. You stole your powers from Luuk van den Hoogenband. And for five hundred years you've used them to spread fear and misery throughout the world.'

'I see you've done your homework. I might ask you to write my Facebook profile.'

'Mrs Van Boxtel told me everything.'

'Ah, Nel! Rather unfortunate timing that was – her telling you about your powers.'

Aldrin began to circle him. Habeas **laughed**.

'Oh,' he said, 'you're going to fight me, are you? Well, first of all, let's do something about the lighting, shall we?'

Habeas raised an index finger high above his head and twirled it around three times. Immediately, the sky turned a dull yellowy-brown colour.

'And let's give ourselves a little atmosphere,' Habeas added, turning his two palms upwards.

It began to rain. But it wasn't ordinary rain. Hot globules of nacho cheese fell from the sky and spattered on the ground around Aldrin's feet. Aldrin continued to circle Habeas, occasionally jumping backwards to avoid the splashes.

He needed a weapon. But what? A sword felt right. He closed his eyes and visualized a long, two-handed claymore. Instantly, he felt his hand gripping a metal handle. But when he opened his eyes, he saw that he was holding a giant stainless-steel fondue fork.

Habeas **chuckled**.

'Sorry,' he said. 'Just my little joke.'

Aldrin had no idea how he was going to use it to fight, but he'd give it a go. He held it up like a two-pronged sword.

'OK, let's make it even,' Habeas said, holding his hand out in front of him with his fingers splayed. He closed his hand quickly and another giant fondue fork – the same as Aldrin's – appeared in his fist.

Without warning, Habeas swung it at Aldrin, who ducked to avoid the blow. Aldrin countered with a lunge, but Habeas blocked it with his own fork and pushed Aldrin back.

'I'm not scared of you,' Aldrin said.

'That's because you have no idea of the many ways in which I can hurt you,' Habeas said, 'and the people that you love.'

'I can protect them,' Aldrin told him. 'Because I'm a Cheese Whizz.'

'Don't overestimate your powers,' Habeas said. 'You're just a boy.'

Aldrin swung his fork at Habeas, who parried the blow with his own blade.

'Why do you care so much about other people?' Habeas asked. 'Agatha will have woken up in her bed by now and realized it was all another horrible nightmare. And here you are, fighting her battles for her, a woman who doesn't care about you, who hates you, in fact – you *and* your father.'

'She doesn't hate us,' Aldrin said. 'You turned her against cheese, that's all.'

Habeas made another lunge at Aldrin, attempting to prong his Adam's apple like a marshmallow. Aldrin jumped to one side to avoid his windpipe being skewered, then he countered, swinging his fork back and forth in a wild, slashing motion, forcing Habeas to retreat slowly.

A huge globule of cheese hit the ground beside

Aldrin, narrowly missing him, but it splashed up and burned his hand. Aldrin grimaced with the pain. Habeas laughed.

'Stealing that cheese from Sir Marmaduke Birtwistle's pantry,' he said. 'That was *her* idea, wasn't it? Little Sisely. She's the brains of the operation, isn't she?'

Aldrin didn't answer.

'I've been saying for a long time, I must see if there's something I can do about her nightmares,' Habeas said. 'That exam one – well, you saw it yourself, it's not really doing anything for her.'

'Leave her alone,' Aldrin warned him.

'She suffers from anxiety. Did you know that? Has panic attacks if she's torn from her routine. Let's see. Perhaps I could give her one where she's lost in a shopping centre and she can't find her mother.'

'**NOOOOOO!!!!!!**' Aldrin screamed, charging at Habeas, holding his fork in front of him like a lance. Habeas jumped to one side. In the same movement, he stuck out his foot, tripping Aldrin, who fell to the ground, dropping his weapon.

Aldrin rolled on to his back. Habeas stood over him with a leering grin on his face. He held his fondue fork in both hands, with the points facing downwards. He lifted it, getting ready to bring it down on Aldrin's chest.

Aldrin closed his eyes firmly and waited for the end to come.

And then he remembered something . . .

The words that Sisely had told him.

'KNOCKDRINNA SNOW!' he shouted.

Suddenly, he heard a clanking sound – like steel hitting steel. He opened his eyes to discover that Habeas's blade had been deflected – by a giant cheese knife!

And then he looked at the figure who was holding the knife. And Aldrin couldn't **BELIEVE** what he was seeing . . .

IT WAS HIS MUM.

He saw the shock register on the face of Habeas, who'd barely had time to see who had administered the block. Cynthia held out her free hand, her fingers spread, and Habeas was suddenly blown backwards, as if struck by some invisible force.

He landed on his back, twenty feet away. Cynthia ran towards him, spinning the giant cheese knife in her hand like a Samurai with a sword. Habeas jumped to his feet. He closed his eyes and, out of thin air, summoned up a heavy steel broadsword.

He swung it at Cynthia, but she ducked away from him, then delivered a perfect roundhouse kick to the side of Habeas's head, knocking him off his feet.

Aldrin, still lying on the ground, was unable to believe what he was watching. His mum, the cheesemonger from Burnett Road, with a manner as mild as Cream Havarti . . . was fighting like a ninja!

Habeas got up again and swung his sword at Cynthia, but she blocked it with the blade of her knife, then she kicked Habeas's legs from under him, and he hit the ground with a thud.

'That's it, Mum!' Aldrin shouted, cheering her on.

But then he saw a look of concern pass over Cynthia's face.

Something was happening. She seemed to be . . . shrinking.

Then Aldrin saw that she wasn't shrinking at all.

She was **sinking**!

Habeas had turned the ground beneath her feet into nacho cheese, and now she was disappearing into it like it was quicksand. Within seconds, she was submerged up to her waist.

Aldrin scrambled up.

Habeas laughed in his usual villainous way and waved to Cynthia.

'Goodbye, Cynthia,' he said. 'Sorry, it's been so short this –'

But then he stopped – and he looked down in horror.

Aldrin had run his fondue fork into Habeas's side.

Habeas **sighed**.

'Just when I was beginning to enjoy myself,' he said,

then he disappeared in a sudden explosion of dust.

Aldrin ran to Cynthia, who was now submerged up to her neck.

'Grab my hand!' he said. **'Quickly!'**

She managed to pull one arm out of the thick, warm goo that was swallowing her up and she took his hand. Then, with all the strength he had in his body, he pulled his mother free.

They stared at each other, neither of them speaking. But everything they wished to say to each other could be conveyed with a simple hug. They stood in the shadow of the now dormant fondue set and held each other, mother and son, crying tears of happiness.

'You know you're going to stink of nacho cheese now?' Cynthia said.

'I don't care,' Aldrin told her. 'I'm not going to let go of you, Mum.'

Cynthia smiled.

'This secret you've discovered about yourself,' she said, 'it's a lot to process, I know. That's why I asked Nel to watch over you.'

'So are you actually –?'

'Dead? Yes, I am.'

'But how are we hugging each other right now?'

'Death ends a life, Aldrin. But it doesn't end a relationship. We all live on in the minds, the memories and the dreams of the people who love us, even after we're gone. Come on, let's go and sit down. You don't have long before the effects of that cheese wear off.'

Cynthia led Aldrin to the adventure playground and they sat down on the roundabout. Aldrin held his mum's hand tightly like he thought she might disappear if he let go.

'We used to come here all the time,' she reminded him. 'You used to love the swings. I'd push you and you'd say, **"Higher! Higher!"** and I'd say, "If you go any higher, you'll do a loop-the-loop!" You never had any fear at all.'

'You knew I was going to be a Cheese Whizz,' he said.

'It's in our family,' she said. 'My dad had the power. And his mum. And my great-grandfather. We've been fighting Habeas Grusselvart for generations.'

'And you're still fighting him?' he asked.

'Of course. When you're a Cheese Whizz, you can't let a little thing like death get in the way.'

'I found your dream journal,' he told her.

'I'm glad,' she said. 'You'll need that.'

'Why is it written in French?'

'Because your dad doesn't speak it. I never wanted him to know about it. I wanted to protect him. Have you told anyone?'

'Sisely. She's my friend. I didn't understand what was happening and she's the smartest person I know, and she speaks French.'

'You know you'll have to protect her now?'

'Habeas said he's going to give her terrible nightmares.'

'He'll try. But you have to stop him. You see, anyone you share your secret with becomes vulnerable. He'll try and turn them against you.'

'Is that what happened with Beddy Byes?' he asked.

His mum nodded.

'He was my best friend in the world,' she said. 'I told him my secret – about my power. I thought I could trust him. But Maurice was in love with me – and, well, I wasn't in love with him. And when I met your dad, he became very bitter. And that was when Habeas got to him.'

An image of a ball of cheese suddenly flashed in front of Aldrin's eyes. It was from the poster on the wall at the end of his bed.

'I can see Mimolette,' Aldrin said.

'You're waking up,' his mum told him.

'**No!**' he said. '**I don't want to wake up! I want to sit here forever!**'

'Don't be daft!' she said. 'You've got the world to save! So, how's your dad?'

'He's good. He misses you.'

'I miss him. I miss both of you. Is he coping?'

'He wasn't for a while – but he is now.'

'I'm glad. I want him to move on. Life can be lonely on your own.'

'He's not on his own. He has me!'

'Yes, he does. And he's a lucky man.'

Cynthia kissed him on the top of the head.

'Will I see you tomorrow night?' Aldrin asked.

'Tomorrow night?' Cynthia said.

'Presumably, if I want to see you in my dreams, I just have to shout, **"KNOCKDRINNA SNOW!"**?'

Cynthia looked away.

'I wish it were that simple,' she said sadly.

'You mean it's not?' Aldrin asked.

'You only get three chances to see me, Aldrin. And you've used up one of those.'

Aldrin's heart sank.

'I'm seeing Pont l'Évêque,' he said.

'You're going to be waking up any second now,' Cynthia told him. 'There's something I want to tell you, Aldrin, before you wake up.'

'What is it?' Aldrin asked.

'Children don't usually have this power. I didn't develop mine until I was eighteen. My dad was twenty-five. Which leads me to think that, well, you might be . . .'

'Might be what?'

'That you might be . . .'

'I'm seeing Bleu d'Auvergne.'

'There's no time. I'll tell you later.'

'I love you, Mum.'

'I love you too, Aldrin.'

Suddenly, Aldrin was staring at the *Fromages de France* poster on his wall, his head throbbing so hard that it hurt to blink.

57

A LONG STORY

Aldrin told Sisely everything that had happened at school the next day. He told her about rescuing Sebastian from the car. He told her about Beddy Byes lifting him up off the ground with one hand and Agatha coming to his aid. He told her about his duel with Habeas using fondue forks.

And he told her about his mum – and how the words **Knockdrinna Snow** had magically conjured her up.

Sisely sat on a bench in the playground and listened to him in silence.

If someone had told her this story just a few short weeks ago, she would have said it was beyond the bounds of credibility. An evil, centuries-old prince who amused himself by creating nightmares for people –

and a boy who could enter those nightmares and help to rewrite the ending?

Sisely would have said that it wasn't logical.

But she had changed – just like Aldrin had changed. Despite herself, she had come to believe the truth in what Mrs Van Boxtel had told her – that there really *is* a world of magic out there that defies rational explanation.

'I just wanted to say thank you,' Aldrin told her.

'Why are you thanking me?' Sisely asked.

'For reading my mum's dream journal. And for helping me to steal Sir Marmaduke's cheese. But mostly for believing me. None of it would have been possible if you hadn't believed me.'

'It's still hard. In a way, it *all* feels like a dream.'

'Sisely, I'm worried that, by telling you about my secret, I may have put you in danger.'

'What kind of danger?'

'Habeas knows about you. He knows you're my Linda Dale.'

'Stop saying I'm your Linda Dale.'

'Well, whatever you are. I'm worried that he might try to get at me by hurting you.'

'How can he hurt me?'

'By playing on your anxieties. If you start having nightmares, will you tell me?'

'I have my exam nightmare all the time. I can deal with it, Aldrin.'

'But if you start having *other* nightmares. If your nightmares become worse –'

'They're just nightmares, Aldrin. They're not real. It's just how our minds process our worries and fears.'

'But he can make them so much worse, Sisely. Please promise me that you'll tell me.'

'I promise.'

'Oh my God,' a voice suddenly said. 'You are in *so* much trouble!'

Aldrin looked up. It was Harry. He was walking across the playground with Frankie.

'Trouble?' Aldrin said.

'Mr Maskell was looking for you yesterday,' Frankie said. 'Where did you two disappear to?'

Oh, no, Aldrin thought. With everything that had happened, he'd forgotten that they had bunked off yesterday.

'It's, um, a long story,' Aldrin told him.

'We'd better get to lessons,' Sisely said.

They headed for the main entrance of the school.

'Uh-oh!' Aldrin said.

Mr Maskell was standing at the door, watching the children arrive.

Aldrin walked towards him, suddenly wishing that his superpower was invisibility.

'Sisely,' the headmaster said. 'Feeling better today, are we?'

'Yes, Mr Maskell,' Sisely replied.

'MiisteerrAaaaaddaaaaammmmmssssss!' the principal said.

Teachers always call you mister and stretch your name out when you're in trouble for something.

'Morning, Mister Maskell,' Aldrin said with a chirpiness he didn't feel inside.

'Would you mind explaining to me,' the principal asked, 'why you weren't in school yesterday afternoon?'

'I was, um . . .'

'Yes?'

'I was, um . . .'

'He wash doing shome work for me,' Aldrin heard Mrs Van Boxtel say. He turned round. She was standing behind him, staring hard at Mr Maskell. 'I shent him to the library to do shome reshearch – for thish book we are writing. I am shorry, it wash my fault

– I should have mentioned it to hish other teachersh.'

'Oh,' Mr Maskell said, disappointed. 'If he had permission from you, I suppose there's nothing I can do about it.'

When they were inside the school, Mrs Van Boxtel pulled Aldrin to one side.

'Thanks for covering for me,' he said before she could say anything. But she ignored him.

'Sho,' she said, 'are you going to tell me exshactly what'sh been going on?'

'I had to get my hands on this special kind ofcheese. To get into Agatha's nightmare. I met him, Mrs Van Boxtel. I met Habeas Grusselvart.'

'You *met* him?' she said. 'What happened?'

'We had a sword fight – using fondue forks.'

'Fondue forksh?'

'Yeah, you sort of had to be there. Anyway, he was about to finish me off when –' Aldrin heard his voice crack with emotion.

'It ish OK,' Mrs Van Boxtel said. 'Take your time.'

'Mum saved me!' he said.

Mrs Van Boxtel smiled.

'You shaw her?' she asked.

'She left a secret code – in her dream journal.

Knockdrinna Snow.'

'You know you can only ushe thish two more timesh?'

'She told me . . . Mrs Van Boxtel, I want to meet him again.'

'Who?'

'Habeas Grusselvart.'

'Only he can chooshe when he appearsh in dreamsh.'

'I'm not talking about in dreams. I'm talking about the real world. He must have a secret hideout somewhere. I want to find out where he lives.'

'Perhapsh we will put our headsh together and figure thish out,' she said. 'But for now I think you have had enough adventuresh. It ish time for you to go back to being a normal boy. A normal boy who ish late for for hish next classh!'

58

HAPPINESS

Aldrin couldn't hide his joy.

'They've GONE!' he said.

Doug and Belinda were standing behind the counter. Belinda was cutting some lovely soft Robiola Bosina for Mrs Monnelly and recommending that she try it with figs later.

'What happened?' he asked.

'It's a mystery,' Doug said. 'Agatha showed up this morning and told the others that she was wrong. She said that their nightmares had absolutely nothing to do with my cheese.'

'That *is* a mystery,' Aldrin agreed.

'I'll tell you something else that's a mystery. That smell last night? It was GONE this morning!'

'You're right. I can't smell it any more.'

'There's been lots of strange things happening lately, hasn't there?'

Mrs Monnelly walked past the three of them on her way out of the shop.

'Thanks, Belinda,' she called over her shoulder. 'You've been very helpful.'

Lots of strange things indeed, Aldrin thought!

'Goodbye, Mrs Monnelly,' said Doug. 'Thank you for your custom.'

Doug turned and caught Belinda's eye then.

'Shall we tell him now?' he asked.

Belinda smiled.

'Now is as good a time as any,' she replied.

'Tell me what?' Aldrin asked.

Doug was blushing.

'Well,' he said, 'you know how I was saying that I thought it was time to move on with my life? And, well, you know that I'll always love your mother . . .'

'Dad,' Aldrin said, 'what are you trying to say?'

Doug blurted it out then.

'Belinda and I are going out for dinner together tonight,' Doug said.

'What, like a date?' Aldrin asked.

'Yes, I suppose it *is* a date,' Doug replied.

Aldrin threw his arms round his dad and sobbed.

'Is he happy?' Belinda asked. 'I can't tell if he's happy or not, Doug.'

'Yes, Belinda,' Doug said, 'you can take it from me that he's happy.'

Belinda stepped out from behind the counter and joined the happy little huddle in the middle of the shop.

They were so lost in the moment that they didn't hear the bell ring to tell them that another customer had entered. It wasn't until they broke away from each other, wiping the happy tears from their cheeks, that they noticed her standing there.

It was Agatha.

'I wanted to say sorry,' she said. 'For being so **GHASTLY** to you.'

Aldrin looked at his dad and Belinda, and wondered if he was hearing her correctly.

'I blamed you for my nightmares,' she said, 'and now I realize that you weren't responsible for them at all. And I want to apologize.'

Doug said nothing. Aldrin gave him a nudge.

'Oh, er, apology accepted,' Doug replied.

Agatha stared at Aldrin for a long moment.

'You were in my dream last night,' she said.

'Was I?' Aldrin asked. 'I hope it wasn't a nightmare.'

'It was at the beginning,' she said. 'But this time it had a happy ending.'

'Well,' Doug said, 'I appreciate you coming here and saying that.'

'There's just one more thing,' Agatha said.

'What is it?'

'I'd like some cheese, if I may.'

'Really? Well, what kind of cheese were you looking for?'

'Do you have the smelly priest one?'

'I think she means the Stinking Bishop,' Aldrin said.

'Yes,' Doug said, 'we've got some of that. I'll cut some for you. And just to show there's no hard feelings, it's on the house!'

59

STORIES

It was Friday afternoon. The children in Mrs Van Boxtel's class were in a state of high excitement.

The books had arrived!

Mrs Van Boxtel distributed them among the class. On the cover was a picture of a short boy with a pudding-bowl haircut and glasses like swimming goggles, wrestling with a crocodile.

He looked remarkably like Harry!

Everyone turned straight to their own story. It was such a thrill for Aldrin to read the title and his name underneath it:

Silas: The Hip-Hop Frog
by Aldrin Adams

He'd decided not to write about Luuk van den Hoogenband in the end. After all, he was part of the story now – a story that was still awaiting an ending.

So, instead, he wrote a fantasy tale about a big green bullfrog named Silas, who escaped from the kitchen of a Parisian restaurant by leaping out of the window and went on to become a world-famous recording artist.

'I am sho proud of you all,' said Mrs Van Boxtel. 'You have all worked sho hard and thish ish the reshult. Now, would anybody like to shtand up and read their shtory to the classh?'

Frankie's hand shot up.

'Frankie,' she said, 'you can go firsht.'

Frankie headed for the front of the class.

'I really loved thish shtory when I firsht read it,' the teacher said. 'Pleashe tell the classh what it ish about.'

'It's about this character I came up with meself,' Frankie told them. 'This is just a taster really. You can follow his further adventures in the comic book that I'm working on with Harry. It's the story of a boy who has the power to enter people's nightmares.'

Aldrin turned his head and looked at Sisely. She was looking back at him and for the first time he saw her smiling, exposing two rows of train-track braces.

'**I can't WAIT to hear this!**' she whispered.

'It's sort of based on a dream I had,' Frankie said.

'You have shuch a wonderful imagination, Frankie!' Mrs Van Boxtel said. 'OK, let ush hear it!'

And Frankie started to read.

'Once upon a time,' he said, 'there was a boy – a very ordinary boy – who had a very extraordinary superpower . . .'

EPILOGUE

It was the darkest of dark, dark nights.

And Habeas Grusselvart was in a foul mood.

He should have been happy. On his gigantic wall full of TVs, he could see hundreds of children experiencing the most **horrible, HORRIBLE nightmares**!

Like Drew Gascoigne from Wheaton Park, who was trapped in an enormous, sticky web, unable to move his arms or his legs – and a horrible, hairy spider was making its way towards him, intent on eating him for its dinner!

'MUMMMYYYYYY!!!!!!'

Like Sally Smiles from Wren Way, who was hiding under her bed while a vampire with sharp fangs, dark, greased-back hair and a long black cloak with a red lining stalked round her bedroom, searching for her. She let slip a small whimper of fear, giving away her hiding place – and the terrified girl heard the vampire laugh: 'M$_W$A$_A$A$_H$A$_H$A$_H$A$_H$A$_H$A$_H$A!!!!!'

'DADDDYYYYYY!!!!!!'

And like Lindsay Walker from Grand Parade, who got out of bed to investigate a noise in her wardrobe – and she opened the door, only to be confronted by . . .

'AAARRRGGGHHH!!!'

All over town – and, indeed, in towns like this all over the world – children were waking up and screaming for their mums and dads. And so were quite a few adults.

Usually this would have filled Habeas Grusselvart with pleasure. But tonight, for reasons he finally understood, he felt no joy at all – just a sense of foreboding.

'The prophecy was true,' he said.

'Prophecy?' asked Beddy Byes.

'The Cheese Whizzes have always talked about the coming of a young Cheese Whizz,' Habeas explained, 'who would have the power to defeat me once and for all.'

'You think he's . . . The One?' Beddy Byes asked.

'I *know* he's The One!' Habeas told him. 'Cynthia knows it too. She's always known it. That's why she asked Nel to look after him.'

'Are you absolutely and totally certain, Oh Wise and Benevolent One?'

'His powers are strong – I've felt them. And they will become even stronger with age. He has his mother's dream journal now. He has Nel to guide him. And he has the girl. This is the moment I've been dreading for five hundred years.'

'What are you going to do?' Beddy Byes asked.

'I'm going to have to destroy him,' Habeas said, **'before he has the chance to destroy me.'**

If you enjoyed the cheesy world of
Aldrin Adams and the Cheese Nightmares,
try these other Puffin books!

A chaotic robbery, plenty of sheep and a
summer of discoveries come together in this
hilarious and heart-warming adventure.

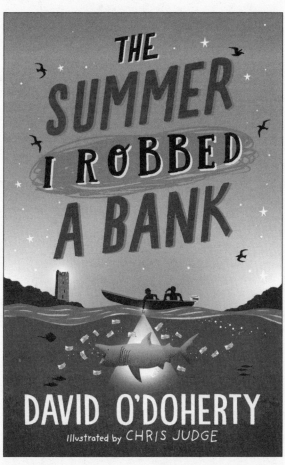

A laugh-out-loud story of dealing with
catastrophe, and how it's OK to be anxious,
scared and sometimes a little bit brave.

'Funniest. Book. Ever.'
Ross Welford, author of
Time Travelling with a Hamster

'Made me cry with
laughter and my heart ache'
Lisa Thompson, author of The Goldfish Boy

WORST.
HOLIDAY.
EVER.

what (MORE) could possibly
go wrong?

Bestselling
author of the
YOUNG BOND
series

CHARLIE HIGSON

Illustrated by Warwick Johnson-Cadwell

Discover all the weird and wonderful things
that go on inside your body with Dr Adam Kay.

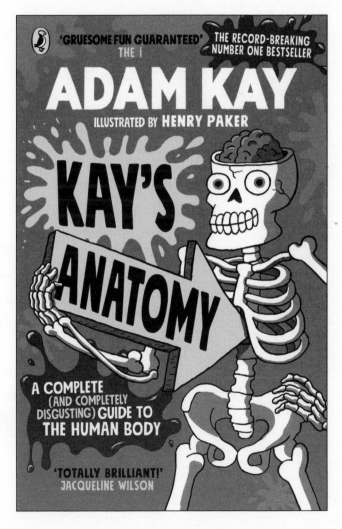

Ready to embark on an INTERGALACTIC adventure?

Discover the incredible series by
Lucy and Stephen Hawking.